BEAUTIFUL DISTRACTION

MCCULLOUGH MOUNTAIN 2

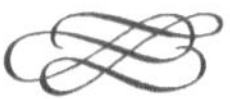

LYDIA MICHAELS

BAILEY BROWN PUBLISHING

BEAUTIFUL DISTRACTION
Copyright © 2019 Lydia Michaels
First E-book Publication: August 2013
First Published as SKIN
All cover art and logo copyright © 2022 Lydia Michaels

McCullough Mountain
Publication Order

Find more McCulloughs in Jasper Falls!

This book is dedicated to you. Yes, you, the one holding the book. Why? Because there was a time when someone said something to or about you that made you feel slightly bad, perhaps slightly ugly, or a little bit fat. And it hurt. I'm dedicating this book to you, because I, too, know what that feels like and I'm here to tell you that YOU ARE BEAUTIFUL! Beauty comes in all shapes, colors, and sizes and don't ever allow anyone to convince you otherwise.

Xo,
Lydia

CHAPTER 1

"Shit."

The uneven flapping of rubber slapped against the dirt road and Finnegan McCullough tugged the battered wheel of his truck, hauling his flatbed to the shoulder. That was the second tire he'd lost in a month. The roads on their family property were eaten up from a long, icy winter.

Climbing out of the truck, his yellow work boots stomped over the dried, packed clay as he took in the damage.

"Bloody hell." There was no patching that.

From the bed of the truck, he grabbed the jack and donut. Heat beat through his flannel as he dropped to his knees and—

What was that sound?

He paused. This far out in the woods there were

only bears and no bear he'd ever seen had made noises like that. His lungs stilled as he tilted his head, focusing on the sound. The slow buzz of insects and then—*there it was*—soft, breathy pants, a steady pulse of soft taps. It sounded like…fucking.

Narrowing his eyes, he squinted at the horizon as the late afternoon sun pierced the green canopy. He turned, but saw no one. Abandoning the jack and spare, he stood and beat the ginger dust off his knees. Whoever was getting their jollies in his family's woods was about to be interrupted. This was private property.

His long, clipped strides rounded the truck and came up short. The noise was coming from a dense part of the woods where a narrow path was rutted into the earth. A twig snapped under his foot as he brushed aside a fern and stepped onto the rough trail. Too late.

Something big slammed into him and white light flashed behind his eyes as he stumbled backward. Pain exploded in his face like when one is blindsided with a basketball. There was a shrill scream.

"Son of a bitch!" His fingers pressed into his eyes as he waited for the sharp smarting to dissipate. The screaming wasn't helping matters.

Cracking his eyelids, he took in the panicked screamer as her body twisted to flee, only to land roughly on the gravel. She twisted again and continued to scream. Her chest moved under a cotton tank top. A trail of sweat worked its way down her flushed cheeks where the threads of earplugs hung.

When she continued to shriek and scrambled to her feet, he yanked out an ear bud and snapped, *"What the hell are you doing?"*

She hurdled back, her breasts heaving as she threw up her arms. "Don't touch me!"

He scowled. "Don't touch you? You nearly broke my nose and you're on *my* property. I could shoot you if I wanted."

Her rosy cheeks paled and her blue eyes went as wide as saucers. Full, pink lips opened and closed like a trout. Scrambling to her feet, she glanced over her shoulder. Her flaxen ponytail, dark with perspiration, swished and smacked him in the face. Her panicked eyes glanced back at him and she bolted past him.

"Hey!"

Her round, little form burst through the trees and he cursed. Where the hell was she going now? Cursing, he took off after her. Nothing like chasing some broad after nine hours of sweating his balls off in the lumberyard.

His truck cut off her escape and his fingers latched onto her arm. Slamming her back into the rusted door, she screamed again and he winced.

Her panicked cries only cut off when he shook her. "Stop screaming!"

"Please don't hurt me!" she babbled.

He frowned. "Who are you?"

"Mmm—Mallory. Mallory Fenton."

"What are you doing on my property, Mallory Fenton?"

"I didn't realize it was private property. I was jogging in the community park and must've gotten confused."

"Jogging? The parks three miles from here."

Her brow rose. "It is? I didn't realize I went that far."

He released her arm and stepped back. "Well…this is private land."

"I'm sorry. I didn't know."

They had to watch for poachers this far out, but she didn't strike him as the type. "No harm."

Her gaze traced over his face and her brow knit. "You're bleeding."

Running a finger under his nose, he drew back his hand and found a dab of red. He'd live. "Yeah, I was nearly bulldozed by a rogue runner."

She winced and lowered her eyes. "I'm really sorry. I didn't expect to run into anyone out here. Literally."

"Well, maybe next time you might want to try running on the high school track."

Her lips trembled and she looked away. In a quiet voice, she mumbled, "Sorry." Her expression shuttered.

Did he say something wrong? Now that the panic was over, she seemed to withdraw. They awkwardly stood there for a moment and she shifted. "Um, I guess I'll just head back the way I came."

He stepped aside. Her fist pressed into her ribs as if she had a cramp. She didn't look like a track star. Her skin was flushed to her chest, which was notable. Her hips filled out her shorts and her thighs jiggled as she stepped back onto the rough path. He frowned. She wasn't jogging. Her steps appeared tired and lagging.

"Are you planning on walking all the way back to the park? It'll be dark before you make it out of the woods."

She sighed and glanced up at the sky. She was still breathing heavy from exertion. "This is what I get…" she muttered under her breath. Then, in a stronger voice, she said, "I'll be fine. Sorry I trespassed on your property."

Center County was a pretty tight knit community. Finn had never seen her before. She must be new. That was probably why she didn't realize this entire mountain was pretty much McCullough land. He sighed. "If you can wait a few minutes I can give you a lift."

Her beaten-in Nikes crunched over the gravel as she turned, her expression weighing his words—as well as his serial killer qualities, he imagined.

Holding out his arms, he said, "I'm not a psychopath. It's easy to get lost in these woods if you don't know where you're going. I'd hate to see that happen. I got a flat. If you can wait a minute while I fix it, I'll drop you wherever you need to go."

Her lips tightened. "Are there really bears and stuff in these woods?"

He chuckled. "You could say that. I definitely wouldn't want to be walking unarmed at night."

Ground scraped under her rubber shoes as she stepped closer. "My car's at the bottom of the trail." She was sweaty. Her skin glistened under the remaining sun.

He nodded, a bit distracted by her soft form. The fabric of her cotton top was darker where perspiration had run between her breasts. Golden beams of sunlight threw shadows over them and the temperature began to drop, the same way it did every night in these parts. Her nipples pressed through her clothing. She was packed into that sports bra under her clothes.

She cleared her throat and his gaze jerked back to her face. "Sorry," he muttered and quickly turned to grab the jack.

She didn't say much as he fixed the tire. The rim fell like a ton of bricks into his flatbed and he stood, wiping the grease off his fingers onto an old rag. His gaze inspected her. She was average height for a girl, sort of plump and curvy, and she definitely didn't look like a runner. "You're not from around here, are you?"

"I just moved here. I'm from Philly." She kept staring at him.

"My brother goes to school there. Villanova. You know it?"

She smiled and nodded. Her teeth were a straight line of pearls. "Yeah—"

His hand went to his hip as his phone started chirping. He held up a finger telling her to hold that thought and brought it to his ear.

"Hey."

"Fin, where are you? I've been sitting here for an hour."

He glanced at his watch. "Sorry, babe. I had to work over and then I got a flat."

"Another flat?" Erin asked, and he grit his teeth at the suspicious tone in her voice.

"Yeah."

His girlfriend sighed. "Well, when are you coming to pick me up?"

He glanced at the girl. What was her name? Melissa? Maloney? Mallory? Yeah, Mallory. "I gotta take care of some shit and then I'll be there. Give me an hour."

She huffed into the phone. "Why don't I just meet you there?" She said this in a tone that spoke nothing of favors and understanding. He wasn't being baited.

"That'd be great. I'll see you when I get there." His thumb rolled over the end call button and he stuffed it back in his pocket. He turned to Mallory and noticed her expression changed as she looked at the ground.

It was getting dark. "You ready?" he asked.

She nodded and silently went around to the passenger side of the truck. The door whined as she pried it open. *Gonna have to get some WD40 on that.*

MALLORY SANK INTO THE BROKEN-IN, leather, bench seat. She was such an idiot. Her doctor had given her a world of crap at her last physical because of her weight. He basically freaked her out, warning that if she didn't get her act together she was going to run into a shit storm of health issues because her family's medical history was a hodgepodge of diabetes and autoimmune diseases. He successfully freaked her out and she'd—like everything else she did—barreled head first into a plan. Like always, she'd wound up embarrassing herself. Now she was lost, getting a ride home from some mountain man who was like a wet dream in flannel.

She sighed. Of course the first time she ran into—literally—a hot guy in Center County, she'd nearly plowed him down like a bull in a china shop. And, of course, she was a fat, sweaty, panting mess when he saw her. And, *of course,* he had a girlfriend, so why the hell did she care? Yeah, that all sounded about right.

She clicked her seatbelt, stretching it as far as it could go. She was all too aware of how the strap hugged and accentuated her ugly parts.

The truck roared to life. Closed in the roomy cab with him she could smell his skin. What was that? It wasn't like the cologne guys wore at home. This was a piney smell, sweet like sap with some briny, manly edge to it.

"We'll have to take it slow so I don't lose the donut too."

His voice was gravelly and distracting. Almost as distracting as the mention of donut. *Mmm...Boston cream—stop! You don't eat that crap anymore. Think of carrots. Delicious, raw, slices of—*oh, fuck it. She wanted a donut.

As they drove over the bumpy pass of road, she eyed him slyly. He was tall. His long, muscled arms handled the steering wheel with evident strength. He was owning that flannel shirt too. Guys didn't dress like that at home. This wasn't the Kurt Cobain type flannel. No, this flannel was his bitch. It was soft and faded, and stretched over his broad shoulders like a second skin. She frowned as she realized she was jealous of a shirt.

Averting her gaze, she stared out the window. Behind the soft reflection of trees going by in the dark she caught her reflection. Dear God, she looked hideous.

Her hand smoothed her ponytail and she winced as her fingers touched the damp, sweaty mop. Yeah, this is why she went to the park and not the gym or the high school. Nothing like working out next to Redneck Barbie to make her feel more like a slob.

Was his girlfriend the Barbie type? She glanced at him again out of her peripheral vision. Yeah, probably.

Her shoulders slumped into the seat. She just wanted to get back to her car and get home. Mallory sighed as she considered the steamed broccoli that waited for her there. God, she wanted a Philly cheesesteak.

"Do you run a lot?"

His question caught her off guard. "Um, I'm trying to. I need to lose some weight." She winced. *Smooth, Mallory. Draw his attention to your flaws. Like he didn't already notice.* She recalled his comment about being nearly 'bulldozed' by her. Nothing like having a hot guy compare her to twenty-ton truck.

"Girls worry too much about their weight."

"According to my doctor, I don't worry enough." Why was she telling him this? *Shut up!*

He glanced at her then back at the road. Thankfully, he made no further comment on the issue. He probably agreed. "What made you move to Center County?"

A chance at a new beginning. "Work."

"What do you do?"

"I'm a secretary. I'll be working at the high school in the fall."

"Oh, yeah? My sister-in-law teaches there. My brother, Colin, is really involved with the afterschool programs too."

"Colin McCullough?" He'd been on the panel of people to interview her.

"Yeah, that's him. You know him?"

"He interviewed me."

"No shit. Small world. You should like it there. They just redid the gym. If you wanted, I could talk to Colin about letting you use it."

Not this again. "That's okay. I'd rather stick to the park."

He nodded like he understood her reasoning when she knew he didn't. "Just make sure you mind the markers. Sometimes people sneak on our land to hunt. You don't want to get inadvertently shot."

No, that certainly wasn't on the agenda. She nodded.

"How often do you run?"

Not enough. "Every day."

His brows lifted. He was probably calculating her weight and calling her a liar. Well, she was trying. She'd only just started this new 'lifestyle'. Like calling it that instead of a diet made it better.

"I don't run unless something's chasing me," he said, and she laughed.

"I hate it." The confession slipped out before she could pull it back.

"Then why do it?"

"Because I don't want to be fat or die from some illness that stems from obesity."

He scowled at her then turned back to the wheel. "You *are not* obese."

"Uh, yeah, I am. Morbidly, actually."

"How much do you weigh?"

She balked. "You did not just ask me that!"

"Sure I did. How much? I bet you can't be more than one-seventy."

Well wasn't he sweet. She hadn't seen numbers that low in years. "You're way off."

"Girls overdramatize things. How much? One-eighty?"

"Stop asking."

"Why won't you tell me? It's just a number."

"You're not supposed to ask girls how much they weigh."

"Why? I'd tell someone if they asked me."

"Yeah, look at you. If I were built like you, I'd probably run around naked." Holy shit, did she really just say that?

He laughed. "That's always an option."

She stared at her lap. What was wrong with her? *So many things...*

"Come on, give me a number."

"No."

"Please."

"No!"

"Pretty please..."

"Why do you care so much?"

He shrugged. "You piqued my interests. I'm of the inquisitive sort."

She sighed and rested her elbow on the door, ignoring him.

"I weigh one ninety."

It was all muscle. She shot him a look telling him to drop it. Finally, when they pulled into the park, he relented. "Is that your car?"

"That's me."

The truck slid beside her tiny Chevy and he put it in park. She busied herself by wrapping the strings of her ear buds around her iPod.

"Well, thanks for the lift."

He turned and nodded. God, he was sexy. His eyes were incredibly blue against his tanned skin. His jaw was strong and dusted with brown shadow from his stubble. He should be doing Bounty commercials.

When she realized she was just sitting there staring and he had better things to do, she grabbed the door handle and yanked it open. It made a loud cranking sound. She jumped out of the truck and her knees nearly gave out. She overdid it today. "Well...thanks again."

"Nice meeting you, Mallory Fenton."

"You too." She shut the door and went to her car. He waited until the engine purred to life before pulling out.

Her head fell to the steering wheel. "You're such an idiot," she mumbled. She glanced back and saw the tail lights of his truck disappear. It was dark and scary in the park at night. Throwing her car in reverse, she quickly made her way home. It wasn't until she got to bed that night that she realized she hadn't even asked his name.

How hard was it to label vegetables? Mallory examined what could be squash or could be cucumber, and glanced around to make sure no one saw her sniff it. She stilled, mid-sniff, when she saw him, her mountain man, talking to another hunk of yummy man flesh and laughing down by the rolls in the bakery section. Where were they hiding these hot guys? Did they have a reservation on the mountain or something?

It had been two weeks since she'd last seen him. Two weeks and four measly pounds. Today she was actually dressed nice in capri jeans and a black T-shirt. Black was her signature color. It hid her lumpy parts best. Should she say hi?

Lowering the cucumber into her cart, she slowly strolled in his direction. Maybe they could be friends. It wasn't like she was winning any popularity contests in her new neighborhood. Most days, she watched television in her apartment until the reality shows pissed her off. Then she either went to bed with a book or Nick at Nite. How sad was she?

She approached the rolls and was accosted by the delicious scent of carbs. There was something wrong with a person who could smell bread through plastic wrappers.

Her mountain man and the other guy were arguing over bagels. She cleared her throat and they both turned.

"Hi." When he gave her a blank stare, she nervously looked to his friend. Glancing back at him, she said, "Remember me? Mallory."

"Uh…" He looked to his friend then back to her. "Sorry?"

"We met in the woods. You gave me a ride back to my car…" Could he have really forgotten her? Mortification crawled up her spine and she fought the urge to turn and go hide in the juice aisle.

Of course he wouldn't remember her. Why would he? It wasn't like he found her attractive. He was rushing off to see his *girlfriend*. She was just an inconvenience, a tiny blip on a hot guy's radar.

"You must have me confused—"

"My mistake," she cut off his excuse. "I thought you were someone else." Her cart squealed as she pivoted out of the bread section and bolted in the other direction.

Idiot!

She didn't stop until she made it to the dairy aisle. What was wrong with her? She probably looked like a complete moron with her big, puppy dog eyes. *Pity me... I have no friends.* Jesus, he was probably embarrassed to have her come up to him in front of his hot friend.

She tossed some Greek yogurt and fat-free milk in her cart as she blinked back tears. No matter how much she could be the funny girl, nothing would ever remove the sad, fat girl inside. The one who always questioned how others saw her and knew boys never noticed her the way they noticed little twiggy bitches. That was mean and she knew it was her jealous conscience talking. She had plenty of lovely, skinny friends with great personalities. They were just at home—in the city—and she missed them.

She was cranky and emotional because she was fucking hungry! Sniffling, she checked out a carton of eggs and placed it on top of her items.

He acted like he didn't know you. Either that or he forgot about you. Both scenarios sucked. She needed to go out and make some friends. The loneliness was getting to her. But at thirty, that was a little hard to do. No one wanted to sit in a bar alone waiting for a stranger to talk to them. If she did that, she'd probably sit there all night watching people go by.

At home she wasn't a wallflower. She had a great group of friends who didn't understand why she'd take a job in the middle of bumblefuck Pennsylvania when she could be a secretary anywhere. She wanted to run away and find a new life. Last year's calendar had been bombarded with baby showers, anniversary parties, kids' first birthdays, and weddings. On the days her friends weren't celebrating their awesome lives, she'd sit at home, forgotten. It sucked being the last man standing.

Tracy's wedding had been her breaking point. When the DJ announced the bouquet toss and Mallory was the only one shoved onto the dance floor, she nearly died of embarrassment. She'd smiled and played the part, made a few sarcastic comments, and caught the damn flowers.

The guy who caught the garter didn't look too excited about having to put it on her leg. The true moment of mortification came when the stupid elastic lace barely stretched past her lower thigh. She'd shoved down her dress and walked right out to the parking lot without saying goodbye.

That night, after tossing her bouquet in the box with all the other dried bouquets she'd caught, she opened her laptop and Googled job listings. Her resume was forwarded to over twenty businesses, all over two hours away from the city.

She couldn't do it anymore. It was so hard,

constantly watching her friends kiss and smile and have babies. She wanted to run away. Then she had her doctor appointment and the last shred of her self-esteem turned to ash.

Her plan was to move away, lose weight, and come back in a year as the *New and Improved Mallory Fenton.* She took down all her pictures on Facebook and packed up her apartment the day after she was offered the job at Center County High. No one understood why she was moving and she didn't bother to explain.

All of her life she'd never been able to borrow anything but shoes from her size two friends. They wouldn't get it. They'd watched her diet since she was a little girl and she couldn't face them after failing again. But this time would be different. She wasn't going to quit. She was getting healthy and changing her thinking once and for all. No one would do it for her, so she was doing it for herself. The problem was…she missed her friends terribly.

THAT NIGHT, she did up her eyes, straightened her hair, and painted her nails. She was going out. There was a pub in town, O'Malley's, which seemed to cater to people her age. Her black spring dress covered just the right amount of leg and the empire waist hid a good amount of the bad. Her white cardigan would be warm, but hopefully the pub was air-conditioned. She made a habit of hiding her jiggly arms and the cardigan wouldn't be coming off.

She waited in the parking lot for some version of her mental pep talk to sink in. *Get out of the car.*

In the city, she and her friends often visited jazz clubs and good restaurants. Things were different here. *Maybe you over-dressed.*

As she watched people enter the pub she took note of the girls. She never really paid much attention to guys, as they never really saw her, but she always watched the girls.

Everyone who went into the bar wore jeans and T-shirts. Mallory had never been able to pull off that casual look. Her T-shirts were always cut too high or hung too wide. If she dressed down she looked like a slob, so she usually dressed up, which was fine in a city like Philadelphia. But out here in the boonies, she felt like a smacked ass in her kitten heels and dress.

Say you were coming from a funeral. Who died? She pressed her head into the steering wheel. *Just go home. Maybe Friends is on.*

There was a tap on her window and she jumped. Holy fuck. It was him. The guy from the grocery store. She turned her key and rolled down the window. Her mountain man smiled.

"I thought that was you. Fun's inside. What are you doing out here?"

Mallory stared, just stared. Did he suddenly

remember her? She frowned. It was an act, in the grocery store. He must not have wanted his friend to see her. Her lips tightened and she scowled at him.

"What? You suddenly remember me?" She couldn't help the snarky tone.

He frowned. "What are you talking about? Mallory Fenton, trespasser and jogger extraordinaire. How could I forget?"

What? Why was he being so nice? She didn't want to like him. Only a complete asshole would act like they don't know someone when they take the time to say hello. He'd embarrassed her. "Well, you sure had a brain fart the other day in the market."

"Uh...I haven't been to the market in months." He made a bashful expression. "I'm a momma's boy. She does all the cooking."

He lived with his mom? Wait, he was lying again! "I saw you. I looked right at you and said hi. You acted like you didn't know me."

He frowned then smiled as though something occurred to him. "When you saw me, did I have this tattoo?"

She looked at the arm he displayed. There was some sort of Irish tribal inked into his skin. How had she missed that before? His flannel had probably been covering it. "I don't know."

"You probably saw Luke, my brother. We're twins."

"It was definitely—wait, twins?"

He nodded. "Identical. People get us confused all the time."

Oh my God, you are such a total idiot.

She laughed nervously. "Oh. I didn't know you had a twin. You two look exactly the same. Might want to think about tagging your ear or something."

"Most people can tell by our tattoos. Wanna come in and have a drink?"

"How about a shot?"

"My kind 'a girl." He smiled and opened her door. She rolled up her window and pulled out the key. Relief repaired some of her hurt feelings as she walked toward the entrance with him, careful not to touch him. He didn't smell as woodsy as before. Tonight he wore light cologne that smelled really yummy.

"Why are you all dressed up? You have some fancy party to go to or something?"

"Or something."

He held the door and she stepped into the entryway. It was the usual pub done in greens and browns with dim lighting and pool tables. Nobody really noticed her coming in, but when her mountain man entered various people waved and called out to him. He nodded and put his hand on her back—causing her to tense—as he ushered her to the bar.

The bartender, a very sexy guy with striking blue eyes to match the blue highlights in his black hair came over and greeted them. "Finnegan, my man. Who's your friend?"

"Kelly, this is Mallory Fenton. Mallory Fenton, this is my brother, Kelly."

She smiled. "Another brother?"

"Aye, we're a big brood," Kelly said as he placed coasters on the bar. "What can I get'chya?"

"Mallory here would like a shot," her mountain man —Finnegan—said.

"Pick your poison," Kelly said.

"Tequila with lime."

Kelly nodded. "Finn?"

"I'll take a shot of Telly."

Kelly turned and prepared the shots. When they appeared in front of them, Finnegan raised his glass and said, "To trespassers and runnin' when something's chasing you."

She laughed and tapped her glass to his. The fiery liquid burned down her throat and she hissed. Her face puckered as she sucked on the lime. Dropping it in the shot glass, she said, "I needed that."

The two brothers smiled at her. "Where you from, love?" Kelly asked.

She hadn't eaten much that day and the booze was swirling nicely in her blood. She grinned. He called her love and she wasn't about to correct him. "Philly."

"Ah, a city girl. How'd you meet Finn?"

She glanced at Finnegan as his brother replenished their drinks. "We, uh, sort of just ran into each other."

"Solute," Finnegan said, raising his glass.

She tapped his and tipped the shot back.

"Where's Erin?" Kelly asked.

"She'll be here eventually. How about a Guinness? You ever try a car bomb, Mallory?"

"When you drop the shot in the beer?"

"Yeah. You gotta chug it."

She laughed. This was the most fun she'd had in weeks. "I'll be picking myself up off the floor soon."

"No," Kelly said, filling two pilsners with dark, black beer. "We'll pick you up."

He slammed down two beers followed by two creamy shots. She took a deep breath. "All right, show me how it's done."

Finn grinned and dropped the shot, glass and all, into his beer. The brew faded with a rising shade of tan. He tipped back the glass and guzzled. His throat was long and tan, rough with stubble. What a nice, little mountain man.

He slammed down his empty pilsner and the shot glass rattled inside. "You're up, Philly."

She grinned at his challenge and dropped her shot in her glass. It was difficult to drink. She wasn't the chugging sort, more of a light sipper. The beer was potent and strong and she wasn't sure she liked it. They cheered and patted on the bar, creating a wild drumroll that made her heart race and her grin tighten. When she swallowed the last sip she gasped and they roared with applause. Kelly reached over and rang a bell.

People looked to see what all the ruckus was and she flushed. Well, she'd wanted to make friends. This was one way to break out of her wallflower status.

Finn threw down a twenty. "Oh!" Where were her manners? She reached for her purse. "Here."

He waved her off. "Those were on me. So have you been running lately?"

Music kicked on and she shouted into his ear. "Why are you so obsessed with my exercise habits?"

He shrugged. "It's what I know about you. You run."

"I do other stuff."

"Like what? Drink?"

"Well, that too. I don't know. I like to go to restaurants…" Watch reality TV, sit at home alone and read, vacuum…" Never mind." *You're such a loser.*

"No, tell me. What else does Mallory Philly Fenton like to do?"

Kelly placed two ordinary beers in front of them and went to help some other customers. "I guess I don't really do anything since I moved here. It's kind of pathetic."

"Well, what did you do in the city?"

She shrugged. "Worked. Slept. Attended uncountable baby showers."

"Aw, women love that crap."

Her face scrunched and she drew back. "Who told you that? Baby showers suck."

"They do? My mom and sisters had one for Sammy last year and they all went nuts over it."

"Who's Sammy?" She was getting tipsy.

"My sister-in-law, Colin's wife. I told you, she works at the school."

"Oh. Right. Well, she may have loved it and maybe your mom, but most women find them tedious and annoying."

"Really?"

"God yeah! There's nothing worse than playing what's smeared in the diaper and wearing beribboned hats."

"Yeah, Sammy wore a hat!"

"Exactly," she said, tipping the neck of her beer in his direction. "They suck. If I ever have kids I don't want one."

"You get a ton of crap."

"True and baby stuff *is* expensive. I should know. I've bought enough over the past year. Maybe I'll have one, but with ground rules."

"There you go. And what are they sniffing out of diapers?"

"Melted chocolate or baby food. Some women even lick it."

"No!"

"Yup. Woman do all kinds of crazy shit when men

aren't around," she informed him, taking another sip of her beer.

He stared at her for a long moment, a half-smile crooking his lips. "Like what? Tell me more secrets about the female species."

"Oh, I don't know…okay. Women can have a closet full of clothes and nothing to wear."

"Even I knew that. Tell me something good," he said, sipping his beer. He had a great Adam's apple. Really nice and defined.

"Women fart."

"I have two sisters—well, three now—I know that too. You're gonna have to do better than that."

She thought for a minute. "When women have sleepovers we wear ugly clothes and old lady granny panties and there's no pillow fights."

His expression sobered. "Why would you tell me that? You just killed, like, hundreds of fantasies."

She laughed and smacked his shoulder. "No man really believes that."

"Sure we do. At least tell me when you girls use the locker rooms you all shower together."

It was her turn to sober. Nope, that definitely never happened. She'd mastered the art of a full wardrobe change without showing a spot of flesh years ago. He was staring at her with those expectant blue eyes. "Sure, we do that."

"Really?" His smile was back. He had great teeth.

She pushed him. "No!"

He tipped his head back and groaned. "You're killing me, Philly. What else you got?"

"There's a magic spot on a girls neck that will make her do whatever you want."

He stilled, beer tipped to his mouth and raised an eyebrow. "Where is this magical spot you speak of?"

"It's a secret."

"Oh, come on!"

She edged off her stool and stood. The alcohol had definitely gotten to her. She leaned close—wow, he smelled good—and ran her finger from his ear, down his stubble, to the curve of his shoulder. "It's right here."

He shifted and she knew she gave him chills. "I can see that." He sipped his beer and the moment was broken. "What else you got?"

"You guys need another one?" Kelly appeared in front of them.

"Shh, she's giving me pearls here, Kelly. Don't interrupt."

"Pearls of what?" Their empties were removed and replaced with fresh bottles.

"Girl secrets," Finn said.

"Oh, I know all of them," Kelly announced and Mallory had no doubt he did. There was something intoxicating about Kelly McCullough that every female probably reacted to, something that said *I'm a bad boy who will break your heart, but make up for it in the sack.*

Kelly turned away and Finn nodded for her to go on.

"Okay, women like a man in charge."

"Right, holding doors and picking up tabs. Got it."

"No, more than that. I mean really in charge."

"Like in bed?"

She nodded. "We work hard and make only a portion of what men make. When it comes to equality we don't want it in the bedroom. We want a man in charge."

"Really? Then why are women never in the mood?"

She snorted. "You're with the wrong woman."

"Story of my life," he muttered. "So you're saying when a woman says she isn't in the mood, she really is?"

"No, but if you get her there and are just the right amount of forceful…"

"That's a fine line."

"I guess. Tell me something about men."

"We love boobs."

"No shit. Tell me something I don't know."

"We love how soft a woman's skin is. What do women like?"

"Hands and arms," she answered quickly.

"Not butts and chests?"

"Well, that too, but not to the degree men probably assume. Hands can be incredibly sexy. I love a strong, calloused hand."

He turned over his palms. "I thought women wanted a soft touch."

"Not me."

"You're a little wild thing, aren't you?"

"Wild, yes. Little no."

"Don't do that," he said in all seriousness. "You're small. I tower over you."

"Yes, but I outweigh you." Her mouth was like a runaway train and she couldn't pull herself in when the opportunity to put herself down presented itself. She hated that. It was a total mood killer, but she always caught herself doing it.

"It's just a number."

"Says the one hundred and ninety pound man."

"Stop. Tell me what else women like."

"You know, I could be strung up for this. I'm betraying my sisterhood by sharing this information."

"Maybe you're helping the sisterhood."

True. "If a woman keeps playing with her hair it means she's horny."

"Women are always messing with their hair," he argued.

"No, not messing with, playing with." She twirled her hair as an example.

"All right, calm yourself."

"Shut up," she snapped, dropping her hair.

He chuckled.

"Finn?" They both turned and Mallory tagged her as

the 'girlfriend' the moment she saw her. Blonde, perky boobs, size negative two waist. This had to be the girlfriend.

Finnegan jumped off his stool and kissed her cheek. "Hey, baby." She shouldered him off and Mallory already didn't like the stink eye she was getting from the other woman.

"Who's this?"

"This is Mallory Fenton. She's from Philadelphia. Just moved here."

"Hi," Mallory said, already missing the fun they'd been having before the girl came into the room. The girl nodded with a tight lipped—oh, so fake—smile.

"Philly, this is Erin."

Awkwardness set in like a brick hurls through a sheet of glass. Mallory sipped her beer and tried to look away, but not before she noticed Erin pouting at Finnegan as she asked him to order a drink. Finnegan turned and did her bidding. It was hard not to curl her lip. *Where'd your balls go?*

Once the girlfriend had a drink in hand, some fruity concoction in a fancy glass, they sort of drifted away. Mallory was left sitting alone and, worse, she was too drunk to drive. A few guys piled into the seats beside her and acted like she wasn't there, repeatedly elbowing her and sloshing her beer as they told stories. The bar got crowded and she ordered water as she waited for sobriety to return.

Kelly talked to her for a few minutes in between customers, but the busier the bar got the less chances he had to check on her. Why did she drink so much? She wanted to go home.

Talk to the guy to your left.

She scanned the bar. Everyone was in pairs, trios, or groups. When her eyes landed on Finnegan and Erin she looked away. They were having a heated conversation by the exit. Why had she told him all those things? He'd likely be kissing Erin's magic spot within an hour. Ugh. She was pathetic.

The group of elbow nudgers left and she was relieved. As she sipped her water she tried to calculate her alcohol consumption in a made-up formula of time and beers per hour to determine how much longer she had to wait to drive.

"Excuse me?"

She turned and found a handsome guy in his early twenties. *Veal.* She looked over her shoulder and realized he was talking to her. Okay, she could do this. "Hi." She gave him her most friendly smile.

"Is anyone using this stool?"

Her smile faltered. "No."

"Thanks." And just like that, he dragged the stool away, and taking with it any hopes of someone else sitting beside her, providing some much needed company.

Fuck it. She was going home. After tossing a few

dollars on the counter, she slid off her stool and left. No one stopped her. No one even noticed she'd left. She should get in her car and drive straight back to Philadelphia.

But she didn't. She made it home safely, stripped off her clothes, pulled on her favorite nightshirt, and climbed into bed. Her fingers curled around the remote and she found Nick at Nite. Maybe she should get a cat —or twenty.

ugust was hot and buggy. Sweat burned her eyes as her soles slapped over the pavement. Her knees quaked with exertion. Fourteen pounds. She was so close to crossing the mini-goal of fifteen pounds by the end of summer. It was the only thing that kept her working.

As she jogged, she ran her slick arm over her brow and panted to the rhythm of Beyoncé. She could do this. Her brain played over images of supermodels and smooth bellies. No matter how hard she worked, she'd never wear a bikini. Her skin was scarred from carrying around too much weight and no diet could un-tattoo that road map. She hated stretch marks.

But this wasn't about being skinny. It was about being healthy. She had to keep telling herself that, because, while her scale proclaimed she was fourteen pounds lighter, her mirror informed her otherwise.

The marker on the park path came into view. Four miles. She should do five, but her heart wasn't in it today. As she approached the little mile marker her steps lagged and she strolled across the finish. Her shaking fingers uncapped her water bottle and she guzzled the lukewarm liquid.

A petite woman walking her dog and smiled. It took every thing Mallory had not to sneer at the skinny thing. God, when had she gotten so bitter? She unlocked her car and chucked the empty water bottle in the back. After rolling down the windows she blasted the air.

One week until she started her new job. Good thing, because she was going stir crazy. It had been weeks since she'd gone out. After the night she was ditched by Finnegan, she lost the urge to be social.

Don't blame him. He's not responsible for you.

When she returned home, she took a shower and bagged up her laundry to take to the Laundromat. Another exciting Saturday.

She didn't bother with makeup or a blow dryer. After lugging her bag down the steps, she carried it across the street to the Laundromat. Once the clothes were loaded and spinning away, she busted out a novel, and settled in to the awkward plastic chair for a long wait.

She was turning to chapter three when there was a knock on the glass. Startled, she glanced up and found Finnegan—or his twin.

"Philly!" The glass muffled his shout.

It was Finnegan. She stuffed the romance into her bag and waited as he entered the Laundromat. The bell chimed and he fell into the seat to her left. "What are you doing here?" he asked.

"Having my taxes done," she said, giving him a sarcastic look.

He laughed. "You snuck out the other night."

"Um, no…I sat at the bar alone for two hours and then went home."

"There were a bunch of guys around you. I thought you were inviting them to your magic spot."

Her brow lifted. "No. They were just next to me. I didn't talk to them."

"Oh, well, you should have come sat with us."

With him and Erin…no thank you. "I was tired."

"So what else is new? School starts soon. You nervous about your new job? I talked to Colin about you. He said he thinks you're gonna be great."

What was he, on speed? Wait, he talked to Colin? About her? It shouldn't have made her feel special, but it did. "I start next week."

He nodded. "Hey, you look like you lost some weight. Still running?"

Earth, swallow me now. "Thanks. I have a ways to go."

"Women," he muttered. "We're heading to O'Malley's tonight. Interested in joining us?"

"Who's us?"

"Me, my brothers, my little sister...Kelly will be there. My one brother's leaving for school tomorrow, so we're sort of sending him off."

"How many siblings do you have?"

"Six."

"Holy crap."

"Don't you have any brothers or sisters?"

"I have a sister."

"Older or younger?"

"Older. She's an attorney. Lives in Maryland. We don't talk much."

"That sucks."

"So, out of six, where do you fall in the line up?" she asked.

"Well, Sheilagh's the youngest, then Kelly, then Braydon, then me and Luke, then Colin, and Katherine's the oldest."

"Do you all live on the same property?"

"Sort of. There's the big house and then my aunt's house. We pretty much own the whole mountain. But it isn't like we're all crammed under one roof. Luke has his own place. Braydon's at school. It's just me, Kelly, and Sheilagh in the house right now. And she was supposed to start school this fall, but...I'm not sure what happened there."

"How old are you?

"Twenty-eight."

She rolled her eyes. "Great. I'm older than you."

He frowned as though he didn't believe her. "How old are you?"

"Let's just say every number I have is bigger than yours."

He nudged her with his shoulder. "You're grumpy today."

She stilled. She wasn't grumpy. Well, maybe a little. She was hungry and tired, but…he didn't know her well enough to comment on her moods. "I'm not grumpy."

"So you'll come out with us tonight?"

She shook her head. "Did you have some pixie sticks earlier or something? You're hyper as hell."

"It's a beautiful day. I'm just being chipper."

Maybe she was grumpy. "It's disgustingly hot out."

"Try working in it."

"What do you do?"

"I'm a logger." Holy shit, he was a real lumberjack. "What? Why are you looking at me like that?"

She shook her head. "No reason. So, you and Erin…"

"What about us?"

"Have you two been together long?"

"Yes and no. We've been on and off again for a few years. Half my family thinks I should just break up with her and call it quits."

"So why don't you?"

He shrugged. "Habit. We've always just sort of been Finn and Erin. I'll probably marry her."

He eyes widened. "You're family doesn't really like her and you are with her out of habit, but you'll *probably marry her*?"

"My family doesn't *dislike* her. At this point they're indifferent. And I want kids. She's a good girl, comes from an Irish family like mine…why not."

"Do you love her?"

"Sure."

Mallory didn't know what to say. He was so casual about it. Where she came from marriage was a big deal. Maybe it was different in small towns.

"Do you have a boyfriend?"

She laughed. "No."

"Why is it funny? You're pretty enough."

She didn't know how to take that. *Pretty enough.* Pretty enough for what? To have sex with? To not throw garbage at? He didn't necessarily call her pretty. Why the *enough?* Why not just *you're pretty.* "Thanks," she said dryly.

"What? I meant it as a compliment. You're funny, fun to hang around with, easy to make laugh."

"Ahh…all the qualities of a fat girl."

He scowled. "Don't call yourself that. You're not fat."

"I'm not arguing with you about this again."

"Then don't insult yourself in front of me." His tone

was sharp and she realized he wasn't playing around anymore.

"All right. Relax."

"You do that a lot, put yourself down. I think what you need is to stop obsessing over your looks."

At that, she took offense. "I do not obsess over my looks."

"How many miles did you run today?"

"Four. So what?"

He looked at his watch. "It's four o'clock. What have you eaten?"

"What do you care?"

"Just answer the question."

She sighed. "I had eggs for breakfast and a salad for lunch."

"That's it?"

"That's a normal amount of food."

"What if I held out a cheeseburger right now? Would you take it? I bet you would. I bet you'd even lick the grease off my fingers."

She bristled. "You're an asshole."

"What? I'm playing around."

All she could picture was her going at his hand, cheeseburger in fist, like Cujo. She stood. "I have to switch my laundry."

The door to the washer swung open with too much force. Her hands plopped the clothes into the hollow basin of the dryer. She slapped the wet clothes down.

"Hey, Philly, what gives?"

She ignored him and continued to scoop up and transfer her clothes. He caught her wrist, mid-toss. "Hey, don't ignore me. You're mad."

Her molars locked. "You make me sound like a heifer."

He made a sound in his throat and drew back. "No. You picture yourself that way. All I was trying to do was get you to go grab a burger with me. You totally mistook my meaning."

She stilled. "You were going to ask me out to eat?"

"Yeah, but I'm not down with rabbit food, so only if I could convince you to have some red meat."

She sucked in a slow breath and mentally called herself a million names. Not one of them nice. "Sorry. I thought…"

"I know what you thought. Look, I like you. I'd like to be friends. Try not to be so defensive. I'm not a mean guy."

No, he wasn't. *Friends.* That's how he saw her. Sure, she could spend days looking at him. He was gorgeous. But he only saw her as a friend, like one of the guys. It wasn't like she could afford to be picky. At the moment she had no friends. Finnegan was it. "Sorry," she repeated.

"Stop apologizing. Here, I'll help you fold."

He lifted the laundry out of the dryer next to the one she'd just loaded and she abandoned the wet clothes she was handling. Her hand snatched back the stuff he'd grabbed. "No!"

"Why?"

"My…private things are in there."

"Ah, some of those sexy granny panty unmentionables you told me about?"

"I should have never told you that stuff."

He laughed and checked her with his hip. "Nah, I'm glad you did. You weren't lying about the magic spot."

Ugh, images of Finnegan necking with Erin bombarded her mind. "Ew."

He chuckled.

They stayed at the Laundromat for another hour waiting for her things to dry. When everything was folded, he helped her carry her clothes home. Mallory slowly forced herself to stop seeing Finnegan as anything more than a friend.

He was fun and made her laugh and she enjoyed his company. He also had a girlfriend and that made him off-limits. There was also the fact that she wasn't his type, or anyone else's for that matter.

Once inside her apartment she awkwardly tucked her laundry in the bedroom and shut the door.

"You're place is nice."

"Thanks. It's small, but I like it."

He went to the fridge and started rummaging around. "Can I eat this yogurt?"

"Um, sure…" He sure made himself at home.

The air from the window unit pumped into the living room and cooled her skin. Her hair was flat because she didn't dry it. Her instinct was to pretty herself up in any guy's presence, but if they were just friends, why bother? It was sort of refreshing to not have to give a shit.

"When are you going to O'Malley's?"

"When are *we* going, you mean? I don't know. Not until later. Wanna watch a movie?"

"Sure."

He plopped down on her couch, his long legs stretching out. He was so damn tall. "You can go on Netflix and pick something. The remotes in the drawer."

He shifted around and grabbed the remote. "Do you like scary movies?"

"No."

"Oh, come on, Philly, where's your adventurous side?"

"I don't have one."

"Pussy."

She stilled and slowly pivoted to face him. "Did you just call me a pussy?"

His broad shoulder lifted. "Watch something scary and prove me wrong."

"Don't be a tit. I'm not going to be bullied into something I don't want to do."

He laughed. "A tit? A tit? That's a new one. Come on, watch a scary movie with me."

She grabbed a yogurt and a spoon. "Jesus, you're needy. Fine. But when I have nightmares I'm calling your ass at one in the morning."

He grinned and scooted over. After he selected a film, he settled in and peeled back the lid to his yogurt. The credits opened and already she was nervous. There was a doll with no eyes sitting on a windowsill while a little girl swung on a swing and sang—her voice just the right amount of eerie and empty. The movie abruptly stopped.

"Okay, what the fuck am I eating, because it's not yogurt?"

She frowned and swallowed the spoonful in her mouth. "Yes it is."

"No it's not. I like yogurt. This disgusting sludge I definitely do not like."

"It's probiotic."

"Probi-what?"

"Biotic. It has microorganisms—"

"Okay, we're ordering pizza." He stood and dug out his phone. He was dialing before she could get out another word. He ordered a large plain and demanded her address then hung up and snatched her yogurt out of her hands.

"Hey, I was eating that."

"Not anymore." He faced her. "Philly, do you know what a microorganism is?"

"Yes. They fight bacteria—"

"They're bugs. Little microscopic bug-like things that belong on a slide in a lab, not in your stomach."

"It's good for you."

"So is pizza."

"No it's not."

"Sure it is. There's tomatoes, dairy, grains…it's got three of your basic food groups."

"I can't eat pizza. I'm on a—"

He held up a hand. "I don't want to hear it. You can and will eat pizza because we're watching a movie and going drinking later and you can't go drinking on an empty stomach. So suck it up. I'm not making you eat the whole pie. Just have a slice or two, but I need real food, not bug-gurt."

Pizza did sound delicious. She hadn't had any in months. Maybe just a slice. That was it. She'd have one slice and that would be her dinner.

Argument over, Finnegan picked up the remote, and started the movie. Mallory settled into the corner of the couch and, while the movie drew her attention, the fact that there was a six-foot man in her home distracted her more.

She'd grown up with guy friends. It wasn't a novel experience being around men. But there was something inherently different about being there with Finnegan, on her couch, in her home, as the sun slowly faded into golden shadows filtered through the curtains, playing over his tanned skin and yummy, supermodel stubble. She should turn on a lamp.

While her head remained turned to the screen where a mother screamed and a father stalked a house with a gun, her gaze kept drifting to the right. Her mind was very conscious of her stiff posture. Knowing they were just friends was not enough to let her fully exhale and slouch. Years of habitually sucking in around anything with a penis weren't going to be rewritten simply because one guy declared a platonic truce.

When someone banged on the door she jumped. Finnegan paused the movie on a startling frame of a little girl going through some sort of exorcism and stood to get the pizza. He had the delivery guy tipped and on his way before she could even get her purse.

"Plates?"

Mallory handed him two plates and a stack of napkins. He carried the steaming box to the coffee table and flipped back the lid. *Sweet mother of cheese!*

"Stop eye-fucking the pie and grab a plate," he said, tearing off a stringy triangle.

She sat down and mumbled, "I wasn't eye-fucking…"

He laughed and dropped a greasy slice onto her plate. She eyed the slice, knowing just one bite could be her downfall. Finnegan inhaled his first piece and tore off a second.

"You gonna eat, Philly?"

Hesitantly, she lifted the floppy slice, heavy with hot grease and cheese, and bit the tip. She moaned almost sexually as the warm tomato sauce and firm crust melted in her mouth and he laughed.

She didn't just eat that pizza, she savored it, eyes closed, senses devouring everything down to the warm flavor on her tongue and the weight of the crust in her hand. It quite possibly could have been a sexual experience, handled with such reverent tenderness and hedonistic gratitude.

Her eyes flew open when her plate grew heavy. Finnegan tossed another slice on her plate and ripped off his third. Only a quarter of the pie remained in the box.

"What are you doing?" she asked.

He shoveled a good four inches of folded pie in his mouth and raised an eyebrow. "What do you mean?" he asked over a mouthful.

She placed her plate on the wax paper in the box and closed the lid. "I can't have anymore."

His brow lowered as he slowly chewed and studied her for a long moment. Once he swallowed, his Adam's apple making a slow bob, he put his plate on the table and turned to face her with his arm resting carelessly over the back of the couch, his knee brushing her leg.

"What?" she asked, jerking her gaze to the floor.

"Why do girls diet?"

"Because being healthy is important."

His lips pressed tight. "Yeah, but you are healthy. You run every day, your fridge is filled with rabbit food and bug-gurt, when's enough, enough?"

It'll never be enough. "I need to lose thirty pounds." *At least.*

"Who says?"

"My doctor."

"Why though? You're not fat."

She winced at his blunt use of the F-word. "Finnegan, there is an extreme difference between me and other girls. Don't act like you don't see it."

When his focused gaze ran over her body, pausing at every bulge and curve, she'd wished she could retract the accusation. "But you don't look bad."

"Thanks," she mumbled, her ears heating under his scrutiny.

"What happens when you lose thirty pounds? Do you eat like a normal person and stop running?" His tone was baiting.

"No. It's a *lifestyle* choice, not a diet."

He was quiet for a long moment and she fidgeted under his inspection. When he spoke his voice was gentle, as though she were something fragile that could break. "Who was mean to you, Philly?"

Her head snapped up. "What? No one." *Liar.*

He eyed her skeptically. Faces from her past flitted through her mind. Taunting whispers of skinny cliques sniggering behind her back but within earshot. The dress rehearsal during high school when her costume barely covered her butt and she pretended to have Mono the entire week of the play so she didn't have to wear it. The uncountable guys in college who were offended she'd even *think* she had a right to bat her eyes in their direction. The way her aunts made comments about how she had such a great personality in comparison to her sister's beauty. The night she was lectured for ordering beer at a take out pub because the bartender assumed she was a pregnant. So many terrible memories, each one a sharp blade slicing through her pride, made it impossible to answer.

"How much have you lost so far?" he asked. She blinked, considering his question.

Why was he so curious? She had no tears on the subject of her weight. Tears didn't count for calories shed so why bother? "Fourteen."

"So you have sixteen to go?"

"No, I have thirty to go."

His brow lifted nearly to the soft hair at his temple. "That's a lot of weight to lose. Why is that your magic number?"

She leveled him with a stare and sighed. "Fine. Here goes. I haven't been small since I was twelve and even then I thought I was fat. My hips were always a bit wider than my friends and my legs a little thicker and my boobs a little bigger. Every year I gained ten pounds like clockwork until I started fanatically counting everything I put in my mouth. I'm overweight, but I'm an expert dieter. When I crossed two hundred pounds I panicked. I didn't always utilize the healthiest solutions. I've done pills, shakes, starvation, cleanses, nothing but produce, and things too dangerous and shameful to mention. Nothing worked."

"All that quick fix infomercial crap is bullshit. That's why."

She stared at the carpet, her fingers wringing on her lap. "I hate what I see when I look in the mirror." Her voice cracked. "It hurts sometimes, physically hurts, when you see yourself and despise it so much."

The warm weight of his palm pressed into her knee. She couldn't look at him. She was too afraid she'd find pity in those sharp, blue eyes. Her voice was a low whisper as she went on. "When I saw my doctor last spring, he scared me. My family doesn't have a great medical history and he basically assured me that if I didn't do something I was going to die."

He scoffed. "That's a little dramatic. You know the difference between God and doctors, Philly?"

"What?"

"God doesn't think He's a doctor."

She laughed, but barely. "He's right, though. I'm not healthy. I'd love to be skinny, but I don't think that's realistic. But there's a part of me that felt like such a fat failure walking out of that office I just wanted to prove that doctor wrong when I went back for my next check-up. I saw the arrogant way he looked at me. He thinks I'll fail and I don't even have the track record of willpower to claim he's wrong."

"You're way too hard on yourself."

"Why shouldn't I be?" she snapped, turning her glare on him. "Look at me, Finnegan. I don't look like a healthy person. I saw your girlfriend and all those other girls at the pub the other week. You have no idea what it feels like to always be the biggest person in a room."

"Mallory, you were *not* the biggest person in the room." His voice was sharp and anger swirled in the depths of his denim blue stare.

"You don't understand. Look at you! How could you understand?"

"You think I don't have insecurities?" He demanded. "You think I don't look at myself and see things I hate? You're crazy if you do. Everyone hates some part of himself or herself. Jesus, I can't even have a functional relationship."

She scoffed. "At least you have a relationship."

"Half the time I think Erin despises me. She breaks up with me almost every month. She never compliments me, but has plenty to say about how I come up short."

Then why are you with her? She didn't understand

why people settled for less than what they deserved. So many times she blamed her unyielding standards for her sentence of singledom. It made no sense that a man like Finnegan McCullough should suffer a dysfunctional love life.

"Sometimes I think I'd be happier without a girlfriend," he quietly admitted.

"Then why don't you break up with her?"

He shrugged, his gaze focused on the ground. "I'm afraid to be alone. My whole family's nuts. Being around them is like being stuck in a biblical outbreak of locusts. They're everywhere. It's overwhelming, but they all seem to know their ranks. Colin's the good boy. Kelly's the rake. Sheilagh's the wild child. Kate's the maternal one. Braydon's the student. And Luke's the…" He shook his head. "Who am I? All I've ever done is log the land under my dad's shadow. That's all I'll ever be. And men like that, they marry and have a league of children so someone can carry on their legacy when they're too old to do it anymore."

She frowned. "You're twenty-eight. It isn't like you have to lock your life in by thirty. If you don't like what you're doing, do something else."

"But they depend on me. My dad's getting older and so are my uncles. I don't hate being a logger. It's good money and eventually the company will be mostly mine on paper. I just begrudge never really being given a choice. It's like my life was chosen the same day they chose my name."

"Is your twin, Luke, a logger too?"

His mouth opened and he hesitated. "Yeah, but Luke's different."

"Why?"

"Because he'll come to a point where he can either pretend to be someone he's not or leave Center County."

"I don't understand."

His lips pursed. "Luke's a private guy and Center County isn't the most accepting community. I just… know there will come a time when he decides to leave and I can't blame him."

His cryptic words weren't making much sense, but she didn't want to press him to reveal more than he was comfortable with. "If you didn't work with your family, what would you do?"

His broad shoulder lifted and dropped. "Don't know. Never really had the option, so I never really gave it much thought. I like my job, don't get me wrong. I'm just saying that my life isn't a bowl of peaches. Most days I'm bored out of my mind and want to just take off and never look back."

"So why don't you?"

"Because my mom would lose it and my dad needs me. I'm just not that guy. I'm Finn McCullough, always there to haul the load no one else wants to carry."

She smiled. "There's nothing wrong with being dependable."

"No. There's not. It just gets old sometimes." He sighed and stretched.

The default screen appeared on the television, sending the movie into sleep mode. She watched the logo bounce slowly from corner to corner as Finnegan rested his head on the back of her couch. Perhaps their heart-to-heart was over.

"When are you going to run once you start work?"

Her lips pursed. She'd been wondering the same thing. "I guess at night."

"What about when it starts getting dark earlier?"

"There will always be an excuse at the ready. I'm trying not to use them."

"We have a field on our property. It's a flat track and no one goes there unless there's a scheduled game. If you wanted to, you could run there. There are lights."

She blinked at him. "Why are you offering?"

"Because I know it's important to you and I know once daylight savings starts it's going to be hard for you to keep up with it. Night's a whole different thing here than what it looks like in the city. You can't see past your nose on some nights. And there are animals you need to watch out for."

Warmth spread in her chest. It was precisely that moment that she realized Finnegan McCullough was, in fact, her friend. "Thank you."

CHAPTER 4

Mallory frowned over the black dress pants and blouse on her bed. Her wardrobe needed to be toned down for nights around town. She had no middle clothes. In her closet hung an assortment of outfits perfect for work and her drawers were packed with loungewear. There was no in-between.

She looked at her watch. Finn said he'd meet her at O'Malley's at eight and she was running out of time. She opened her closet and inspected the hanging garments once again, as if something perfect would magically appear.

Her gaze snagged on the big plastic bin of items she had yet to unpack. There were skinny clothes in there from years past, items she loved and didn't have the heart to let go of.

She moved a few boxes and dragged the tub out of the closet. The top popped off with a sealed snap and she tossed it to the floor. Her hands sifted through a hodgepodge of shirts and jeans that were likely out of date, but she loved them all the same. When she landed on an old pair of perfectly worn-in jeans, she smiled.

She loved those jeans. It was ridiculous for a piece of denim to hold so much nostalgia. Her heart steeled itself for the emotional disparaging that usually followed when trying on clothes.

Slipping out of her sweats, she stood and slid the jeans over her legs. She fell back on the bed and hiked them over her hips, sucking in to do the buttons. She stilled, her mind hollow without a thought as the zipper glided up without a hitch.

Frowning and blinking, she tucked her chin against her chest and tried to see over her boobs. That wasn't right. She rolled off the bed and went to the mirror. They fit. Holy shit, they fit!

Her hands gathered up her shirt as she twisted in front of her reflection, admiring her hips and hating the bulges that haunted her since adolescence. If she could hide those nasty parts she could wear the jeans.

She returned to her closet and tugged down a loose fitting, swoopy shirt that had a swatch of lase sewn in over the chest. The purple top slid over her skin and she returned to the mirror. She actually looked pretty good. Her fingers tugged the top over her hips and she nodded.

The shoes she intended to wear wouldn't go and there was a vain part of her that could only go so casual. She dug in her closet and produced a pair of peek-a-boo toed black pumps. Wedging her feet into the heels she stood and smiled. This was an improvement indeed.

As she drove to the bar, the radio gods seemed to be celebrating with her. Nothing but great songs played as she consistently reminded herself she was in her skinny jeans.

As she parked, she looked for Finn's truck. When she didn't see it, she hesitated. *You can go in without him.*

She lamented her lack of wingman only a minute or two before her bolstered, skinny jeans pride insisted she make a move. Locking her car, she grabbed her purse and headed into the bar.

The atmosphere was familiar and unfortunately a reminder of how she'd invisibly slinked out the last time she was there. *You can do this.*

When she spotted Kelly at the bar, she smiled and made her way in that direction.

"Hey, Philly! Long time no see, m'lady."

"Hi, Kelly." She settled onto one of the many vacant stools and checked her watch. It was ten after eight. Finn should be here any minute.

"What are you drinking tonight?"

She ordered a glass of wine, thinking the narrow stem would add a level of sophistication to her look. *You're insane.*

Kelly produced a glass of merlot and went to help another patron. Mallory turned and surveyed the bar. Sitting at the bar on the tall stools felt a little like she was on display.

She recalled how Finn had eventually migrated over to one of the booths the last time they'd been there. O'Malley's was somewhat empty at the moment so she had her pick of the litter. Her gaze settled on the table in the back corner and she plucked up her glass and headed that way.

After sliding into the booth, she placed her glass on the table and settled in for some people watching. The door continuously opened as new people arrived. Each time the bell rang she held her breath waiting for her friend, but suffered a bite of disappointment when a stranger appeared.

The bell rang and in walked a face she recognized. Mallory slumped a little lower, ducking into the shadows and watched as Erin made her way to the bar. Kelly's welcome of his brother's girlfriend was indifferent. He handed her a beer and quickly moved on.

Erin wore tight jeans and a fitted, pink flannel with cute tucks over her thin arms. Her shoes were nothing more than flip-flops and her hair was straight and pale gold. Somehow Mallory knew she was one of those girls who didn't have to bother with straighteners and blow dryers. She was very pretty in a low maintenance way Mallory envied.

She frowned as Erin sidled up to a man in a green T and rugged Levis. Mallory's frown turned to a protective scowl as Finn's girlfriend nudged the other man with her hip. The man drew her close, draping his arm over her hip and whispered something in her ear.

The bell above the door rung and Erin immediately put space between her and the man. Her eyes darted to the entrance and she relaxed when a man Mallory didn't recognize walked in.

Erin whispered to the man. He glanced at the door and whispered something back. Erin smiled and batted her gold lashes, then sauntered away to the bar. Mallory glanced at Kelly who was preoccupied at the bar. Her gaze returned to Finn's girlfriend who sat alone at the table in the front, her fingers rapidly moving over her phone. Was she texting Finn?

The door opened again and a group of guys came in followed by one young girl with striking red hair. Mallory ducked a little more into the shadows. If Erin was pretty this girl was breathtaking.

The guys all seemed to surround the redhead with a protective air and Mallory wondered what made a girl so lucky. The redhead laughed and slid onto a stool at the bar, resting her arms over the edge of the counter as she shouted for Kelly.

Finn's brother turned and smiled as a rowdy cheer broke out from the group surrounding the redhead. They were all obviously very close. Drinks were served and the group sidled around the bar like puppies in a barn, each person crowding over the other and reaching for whatever they needed.

Mallory drew back as she saw Erin roll her eyes and shove her phone in her purse. She didn't look happy. The girl stood and strolled over to the group of newcomers, a fake smile taking the place of her frown just before she made her presence known.

The group turned and Mallory gasped. Every single one of them was beautiful. The redhead glanced at Erin then rolled her eyes, turning back to the bar as if she had better things to do. The men all smiled politely.

Mallory recognized some of them. The blond man she'd never seen before, but the rest of them seemed familiar. Her shoulders tightened when her gaze landed on the man she saw at the market with Finn's twin.

The bell rang and the door opened. Finnegan and his twin walked in. It was odd that she suddenly had no problem telling them apart. It wasn't the difference in their tattoos or clothes. It was the glint in their eyes and the set of their shoulders. They were identical, but very different in subtle ways.

Finn had a kindness to his gaze that was absent in his twin's eyes. His twin looked like a man burdened by secrets. He lacked the ease Finn displayed, as if he wasn't comfortable in his own skin.

She watched from the shadows as they joined the others at the bar. The redhead, when she spotted them, lit up with a stunning smile, nothing like the uninterested way she greeted Erin.

They were each handed a beer and Finn draped his arm over Erin's shoulders. His date scowled at him and he seemed to tease her. She shouldered off his touch and he visibly sighed. Was this what his life would be like if he married her?

Mallory searched the bar and saw the guy Erin had first talked to before Finn's friends arrived. He was watching the group as closely as Mallory had been.

"Hey."

She turned and found Finn standing beside her table. "Hey."

He slid into the booth and she glanced nervously back at his group of friends. Erin was leering at them. She cleared her throat and sipped her wine. "Are they your siblings?"

"Yup. Colin and Sammy are coming later. They have to get Tallulah to bed first."

"Tallulah?"

"My niece. Little devil. I think she's God's way of smiting Colin for giving up his priesthood."

She choked. "Colin was a *priest*?"

Finn chuckled. "Almost. He was in seminary for almost ten years. Then he met Sammy."

"Wow, he must really love her to give up something so meaningful."

He smiled softly and she recognized the envy in his distant gaze. "Sammy's something special. She makes Colin a better man than any white collar ever could."

"Were your parents upset?"

He sniggered. "No, but Braydon was. She was his girlfriend first."

"Braydon, your brother?"

He tipped his beer, pointing the neck to the blond at the bar. "Yup. He's over it, though."

Her eye's returned to Erin. She didn't look pleased that her boyfriend was talking to her. "Maybe you should go back over there with your friends."

He frowned. "They know where I am. If they want me they can come over here." He eased back, making himself comfortable and stretching out in the booth.

The redhead picked up her beer and flitted over to them, a young guy with blond hair on her trail. "Who's this?"

Finn shifted his legs, making room and she slid in beside him. "Sheilagh, this is Philly, a.k.a. Mallory Fenton. Mallory, this is my sister, Sheilagh, and my cousin, Patrick."

"Hi."

Sheilagh nodded, smiled kindly, and then turned to Finn. "What's up Erin's ass?"

He rolled his eyes. "I was late and she had to sit alone for twenty minutes."

Sheilagh snorted. "Oh, the horror."

Mallory wanted to point out Erin was only alone for about five minutes in reality, but it wasn't her place. Patrick straddled a chair at the end of the table and they talked about people Mallory didn't know.

After about twenty minutes of casual chit-chat, Finn's sister finished her beer and stood. "Are we ready to kick this off? I want one picture of Braydon hugging the toilet before he goes."

"You're evil," Finn commented, sliding out of the booth behind her.

"You love it."

The three of them stood and Mallory had to bite back her panic that they were leaving her.

Finn turned. "You coming, Philly?"

She smiled, completely relieved, and slid out of the booth.

He briefly looked over her outfit and smiled. "You look nice."

"Thanks. So do you."

They went to the bar and Kelly gave a Cheshire grin as he lined up several shot glasses. Erin sidled up to Finn and hissed something in his ear. He frowned and shook his head, whispered something back and then she stomped off toward the ladies' room.

Finn pasted on a smile, but Mallory saw through it. Shots were poured and there was a great sense of camaraderie that came with the weight of a shot being pressed into her palm.

"To our golden boy, Braydon. May his last year of school be the best he's seen yet!" Luke toasted.

The others raised their glasses and shouted, "To Braydon!"

Braydon, who of all the McCulloughs was the fairest of skin and hair, grinned and tipped back his shot. "Solute!" he said, slamming the empty glass back on the bar.

Mallory's eyes watered as her shot burned a path to her belly. She gasped and slipped the glass back on the bar with a shaky hand. "What was that?"

"'Tis the best Irish whiskey O'Malley's has to offer," Finn said.

"It tastes like shit," she grumbled, wiping her lips with the back of her hand.

He laughed. "Only the first one tastes of shit. After that your taste buds burn away and it's smooth sailing until morning."

"How can you drink that?"

"I'm Irish. It's expected."

She laughed. "Nothing like proving a negative stereotype wrong."

He nudged her with his hip. "We try."

"Hey, I know you," Luke said, coming to her side.

Finn tipped his head and said, "Yeah, I heard you two met at the market."

"You thought I was Finn, didn't you?"

"Sorry about that," she said, her face heating as she recalled how much of an ass she made of herself that day.

"No problem. So, where'd you come from?"

She, again, explained about how she recently moved from the city and the same connection was made that she would be working with Samantha McCullough in a few days. She hoped the mysterious Samantha would get there soon so she could put a face to the name and maybe have a work ally before her first day.

Mallory finished her wine and excused herself to use the bathroom. She headed past the pool tables in the back and turned down a dark, narrow hall and came up short.

Erin stood, back to the wall and a smile on her face, as the man from earlier braced his arm on the wall above her head. There was no mistaking the intimate pose for anything else. Mallory flushed and pivoted, going back the way she'd come and nearly plowing into Finn as she turned the corner.

"Whoa, Philly. No runnin' in the bar. Did you find the bathroom? That was fast."

"Finnegan," she said, enunciating his name louder

than necessary. Hopefully Erin heard her and knocked off whatever she was doing.

He frowned. "You all right?"

"Uh, yeah. That shot must've gone to my head."

"'Excuse me." She turned as the man who had been practically groping Erin in the hall came out looking innocent.

"What's up, Tim?" Finn said.

The man—*Tim*—nodded. "Hey, Finn." He kept walking. *Great. They know each other.*

Finn turned to her. "Did you see Erin in there?"

Lie or no lie? Thankfully she didn't have to answer. Erin came around the corner that very moment. She, too, took on an air of innocence that quickly turned to disapproval when she spotted Mallory. She had some nerve!

Finn smiled and took her hand. Mallory had to look away. She also had to pee since she never made it to the bathroom. "I think I left something in the bathroom," she mumbled and fled.

When she returned to the bar, the McCullough clan had acquired a large, round table. Erin perched on Finn's lap, her posture and touch affectionate. Mallory turned away and saw a woman she didn't recognize.

"Sit here," Sheilagh called to her, and Mallory settled in to a seat.

Colin turned and his face lifted in surprise. "Ms. Fenton. How are you?"

The formality was awkward and she wondered if it was in bad taste to drink with the man who'd hired her. "I'm good. How are you?" She couldn't bring herself to call him Mr. McCullough.

Sheilagh shoved him. "Don't be all formal. Mallory's a friend."

Colin looked contrite. "I wasn't being formal. I was being polite."

"Whatever. I'm getting a drink. You want another glass of wine, Philly?"

She handed Sheilagh some cash and thanked her. Colin scooted back. "Mallory, this is Sammy, my wife. She teaches AP English at the high school."

Mallory extended her hand and said, "It's nice to meet you. I've heard a lot about you."

"All good I hope," Sammy said. She was an all-natural beauty with dusty lashes and freckles. "Don't judge me. Tonight's my last night to let loose before I'm overwhelmed with grading papers."

Mallory smiled. "Not judging. I plan on doing the same, since I start a new job on Monday."

FINN WATCHED Mallory chat with his sisters and admired how easily she smiled and laughed. Erin was being awfully lovey and he wasn't sure what changed. Sometimes she was like dealing with a bipolar patient off their meds.

Her breath coasted over his ear, but it didn't have the same effect such affection normally did. On the contrary, it annoyed him. Tonight was all about hanging out with his siblings before Braydon left for school. He had the sense she was trying to get him to leave early, which would turn into an argument about him picking his family over her.

"You smell extra good tonight," she whispered, her breath soft and warm on his neck.

He shifted in his seat and gave her hip a squeeze, not seeing the need to comment.

She sat up, pressing her breasts into his chest. "We should sneak out to your truck for a bit."

He frowned, pulling his gaze from Mallory who was laughing heartily at something Braydon said. He looked down at Erin. She never—*never*—made offers to screw around in public places. It wasn't her style. He, on the other hand, didn't have a style when it came to sex.

"You're in rare form tonight," he teased and she bristled.

"So? Maybe I just want to have some fun for a change."

She made the comment as if nothing they ever did was fun. "I'm having fun here."

She groaned and pulled back, her breasts no longer flirtatiously close. "It's the same shit every Saturday."

He gave her a warning glance. "It's Braydon's last night."

"And last week was Kelly's birthday and next will be Sheilagh's and then your parents' anniversary and then some other lame reason to come here."

He stared, unsure how to respond to such clear contempt for his family. "If you don't want to be here you can go."

She scowled at him. "Why, so you can cozy up with your new friend? Where did she even come from?"

He drew back and grimaced. His eyes flickered over to Mallory who caught his glance and gave him a questioning look. She couldn't have heard Erin's comment. He nudged Erin off his lap. "Come with me."

He led her out of the bar and into the parking lot, turning her back against the brick siding. "What's the problem, Erin?"

She snatched her hand away and glared at him with nothing more than contempt. "What do you think? Every time I turn around you're talking to that girl."

"So? She's my friend."

"Since when, Finn? You have a girlfriend. She can go find another guy to pester."

He drew back. "You're jealous."

That seemed to outrage her. "*Of her?*" She scoffed. "Hardly."

"Well, maybe you should be. She's a nice person."

"What's that supposed to mean? That I'm not? If she's so damn nice, Finn, why don't you go out with her?"

"It's not like that!" He turned and shoved his fingers through his hair. "God, why are we always fighting?"

"Probably because you can't be on time for anything and when you finally do show up, you spend your time talking to everyone *but* me!"

"I talk to you all the time!"

"It's not the same, Finn. You laugh with you brothers and sisters. You don't laugh with me like that. And now you're laughing with some girl I've never seen before who hangs on your every word."

"That's not true," he argued, but his mind called him a liar. He did laugh with his siblings. He also laughed with Mallory. He couldn't recall the last time he and Erin actually had fun and laughed together, just the two of them.

He sighed. "Maybe I've been a little preoccupied with family stuff lately. My dad hasn't been feeling real well and my mom's overwhelmed with my grandmother. I'm sorry I can't always be there when you want me to be, but I can't just ignore my responsibilities."

"You have six siblings. Why don't your parents ask one of them for a change?"

It was the same argument they always had. "Colin's busy with his own family. Sheilagh helps out and Bray is leaving soon."

"What about Kelly?" she demanded.

"He's always working."

"They don't bother Luke, because he had the sense to move out, but you won't!"

"I'll move out when I'm ready to buy my own house."

She rolled her eyes. "When will that be, Finn? You've been making the same excuses for years. You're twenty-eight years old. I wish you would for once act like it."

He drew back as if she slapped him. "Is that what you think, that I don't act my age? What do you do, Erin? You work at the same place you did in high school and you wait around for me to come and entertain you. Why is it always me? When do I ever judge you as harshly as you judge me? You're right, I won't move out right now for the same reasons I wouldn't move out last year. My parents need my help with my grandmother. It falls on them, because my aunt and uncles are busy and have their own relatives to tend to. That's what family does."

"So I have to wait for your grandmother to pass away for you to make a move?"

He stilled. In a hushed voice, he said, "You don't have to wait for anything. Go buy a house if you want one so badly. I'm not stopping you."

Her eyes narrowed. "Maybe I will."

He'd like to see her try on her salary. There were times Erin came off as such an entitled princess it blew his mind. He sighed. "Why do we always fight?"

Her gaze drifted away for a moment. "Maybe we should consider seeing other people."

He jerked his gaze back to hers. "Where the fuck did that come from?" They'd broken up in the past over dumb shit, but never had either of them ever made mention of seeing—or wanting to see—other people.

"I'm just saying maybe this isn't working."

"You want to see someone else?" he demanded.

"Finnegan, don't act like you aren't checking out other girls."

He scoffed. "I have eyes like everyone else, but I've never been disloyal to you."

"Really? Where were you this afternoon? I called you five times."

His gut clenched. "I was with friends."

"What friends?" When he didn't answer, she snapped. "You were with that girl! Oh my God!"

"We're just friends!"

"Okay, well, I'm going to go make some new friends and you tell me how you like it."

She turned to leave and he caught her arm. "Don't. I'm not playing games."

"Neither am I," she sneered and tugged her arm away.

As she stormed off to the bar, he yelled, "So that's it?" He wished he had something better to say, but that was all he could come up with in that moment.

"Until you're ready to grow up and give me as much

—if not more—of your free time than you give your *friends* then yes, that's it. This isn't fun anymore and I'm sick of begging for your attention."

She disappeared into the bar. Music interrupted the silent night as the door opened and closed. He growled and pressed off the brick wall. If it weren't Bray's last night in town, he'd leave.

A door at the back of the bar opened and the sound of trash being thrown in the dumpster rattled in the silence. He turned and found Kelly brushing off his palms.

"Hey, Finn. Whatch'ya doin' out here?"

His head shook. "Erin and I had a fight."

"What else is new?" His brother must have seen something in his face that told him it wasn't a joke. "Sorry. You okay?"

He shrugged. "I'm so sick of being told I'm not doing enough."

"Does anyone ever do enough for Erin? She isn't exactly easy to please."

That was true. "Do you think I'm irresponsible?" he asked his younger brother.

Kelly laughed. "Finn, you're the most responsible McCullough I know next to Colin or Dad. Don't listen to anyone who says otherwise."

"Thanks."

Kelly eyed the back door of the bar. "I gotta get back

in there. You should too. You're little friend's no longer tasting the whiskey, if you know what I mean."

He laughed and headed back inside. Music belted from the speakers and his family overran the middle table. Bray looked like he'd gone through the ringer over the past thirty minutes. Sammy was slurring her words and petting his brother in a way the rest of them were still not used to seeing Colin touched. Colin didn't seem to mind in the least.

His gaze snagged on Mallory. She was laughing hysterically, her hair kinking under the heat of the bar and her skin glossy. She looked…nice.

He turned and scanned the bar for Erin. When he found her she was standing in the corner whispering to Tim. He frowned. Since when did they talk? He debated pulling her aside and apologizing, but the sound of his family laughing and enjoying themselves tugged at his attention.

"Hey, Finn," Luke called from the table.

He turned and pasted on a smile. "Yeah?" he said, heading over to finish his lukewarm beer. He settled into his chair.

"What was that teacher's name who always wore the lacy slip we'd peek at in middle school?"

"Ms. Fitzpatrick."

Luke clapped his hands. "That's it! She had a set of legs on her."

Finn gave a charitable laugh, feeling sorry for his

brother. Being his twin, they were somehow closer than the rest of them. Finn had known Luke was gay since they were thirteen. Fifteen years later, he'd hoped his brother would have the confidence to come out.

He wasn't sure how many of his siblings knew or if his parents were aware, but he was certain Tristan knew, as Finn was certain the two had been in a relationship for some time. It was one of the reasons Luke moved out.

Tristan lived with his cousins. He'd moved to Center County from Texas after college. From there he started working in the log yard with the rest of them and more nights than not, Finn caught his truck at his brother's.

Luke had been devastated when he blew out his knee in college thereby blowing his free ride. For two years, Finn worried his brother might never smile again, and then Tristan showed up and something changed.

It took Finn a few months to realize what was happening, especially since Tristan flirted with women constantly and Luke made jokes as though he were a hound with the ladies. But it was there, in the way the two glanced at each other, the subtle way they seemed to look out for the other, and in the not-so-subtle way they always left together.

What bothered Finn was the secrecy. Did Luke think they wouldn't accept him? All they wanted was for him to be happy. If Tristan made his brother happy then he was happy for them. Sometimes he wondered if any of his other siblings knew Luke was gay.

Finn glanced at Sheilagh. She was doing better. Finn suspected she'd found out their brother's secret as well. Since meeting Tristan, she'd had a crush on the man. Something happened about a year ago that changed her. She no longer seemed like the baby she'd always been. There was something a little colder in her green eyes that had never existed before, sort of like when a child learns the truth about Santa.

One of the waitresses appeared with a tray of shots. "This round's on Kelly. He said to wait for him."

They dealt out the shots and Kelly came to join them. The lot of them were rowdy and beyond manners at this point. Finn wasn't feeling it anymore, but tossed back the shot anyway.

Luke nudged him and whispered, "Hey, what's up with Erin? She's getting awfully cozy with Tim over there. You gonna say something?"

He shrugged. "She can talk to whoever she wants."

"You're way more forgiving than I am."

Finn gave him a look, tempted to ask how he could declare such a thing when every bit of Luke's private life remained private and Tristan flirted with his share of women, but never men. Maybe it didn't mean as much because they were only women.

His gaze snagged with Mallory's. She tipped her head

and frowned. He shook off her questioning glance. Her mouth moved. *You okay?* He nodded. She turned to say something to Sammy, but her eyes kept returning to his.

The night went on until the bar was ready to close. Finn was sober, so he took Sheilagh's keys to her SUV and shuttled out the first group of drunks. When he returned, it was only Kelly and Mallory sitting at the bar.

"What happened to everyone else?"

"Pat called Aunt Colleen to take the lot of them home."

"I told him I was coming back."

Kelly shrugged and bent to carry a tray of clean glasses to the back. Mallory was resting her head on her arms over the bar. "Hey, you alive?"

She grumbled something and lifted her head. Her lashes fluttered as she focused on him. "Your family got me drunk." She hiccupped and he laughed.

"They have a tendency to do that. Come on, I'll drive you home."

"Thanks," she slurred, stepping off the stool and losing her balance. He caught her elbow and steadied her.

"We're taking off, Kel."

"Drive safe," his brother called from the kitchen.

He ushered Mallory out the door and helped her into the SUV, figuring Sheilagh could take him to get his truck in the morning and he'd run Mallory to get her car.

She stumbled and cursed. "The ground's wobbly."

He chuckled. "You're wobbly. Those shoes probably aren't helping."

"I like my shoes," she announced then giggled. "Wanna know a secret, Finnegan McCullough?"

"What's that, Mallory Fenton?"

She leaned in and whispered, her whiskey scented breath a warm tickle at his cheek. "I can tell you because we're friends."

"What?" he whispered back.

"My jeans fit."

It took him a minute to follow and then it occurred to him that this was something monumental for her. He assumed they hadn't fit before she'd started starving herself and training like she was preparing for the Olympics. "That's good."

"That's great!" She corrected then informed him in a serious voice, "These are great jeans."

He looked down and evaluated said jeans. They were blue and denim, like every other pair to ever exist. "They sure are. Here, let me help you in the car."

He opened the door for her and she slid in. Her head rolled on the headrest. She was like a fish out of water on its last flop. His lips twitched as he fought the urge to laugh. Reaching over, he buckled the seatbelt and stilled when his hand accidently grazed her supple chest.

He cleared his throat. "Sorry." Backing up, he realized she'd passed out.

The ride back to her place was silent, being that his passenger was comatose. When he parked Sheilagh's car out front, he pulled the key and nudged Mallory. "Philly, wake up. We're home."

She snuffled and shoved him away. He got out and went around to her side. She was snoring softly when he opened the door. He undid her seatbelt and shook her knee. "Hey. Mallory. Come on, we have to go in."

She sighed. "Thanks for getting me to go out tonight. I had fun."

Leaning into the car, he stared into her eyes. They were blue like the ocean off the coast of the Caribbean. A small sprinkling of freckles showed through the powder on her cheeks and she smelled like soft flowers. Everything about her was soft.

He tugged her hand. "Come on. I'll help you up the stairs."

She climbed out of the car and stumbled as she plucked off her shoes. Once she removed her heels she shrank a good five inches, coming only to his chest. He followed her up her steps and waited as she fumbled in her purse for her keys. The task seemed to exhaust her. When she finally fished them out she had a hard time unlocking the door.

"You got to put it in the hole," he commented.

She snorted. "That's what she said."

He laughed and took the keys, making quick work of opening the door. She stumbled in and went straight through the door he assumed was her bedroom. He placed the keys on the counter and waited. "You gonna be all right?"

Something fell to the floor in a clatter and she cursed then burst into peals of laughter. He ran into the room. She was flopped over the mattress and her lamp was lit, but lying cockeyed on the floor. She laughed and then moaned. He knew that moan. That was the moan that came when your insides decided they wanted to be on your outside.

He quickly righted the lamp. Her bedroom was cute and neat. Teals mixed with lime greens in geometric shapes. It was girly, but cool. Not too frou-frou. "Come on," he said taking her hand and hoisting her up. "Let's get you to the bathroom."

"Don't wanna…" she mumbled as he brought her to her feet.

"I don't think you have much of a choice."

He ushered her into the small bathroom and propped her down on the lip of the tub. Let her wait it out a moment. If nothing happened he'd take her back to her bedroom.

Her head hung like dead weight between her shoulders and her soft brown hair teased at the pink bathmat. Her shower curtain was black with white and pink polka dots.

"Whiskey's the devil," she grumbled.

He laughed from where he stood propped against the doorjamb. "I've been there."

"How come you're not drunk?"

"Someone has to look out for the rest of them."

She peeked through the curtain of her hair and smirked. "You're a nice guy, Finnegan McCullough. I'm glad you're my friend."

"Me too."

Her hand swatted at her hair, pushing it over her shoulder. "I really should—" her shoulders jerked and she swallowed. Her face paled and then she fell forward and gripped the toilet.

"Fuck." He went to her side and gathered her hair as she emptied her stomach. Once he had her hair wrapped around his fingers and out of the way, he ran a hand over her back.

She whined and gripped the bowl. "Get out…"

"It's fine. I've been there. Just get it all out."

"I can't puke in front of you!" Her next sentence was cut off as her body proved her mouth a liar.

He waited there, rubbing her back and offering her tissues until the worst of it seemed to pass. "I'll be right back." He went to the kitchen and poured a glass of water. He looked in her cabinets for crackers, but found none.

When he returned to the bathroom she was sprawled over the toilet, her face pressing into the cool lid. "Here, drink this."

She took the water and guzzled it down. "I can't believe you just heard me puke."

"Saw you puke too."

She shot him a mutinous glare and finished her water.

"Do you have crackers?"

"No crackers. Carbs are the devil."

"I thought whiskey was the devil?"

"They're both evil."

He lowered himself to the floor, figuring he should wait a few minutes before moving her. "Did you have fun tonight?"

"Yes. You're family's really cool. I like Samantha a lot."

"Sammy's great. You'll have fun working with her."

"We're gonna have lunch together on Monday."

"That's good."

She sighed and snuggled into the toilet as if it were a down pillow. "Hey, what happened to Erin?"

Finn sighed. He stretched his legs over the narrow space of tile. "We had a fight and sort of broke up again."

"What did you fight about?"

"The same old bullshit. Me not giving her enough

attention. Her wanting me to move out of my parents' house."

"To live with her?"

"To buy my own place."

She frowned. Her lashes drooped over her eyes and he knew she wasn't at her cognitive best at the moment. "How does you moving out of your parents' house affect her?"

"Because I think she assumes my house will eventually be hers."

"Does she live with her parents too?"

"Yeah."

"Well then why doesn't *she* move out?"

"Exactly."

She rolled her eyes and mumbled something he didn't catch.

"What?"

"Nothing. If you ask me…"

"What?"

"Nothing. Never mind. It's not my place."

"Say it. We're friends. I want to know what you think."

She seemed to hesitate. "I think you can do way better than her."

He frowned. "You don't really know her."

"I know the kind of girl she is."

Erin was someone he cared about on some level. It

was hard not to come to her defense. On the other hand, Mallory had never been anything but honest with him and she wasn't the type to put people down for no reason. In truth, he'd never heard her say a bad thing about anyone aside from herself. "What kind of girl is she?"

"The kind who is always looking for a better, faster solution."

"What do you mean?" For not truly knowing Erin, she seemed awfully insightful.

"I saw her talking to some guy before you got there tonight."

He stiffened. "Who?"

"The guy who came out of the bathrooms after me. Should I be telling you this?"

"Yes. What was she saying to him?"

"I don't know. I wasn't close enough to hear, but they were real cozy and she kept checking the door. The minute your family showed up they acted like perfect strangers and she sat alone for a while. Then when I went to use the bathroom…"

He forced himself to breathe slowly. "What happened at the bathrooms?"

"I found them in the hall. He was leaning over her like he was about to kiss her or just had."

His teeth clenched. "Did she look angry?"

Mallory's lips tightened into a sympathetic smile. "No."

He looked away. He was pissed, but not that some

guy was hitting on Erin. Strangely, he was pissed she'd made a fool out of him. He really didn't feel any sort of jealousy for her when he pictured her with Tim. The two of them actually made sense as a couple on some level. It was weird that he could admit that to himself.

"Are you mad I told you?"

"What? No, of course not. You're just being honest and telling me what I asked."

"I'm sorry."

"You didn't do anything."

"But now you're sad."

"Mallory, I'm not sad. I'm angry and curious how long whatever they have going has been going on, but I'm not really sad about it."

"Are you going to go back to her if she asks you?"

He sighed and pressed his head into the wall, staring up at her ceiling. "I don't know."

"Finn, she's cheating on you!"

"You don't know that. You didn't actually see them kissing, right?"

She scoffed and sat up. "No, but it was obvious they'd kissed before."

He was silent for a while. Over the years it had always been Erin. She'd become a fixture in his life he sort of depended on to always be there. In the beginning he'd wanted to do things one on one with her, but over time that urge sort of fell away. They barely even had sex anymore and when they did it was nothing to write home about.

"Did you ever do something habitually even though you knew it was bad for you each time you did it? You get so used to doing it you don't even really enjoy it anymore, but you can't stop for some reason."

She snorted and sat up. "Hello? I eat."

"That's not the same—"

"Of course it is. I don't even really like donuts, but if you put one in front of me it has about a thirty second life expectancy."

He frowned. "Then why eat it?"

She shrugged. "Because I know I shouldn't and knowing that tells me I may never have one again so I better take it before the offer's off the table."

"That doesn't make any sense."

"I know. Neither does dating someone you don't enjoy when you can do a hell of a lot better."

He shifted. His ass was going numb. "Do you think you're going to puke anymore?"

"No. But hey, I gave back my pizza so that means we can eat the rest of it."

He frowned. "That's not funny, Philly. I better not find you messing around with that shit. Bulimia can kill a person. You're smarter than that. "

She drew back and scowled at him. "I don't make myself vomit, Finnegan. I'm not thirteen anymore."

Her answer should have reassured him, but it didn't.

It only told him that once she'd been desperate enough to try something as dumb as purging.

He stood and held out a hand. "Come on, let's get you to bed."

"I'll be there in a minute. I gotta brush my teeth and pee."

He stepped out and shut the door. As he waited he looked at the pictures scattered throughout her apartment. There was one with three other people he assumed were her family. Her sister looked nothing like her. She was tall and all sharp edges, while Mallory was small and soft. She had a smile that was contagious.

The toilet flushed and the sink turned on. He replaced the picture and turned as the door opened.

"You are so lucky we're just friends. I look like death."

He smiled. She didn't look like death. She looked cute. Her hair was twisted up in one of those sexy, sloppy knot styles girls did and her face was scrubbed clean of all traces of makeup. She smelled like floral soap and mint.

"I'm going to change into pajamas. I'm not really tired anymore. You want to finish our movie?"

"Sure."

She was still intoxicated, he noted, when she tripped over the lip of the rug and cursed and giggled. He had nothing better to do, so he settled onto the couch and set up the movie where they'd left off.

She returned from the bedroom wearing cotton pants with candy canes on them and a sweatshirt that was way too big for her. In her arms she held a fluffy blanket and two pillows.

"Here," she said tossing him a pillow.

He wedged the pillow under his shoulder and waited as she fluffed the blanket and maneuvered around. She seemed to be having a hard time of it. "You all right over there?"

"I…I can't…I can't get the damn blanket to open."

He laughed and gave the corner a tug.

She plopped down and let out a breath. "Thank you. The stupid thing was fighting me."

He eyed the blanket. "It *was* being quite ferocious."

She gave him the finger and he started the movie. He knew this was where they'd left off, but he had no idea what was going on. The woman on the screen screamed as some guy ran through the house with a rifle. Was he the killer? No, wait, that was the husband.

This movie sucks.

Mallory's feet brushed his knee. "Sorry."

"It's okay. Stretch out. I don't mind. Here." He rested a throw pillow over his lap and pulled her feet on top.

She sighed and shut her eyes. The people on the screen carried on. It seemed like the climactic moment of the movie when all hell breaks loose, but he found her little pudgy toes more interesting. They were painted bright pink and had daisies drawn on them. Who could paint a flower that small?

"You know what would make this perfect?" she asked and he jerked his gaze away from her feet, a guilty flush heating the back of his neck.

He cleared his throat. "What?"

"Ice cream."

"You *are* drunk."

She laughed. "Yeah, but ice cream would be damn good right now, drunk or not."

"Do you have any?"

She snorted. "No."

"Want me to get you some bug-gurt?"

She made a gagging face. "That is so not the same thing and you know it."

He laughed. "What happened to Little Miss Superior?" He mimicked her city twang, *"Tastes fine to me."*

She scrunched up her face and stuck out her tongue. He pinched her toe and she yelped, drawing her feet back. They turned their attention to the television. He was sure she was about as interested in the movie as him.

Each time he peeked at her, the lashes of her eyes hung a little lower until finally they remained closed. He rested his head on the back of her couch and shut his own eyes, not bothering to open them again until morning.

Mallory stretched and grunted. She couldn't move. And she was burning up. What the hell? She opened her eyes and made a sound of panic. Someone was on top of her!

Squirming and scrambling upright, the man grunted and mumbled into the couch, "Chill, Philly, before you kick me in the nuts."

She stilled. "Finnegan?"

"What?" came his muffled reply.

"What are you still doing here?"

"I passed out after the movie. You hog the covers."

Oh my God, he spent the whole night. You slept the whole night next to a guy and were too drunk to even enjoy it!

Her mind chased over memories from the night before. The trip from the bar to her place was all a blur.

Then she remembered talking in the bathroom for a long time. Why were they in the bathroom? Oh, God… she'd puked.

She groaned. "I guess I was the asshole last night."

He sat up. Finn was a cute guy no matter what, but in the morning he was scruffy and encroaching on a whole new level of yummy. She had to look away.

"No, you were fine."

She groaned and covered her face. "I can't believe how drunk I was."

"A group of rowdy McCulloughs and unlimited whiskey has that effect. Are you hung over?"

She took inventory of her body. "No."

"See, that's because you threw up. So stop worrying about it."

She stood and went to the bathroom. After brushing her teeth and washing her face, she headed into the kitchen. Finn was sprawled out on the couch under her comforter.

"Are you hungry?" he asked, watching her start the coffee. It was strange having an audience.

"I was going to make an egg white omelet with spinach and tomato. Did you want one?"

"Is there cheese on it?"

"I don't have cheese."

"You're killing me, Philly. How about you come with me to get the cars? We can get yours and then you can drive my truck back to the house while I drive

Sheilagh's SUV. My mom always makes a big breakfast on Sundays. You come eat there with me and I'll run with you on the field I told you about."

She arched an eyebrow. "You'll run with me?"

"Sure."

"I thought you didn't run unless something's chasing you."

"So you'll have to chase me."

There was something very tempting about running behind Finn, his back all sweaty, shirt clinging to his broad shoulders, strong legs pumping…"Okay."

"Really? There might be carbs there."

"It's fine. I'll eat a banana on the way so I can be selective."

They drove to the bar and retrieved her car. She left it at her apartment and then went back to the bar for Finn's truck. It was tricky driving so far off the ground, but she did fine. Once they turned onto the road leading up the mountain, she noticed the signs declaring it private property that she'd missed before.

Mallory followed the SUV up a long, windy road and the pavement gave way to packed clay thorough-fares. The property was mostly woods, but she caught glimpses of a few lakes.

She turned down a narrow drive after Finn. The shoulders of the road were dusted with fallen pine needles. As they drove over the bumpy terrain, shel-tered in a canopy of green, a large, log cabin came into view. It was so picturesque she wondered if Betty Crocker lived there.

A variety of trucks were parked in the drive and a smaller cottage like house sat in the distance. She pulled in beside the SUV and Finn opened her door.

"Are you sure this is okay? You're family already has a full house."

"We're McCulloughs. Our house is always full. Come on."

She followed him up the porch steps, wishing she'd dressed a little better than her black stretch pants and sneakers. At least her sweatshirt covered most of her upper body.

As he threw open a screen door, voices greeted them. Several people were shouting and she had the sinking sense they were walking into an argument. Before she could suggest maybe they skip breakfast, Finn announced their arrival.

Everyone in the kitchen stilled and stared at them for a split second that felt like an hour. She recognized the McCullough children, but they'd multiplied like gremlins over night. There were several children, a baby, two older women, and many other adults she didn't recognize.

Kelly, who was shirtless and still in his pajama pants, was the first to greet her. "Hey, Philly, you made it through the night!"

The talking picked back up with a roar of chatter

and she instinctively took a step back. Finn abandoned her to kiss the woman at the stove who could only be his mother.

Braydon, who looked a bit green, hugged a mug of coffee and slid over. "Here you go, Philly. Take a load off."

Their welcome was surprising. She hadn't expected to feel so accepted. She stepped closer to the table and Finn caught her arm, stilling her progress. "Philly, let me introduce you. This is me mum. Mum, this is Mallory Fenton, a friend of mine."

"It's nice to meet you, Mrs. McCullough."

Finn's mother eyed her as if she was trying to ask where she'd come from, but then her curious expression split with a grin and she said, "Welcome to our home. Had I known we'd be havin' company I would have fixed myself up a bit. Excuse my appearance."

"Do you need help with anything?"

Her copper brows rose and her smile widened. "Well, well, a woman who actually offers assistance in the kitchen." She slapped Finn's cheek affectionately. "That's a nice change, dearie. No, you two go sit. Breakfast will be done in a few minutes. Finnegan, get your friend some coffee. Juice is on the table."

Finn turned to her. "You want coffee?"

"I'll just have water if you have it."

He twisted his lips like he had to stifle a comment on her choice, but he went to the sink and got her a glass of water. She sat down next to Braydon and soon was immersed in regaling stories from the night before.

Finn slid in beside her and Mrs. McCullough began to cover every square inch of the long, wooden farm table with food. The scent of succulent sausage, crispy, fried bacon, and shingles of home fries wafted up from the surface. Mallory's mouth watered.

An enormous plate was settled in the middle, over-flowing with hot, fluffy, yellow scrambled eggs. Next came a teetering stack of pancakes. "Dig in, loves," Mrs. McCullough announced as she settled into the seat next to a man who had to be Finn's dad.

Mallory hung back as elbows knocked and hands grabbed. Siblings shouted and babies cried and a parade might have passed through. Then all was quiet as everyone dug in. She held her plate protectively to her chest and—once everyone else seemed served—she reached out to scoop a small pile of eggs on her plate.

"Is that all you're gonna eat, dearie?"

Mallory stilled at Mrs. McCullough's question and felt everyone's gaze. "Um…I had some fruit earlier."

"Leave her alone, Mum."

She wanted to tell Finn it was fine, but she was grateful for his interception. He gave her knee a conspirator's nudge under the table and she smiled.

Once everyone's bellies were full, the chatter continued. McCulloughs, she realized, only spoke in one volume. Loud.

"I'll be right back," Finn said close to her ear.

She watched as he stood and walked over to the little old woman falling asleep at the end of the table. Something inside of her chest pinched at the gentle way he woke her and squatted close to the elderly woman's ear. "Morai, do you want to go to your room to lie down?"

The woman gave him a startled look and then smiled softly. Her gaze was innocent and trusting like a confused child. Finn stood and carefully took her elbow as she shuffled away from the table.

When he disappeared with the woman who was likely his grandmother, Mallory stared into her glass and wondered if she'd ever seen something so beautiful or chivalrous. Part of her mind replayed the soft way he'd spoken to her and she wanted to lock it away as one of those Kodak moments one caught too rarely, like seeing a couple that's been married over half a century holding hands in the grocery store. But another part of herself warned that seeing those sides of her friend were dangerous and would only confuse their platonic status and get her hurt.

Finn returned and she was quiet. He hadn't changed or even cleaned himself up, but for some reason he looked different. A protective urge rushed through her as she thought about Erin.

Finn was a good guy and if Erin couldn't see that she didn't deserve him. There was no way Mallory would sit idly by and watch him go back. No. She'd make it her personal mission to find him someone who could appreciate his humor and kindness, not find fault in those admirable qualities.

"You ready?"

She turned to the man who had monopolized her thoughts over the last twenty minutes. "Yes."

"I just have to run upstairs and change. I'll be back in five."

While Finn was gone, Mallory helped clear the table, and started rinsing the dishes.

"Oh, I'll do that, love," Mrs. McCullough said, appearing at her side with an armful of plates.

"It's okay. You cooked."

She smiled and took up the rag to begin drying. "You and Finnegan going out somewhere?"

"He's going to take me to the field. He said I could run there, if that's all right with you?"

"What's chasin' you?"

She smiled. "That's what he always says. I'm trying to be more active."

Finn's mother, who was rounded in an expectable way for her age and the fact that she'd birthed a gazillion big men who likely started as big babies, gave her a scrutinizing inspection. "Nothin' wrong with being active. It's good for your heart. But don't lose too much of those feminine curves, love. A man likes a bit of meat to hold onto."

A rush of blood heated Mallory's cheeks. She focused on the dish she was washing and prayed Finn would return soon.

When the last dish was put away, Finn came down. He wore loose fitting charcoal gray sweats and a faded green baseball T-shirt. He laced up his sneakers with a few quick tugs and stood. "Ready, Philly?"

Words. Say words! She swallowed. He looked hot as hell. "Yeah," she croaked.

The field was only a short drive from the house. She was amazed to see it was actually a baseball field, complete with bleachers and all.

"We have a league with the bar. It's sort of a tradition, generations old, that we play every year, so my dad and my uncles made the field."

"Wow." What else could she say? How many people owned mountains and baseball diamonds?

He climbed out of the truck and handed her a bottle of chilled water. She was grateful he remembered. She'd been so out of sorts that morning it had slipped her mind to grab anything.

Taking the water, she walked over to the bleachers, placed the water on the first step, and then proceeded to stretch. He watched her for a moment as though he'd never seen stretching before.

"Are you going to stretch?" she asked as he continued to gawk. Her face and shoulders were warm under the sun, but she knew part of her flush was the result of him continuously watching her.

He twisted his torso a few times carelessly then seemed to think that was enough warming up. "I'm thinking four diamonds makes a rough mile. How many laps do you want to do?" he asked.

She did some quick math in her head. "Let's walk four, run eight, and walk the last two."

His eyes bulged. "That's like four miles!"

"Yeah. That's what I usually do."

He drew in a deep breath. "You're gonna kill me."

She slapped his shoulder and loped off toward first base. The sound of his sneakers beating against the sand crept up behind her. Her ponytail was yanked and then Finn passed in a flash of green.

"You're gonna get a cramp," she called as he rounded second.

She was crossing home plate when he lapped her again. Her heart rate was picking up by her second lap and he was running out of breath. She picked up her pace and began pumping her arms.

Finn was walking beside her. "We should've grabbed a radio."

"My iPod's in my bag."

"It's called an *I*-pod because it's only meant for one person, Philly."

She crossed home plate, shrugged, and broke into a

jog. He kept pace with her and she sensed his eyes on her. "Why are you being so quiet?"

Her breath punched in and out of her lungs. "It's…hard…to…talk and…run…"

They made the next few laps in silence. When she passed the bleachers she stripped off her sweatshirt. It was too damn hot to worry about vanity. She jogged off and he seemed to lag behind, but she never lost track of his pounding footsteps on her tail.

"You tired, Irish?" she teased as she doubled her pace.

"Just enjoying the view."

Her steps stumbled and she shot him a look over her shoulder as soon as she righted her footing. He smirked and she slowed. Was he looking at her ass? Good God, why?

She fell back until she was running beside him and his gaze remained resolutely straight ahead. Sweat trickled down her cleavage and her neck was slick.

It was strange exercising in the presence of others. She'd thought it would bother her more, but she was actually a little proud she was keeping pace with someone as fit as Finn.

When they passed the bleachers again, he veered off and returned to her side a minute later. "Here," he said, handing her a bottle of water.

She uncapped it and took a few swigs. "Thanks," she gasped.

Her legs burned as they made their fourteenth lap. Her heart was racing and her shirt was soaked. Finn kept snagging glances as she ran that last quarter mile and she was extremely conscious of how little a sports bra did for a woman her size.

When they crossed home plate, she fell into a clipped walk, and started to catch her breath. Her sides burned and her blood pumped as she began to cool down.

"That's was intense, Philly. You do that every day?"

"Unless it's raining."

"You could use the track at the school gym when it rains."

He was in such good shape his voice didn't even struggle after running nearly four miles. She gazed at his chest. He was breathing heavily and the fabric was soaked with a "V" of perspiration, but otherwise he looked perfect.

"I do sit-ups and stuff on the days it rains. But thanks for the offer."

He drank the rest of his water and tossed it into a receptacle by the bleachers. "What are we doing after this?"

We? "I have to get my clothes and stuff ready for tomorrow."

"So after you spend five minutes doing that, what are you doing?"

She snorted and mopped the sweat off her forehead.

"I need to shower and it takes me a lot longer than five minutes to put together an outfit."

"You look good in jeans. Look good in dresses too."

She eyed him skeptically. Her clothes were decent, but she rarely thought she looked good in anything. As she finished her last lap, her legs quivered from exertion. In an hour there would be that rewarding burn that came with hard exercise. She finished her water and threw the bottle in the recycling can.

"Ugh, I'm disgusting. I hate sweat."

"You look good in sweat."

She blinked at him. "What?"

"What?" he echoed innocently. "You look good in sweat."

"Ew. No I don't!"

He stepped closer and she frowned. "Sure you do. Your cheeks are all rosy and your lips are parted. You're breathing heavy. You look like a woman who's been…"

Her brow lowered and she stepped away. "Stop looking at me like that. And get your head out of the gutter. Come on. I need to go home and shower and you're my ride. I stink."

It wasn't fair for him to look at her like that and make sexual comparisons when they were friends. It complicated things. As much as she could whip up some fun fantasies about Finn, that's all they would ever be. Fantasy.

It was dangerous to even entertain ideas like that

regarding him. One, because it would never happen. Guys like that didn't go for girls like her. Two, even if she could convince him to give her one night of no strings great sex, he'd eventually find Mrs. Right and she'd have to stomach it. And three, she really liked having him as a friend and didn't want to ruin it.

When they returned to her apartment she assumed he'd just drop her off and go on his way, but he followed her inside. "I need to shower."

"So shower. Get your stuff together for tomorrow and then we'll go grab lunch. I'll even go somewhere with salads if you want."

Was this because he and Erin had broken up and he didn't know what to do without her? Was she filler? "What would you normally be doing right now?"

"Hanging out on my own couch watching television with my dad."

"And Erin?"

He grunted. "No. She never comes to my house. Says it's too much chaos and gives her a headache."

"Didn't you go to her house sometimes?"

He shrugged. "Sometimes. Not much."

"What did you guys do for fun, like couple stuff?"

His shoulder lifted as he stared at the TV, remote targeted in that direction, thumb casually flipping channels. "I don't know. Went to O'Malley's. I'd drive her to the mall now and then. Nothing really."

"Didn't you go on dates?"

He stared at the ceiling for a moment. "Not really. At least not for a while. She always had something going on and I never really was into the stuff she was. Come to think about it, if we go to lunch it will be the first time I took a girl to a restaurant in a long time. Funny, Erin and I dated but we were never really friends. It's a lot easier to hang out with friends. Less expectation, more of just being ourselves."

They went to a little diner in town. She had a salad and Finn had half a cow shoved between a roll. They talked about his time growing up in Center County and her time growing up in the City of Brotherly Love. It amazed her how differently outsiders saw Philadelphia. Finn knew all about the museums and the steps Rocky climbed, from visiting his brother at school. He didn't see the poverty and rough parts she'd come to know as her home.

"I had one of those cheese steaks when I was there," he said as if it was a major accomplishment. "That was good."

"From where? Geno's, Pat's, or Tony Luke's?"

"I don't think it was any of them."

"Then it wasn't a real Philly steak."

"It was still better than any steak sandwich you can get around here."

"It's been four months since I had a cheese steak."

"You gonna have one when you visit home?" he asked, popping a fry in his mouth.

"No, but I might run the steps of the Museum of Art."

"Yeah, Balboa? I'd like to see that. You could do it."

She grinned at his belief in her. "Thanks."

After lunch they drove to the mall because she needed stockings and the kind from the pharmacy always ripped. She didn't want to be anywhere near a plus sized store with him, but he was turning into a rash she couldn't shake.

As she evaluated the selection in the women's department Finn nudged his way through a sales rack. "Hey, Philly, this would look nice on you."

She hated shopping for clothes. It was always depressing. "I only need stockings."

He held up the top. It was way too small, she noticed right off the bat. Also, it was bright blue. "I don't wear blue."

He frowned. "Why not? Blue's a nice color. It would match your eyes."

Flustered that he knew the color of her eyes, she turned and found the size stockings she needed.

"What size are you? I'm gonna buy it for you. You wear black too much."

"You aren't buying that for me."

"Why not? I want to."

"No, Finnegan."

"I'm getting it."

She huffed and turned. "No. Now put it back." She continued walking to the register.

"Come on, if you don't tell me what size I'll just guess—"

Mortified and highly annoyed, she pivoted and snapped, "I said no! I'm not telling you my size, so drop it!"

His expression fell and she felt horrible. "Sorry. All right, I'll put it back. I just wanted to do something nice for you."

He turned before she could apologize and she cursed under her breath. "Finn."

He held up his hand, but didn't turn. "Forget it."

They walked back to the car in silence. She berated herself for being a shrew the entire drive home. When he pulled up at her apartment, he didn't shut off the car and she was sad the moment she realized he wasn't coming inside.

Her hand went to the handle on the door and she paused. "I'm really sorry for the way I spoke to you."

His eyes narrowed, his lips set impatiently. "Tell me this, was it because you didn't want me to spend money on you or because you didn't want me to know your size?"

She lowered her head, embarrassed on so many levels.

"That's what I thought. Why do you make it so hard

to compliment you? I wanted to do something nice for you Mallory and you—"

"It isn't nice if it makes me feel bad."

"It's just a number," he snapped. "Who cares if it's two or twenty?"

"I do! You don't understand what it's like to hate yourself the way I do. It's—"

"You're right, I don't! Because when I look at you I see a fun girl who's beautiful and smart and I can't understand how—when it comes to her self-image—she can be so dumb."

Her mouth fell open and she blinked as her eyes suddenly started to sting. "I'll add dumb to the list of my faults." Her fingers trembled as she wrenched open the door.

"Damn it, Mallory, don't take what I said out of context."

"Thanks for taking me to the mall." She slammed the door.

Mallory's first day of work was busy enough that she barely thought about Finn. She told Samantha, during lunch, what they'd fought about and Sam was very understanding.

"Finn is probably the least judgmental of his whole family. And none of them are really judgmental to begin with. He wouldn't have batted an eye at your size," Sam had said.

"I know, but I'm a private person. I hate drawing any attention to my weight."

Sam scrunched up her face. "I get that. I put on almost fifty pounds when I was pregnant with Lula, fifteen of which I'm still trying to get off. Colin swears it makes no difference, but I see it every time I look in the mirror."

Mallory narrowed her eyes at the other woman. She

couldn't weigh more than a hundred and twenty pounds soaking wet. She decided she was preaching to the wrong choir and let the topic drop.

After work she raced home and changed into her running clothes. She was tired and had to drag her ass all the way to the park. She planned on using the McCullough field, but after yesterday she didn't know if the invitation still stood.

She cranked up her iPod and took twice as long as she usually did, as her heart was just not in it. When she was finished, it was nearly dark. She pulled up outside of her apartment and stilled when she saw Finn's truck.

Her heart stuttered when she found him waiting on her steps by her front door. He was dressed in sweats and sneakers. "You weren't at the field," he said by way of greeting.

"I went to the park."

His eyes bore into her, but he didn't say a word. She shifted, unable to make it to her door with him in the way.

"How was your first day?" he asked.

"Fine. Good."

"Good."

"What are you doing here, Finn?"

"I felt bad about yesterday."

"It was my fault. Sometimes I'm overly sensitive—"

"I should have listened the first time you told me no. I didn't mean to upset you."

She smiled, but his apology made her feel ashamed. Deep down she knew he was only trying to be nice and now he was apologizing for it. "You don't have to apologize. Let's just drop it. Do you want to stay for dinner? I'm making fish."

"Sure." His legs unfolded and he stood.

They went into her apartment and she pulled out the ingredients for dinner. "I need to shower before I can eat. Can you give me ten minutes?"

"Sure."

She grabbed her pajamas and went to the bathroom. Ten minutes later she returned, hair tied back in a bun, skin freshly cleaned. She threw together some fresh salsa while the Tilapia baked. It was an easy meal and they were sitting down at the table in no time.

"There's a girl at my work you might be interested in," she said as they started to eat.

His fork stilled halfway to his mouth. "Oh?"

She took a bite and nodded. "Her name's Kelsey Stevens. She teaches intermediate math."

"Sounds right up my alley."

She frowned at his tone. "She's single. I told her about you and she seemed interested. She knows of your family and I think Sam's had her to the house. You probably saw her before at your niece's birthday."

He scraped up another bite and made a noncommittal sound.

"She's cute. Slim, short, dark hair, pretty smile. You think you'd want to go out with her?"

His fork clattered to his plate. "What are you doing, Mallory?"

"What?" she asked innocently. "I just figured since you and Erin—"

"Since we broke up you just figured you'd fix me up with the next best thing?"

"I don't want you to go back to her, Finn. She doesn't appreciate the good catch you are."

His brow arched. "You think I'm a good catch?"

Duh. "You're a great catch."

"And this Kelly is good enough for me, but Erin's not?"

She cleared her throat and wiped her mouth on her napkin. "Kelsey," she corrected. "And yes, I think she'd be more your type than Erin."

"And what's my type?"

She shrugged. "I don't know. She's nice."

"There are lots of nice girls in Center County. What makes this one right for me?"

"She's pretty."

"Lots of pretty girls too. I want to know what—specifically—made you see this girl and think, oh, she'd be perfect for Finn."

She frowned. "I don't know. Forget I said anything."

"I don't want to forget about it. I'm curious. Is it because I'm a charity case?"

"No! Of course not! I just thought you might want to take her out."

"I don't." He eased back in his chair and crossed his arms.

"You haven't even met her. How do you know?"

"Because I already have my eye on someone else."

Her nose crinkled. "Who?"

"Don't worry about it."

Her mouth opened and closed. "Okay. Fine."

She stood and collected their plates. At the sink she turned on the faucet and began scrubbing the remnants of dinner down the drain. She jumped when Finn stepped behind her. Close. Very close.

"You forgot my fork," he said, voice husky as he leaned around her shoulder and dropped it in the sink.

Her body tightened and her eyes widened as she stared at the water rushing over her soapy hands frozen in place. Her breath quickened as he seemed to lean into her a moment longer than necessary.

When he pulled back, she let out a breath and needed a moment to find her bearings. She was overreacting. She was totally overreacting. All he did was bring her a utensil and her whole body was on fire.

Maybe she needed to masturbate. That was it. She just needed sex. It had been a long, long time since she'd had any action and she was being overly sensitive. He probably didn't even realize she'd had that reaction.

You're pathetic.

After the dishes were done she sat on the couch and watched the news with Finn. He wasn't sitting on the side like he usually did. He was hogging the middle and she remained stiff so as not to inadvertently touch him.

When the news was over she stood.

"Where you going?"

"I have to get my clothes ready for tomorrow."

"You spend an abnormal amount of time thinking of things to wear." He lounged over the other two cushions, making himself at home.

She really wanted to see if she had batteries, but she couldn't tell him that. "I'll just be a minute."

A minute turned into twenty. She was debating over a pair of shoes when Finn walked into her room. She jumped as he approached her.

"Minute's up," he said and she blinked up at him. He was acting strange.

"Sorry. Which shoes do you like better?"

He stepped close and removed the shoes from her hands, glancing briefly at each one. "The gray ones." He tossed both shoes on the floor.

"Wh—what are you doing?"

"You're making me crazy, Philly."

She shook her head. "What…what do you mean?"

"Stop talking." His head lowered and his mouth found hers.

She jerked back, her fingers trembling over her lips. *"What are you doing?"*

"I'm trying to kiss you?"

Oh my God he's horny and Erin isn't around. She stepped back. "Don't."

He frowned. "Why not?"

"Because I'm not Erin."

His head drew back. "Oh, I'm quite aware you're not Erin."

Yes, it wasn't likely he'd confuse the two of them. That would be like mixing up a penguin with a water buffalo. Suddenly something deep in her chest began to ache. She stepped back again and her knees met the bed. He caught her elbow and she quickly tugged her arm free. "Why are you doing this?"

He frowned. "Because I want to and I thought you might've wanted me to."

Her head shook like an imbecile. "I don't." If they crossed that line, their friendship would be over and it would only be a matter of minutes before he realized she wasn't at all what he was used to.

His lips parted and his expression shuttered. He stepped back and dropped his hand. "Oh. Then I'm sorry." He turned and grabbed the back of his neck, which was flushed. "I should probably get going."

He wouldn't look at her. No! This couldn't happen. She said no, so nothing should change, but her stomach knotted as she realized it was too late. Her lashes fluttered as her vision blurred.

Should she call him back? Maybe she should just let

him use her. She'd enjoy it. *Have some self-respect, woman!* "Finn, don't go…"

He held up his hand, much like he did at the mall when she'd offended him. It must not make any sense for a man like that to be rejected by a girl like her.

"I gotta go," he said and the next thing she knew her front door was shutting.

FINN DROVE until he reached his property then he pulled over to the side of the road and punched the steering wheel. *"Fuck!"*

Why did he do that? He was so damn stupid. Of course she wasn't into him. He wasn't any prize. He'd just thought he'd seen something in the way she looked at him. No one had looked at him like that in a long time. But he was wrong.

She thought of him as just a friend. He'd thought of her as the same, but sometime over the last few days that changed. Erin disappeared from his life like she'd never existed. He'd barely given her absence a moment's thought. Yet, when he'd upset Mallory at the mall, he could think of little else. He rushed through his workday just to run with her at the field. When he arrived and waited for her, only to have her never show, he suffered the terrible fear that he'd ruined their friendship.

But it was more than that. When she showed up

after her run at the park, she looked beautiful. Her hair was a mess, her cheeks flushed, her breasts pressed against her fitted tank top. His eyes had roamed over her shapely thighs and he had to fight the entire way through dinner not to kiss her.

Listening to the water run while she'd showered was pure torture. He'd imagined her naked and wasted at least six minutes debating if her nipples would be soft pink like her lips or tan. But none of that mattered.

Yes, she was a beautiful woman, but she was so much more than that. Finn didn't have *girl* friends. He got along with his sisters, but other than that, they were it. The way he was around Mallory was a totally novel experience. He liked her, really liked her. And now he was thinking like a fifth grader.

"Gah, no wonder she shot you down."

The worst part was he might have seriously fucked up their friendship. He glanced at the clock on the dash and considered going back and asking her to forget the whole thing, but it was late and she had work in the morning.

He threw the truck into gear and barreled over the road, heading home. When he went to sleep that night his bed seemed a little colder, a little less comforting, and lot lonelier. Maybe he wasn't meant to have a partner in this life. Maybe he should go back to Erin.

His mind immediately rejected that idea. Erin's long legs and trim hips were no longer what he wanted.

After seeing how Mallory actually listened to him when he spoke, he had no desire to return to a girl who had mastered ignoring him. Erin never cared about what he thought or what motivated him.

Mallory cared. Or she did. His last hope before sleep took him was that he hadn't ruined what friendship they'd had together.

CHAPTER 7

The first week of work did wonders for Mallory's spirit. Everyone was nice to her and she was glad she talked herself into moving. The weather this far west of Philadelphia was preferable as well. It was still sweltering, but she took pleasure in the bursts of fall she caught here and there. Such things only presented themselves in temperature drops in the city, but here there were bursts of color in the foliage and cool breezes that snuck in.

That was the crap she forced herself to focus on every time she missed Finn. The day after he'd kissed her, she was confused. Then she was angry. How could he do that? There was no question in her mind that he was using her. He was horny, lonely, or looking for an escape to forget Erin. No way would she believe this actually had anything to do with her. Mallory was simply convenient and, maybe in Finn's eyes, desperate enough to agree to a meaningless fling. That thought hurt, because it was clear how little he valued their new friendship.

When Thursday came she was sad. He hadn't stopped by and no matter how much she *didn't* expect him to, each day when she came home there was a sting of disappointment that he hadn't been there waiting for her like he had the time after the mall fight.

Saturday morning it was gloomy. Rain softly pelted the windows of her apartment as she stared mindlessly at the Morning Show on the television. Some skinny blonde was being gifted with a dream wedding and her sweet, emotional story made Mallory want to fling her yogurt at the screen.

Her phone rang and her heart pinched, letting go with a sad little exhale as she realized Finn didn't have her number. She picked it up and saw Ally's number on the screen. Smiling, she slid her thumb over the face and brought it to her ear.

"Hey, girl."

"Hey! How's bumblefuck?"

Mallory laughed. "It's good."

"Did you start your job?"

Mallory poked her spoon through her yogurt, no longer enjoying it. "Yeah. I love it. Everyone is so nice."

"Do they have all their teeth?"

She snorted. "How deep in the boonies do you think

I am? Yes, they all have teeth." Ally giggled and Mallory heard Savannah, her friend's newborn, coo in the background. "How's the baby?"

"She's…" Ally sighed. "Perfect."

"Good. Getting big?"

"Yes. She's a little piglet."

Mallory fought the envy tightening her stomach. "How's Joe?"

"He's good. He got that promotion."

"That's great, Ally! Things sound like they're going really good for you guys." She stood and chucked her half-eaten yogurt.

"Okay, now really tell me. How are you? You sound shlumpy."

Mallory returned to the couch and flopped onto her back. "I'm fine. It's raining here, so the weather's just getting to me."

"Mallory Fenton, don't you dare feed me a line of bullshit when I ask you a question. What's going on? I can tell you're upset. Do I need to come there?"

She laughed, imagining the arsenal of baby paraphernalia Ally would need to make the trip. "No." She huffed. "I made a friend and I think I already lost him."

"*Him?* Do tell."

"His name's Finnegan McCullough and—girl—he is a *real* mountain man."

"Sounds delicious. Tell me more."

Mallory spent the next twenty minutes catching

Ally up on her past few weeks. When she finished Ally was quiet for a moment. "Let me get this straight. He kissed you and you automatically assume he's just trying to get laid and that's it?"

"He just broke up with his girlfriend, which, from what I hear, is a normal occurrence. He doesn't see me that way."

"How the hell do you know, Mal? Maybe he realized you're a cool girl. You're beautiful, funny, and people love you. There's no reason he shouldn't like you."

She pursed her lips. "You don't understand, Ally. You'd have to see him to get it. When I say he's hot, I'm not talking turn your head and bat your eyes for a smile. I'm talking Adam Levine and Brad Pitt's lovechild hot. Sometimes it hurts to look at him."

"So? Mallory, you're gorgeous."

"No, I'm not," she mumbled. "I'm a fat she-beast."

"*Do not make me load up the car and come kick your ass! You are not fat and you are not a beast!*"

She silently ignored her friend's reassurance. It was always flattering to hear people say she had pretty eyes or a nice smile, but when they flat out argued that she wasn't fat it made it all bullshit. She was fat. Her doctor, who didn't give a shit about being her friend, told her so. He even had a chart that put her in the 'danger zone'. The truth was, unless she dropped down to one hundred and forty pounds—which was light years away —she'd remain in the obesity category.

Who was a hundred a forty pounds? She couldn't even comprehend what that would look like on her. Currently, she was focusing on getting herself out of the red zone that classified her as 'morbidly' obese.

There were people who could barely walk or get anything besides sneakers on their feet. She wasn't quite there yet, but the facts were the facts. According to the American Association of Health, she was among the thirty-three percent of the obese population.

"*Mallory!*"

She flinched. "What?"

"Are you even listening to me?"

"Sorry, I zoned out. What did you say?"

Ally sighed, her voice softening. "Honey, don't go there. I know how you get. You're perfect, just the way you are. Don't dismiss this guy just because you have some demons to work out. See where it goes. You deserve to be happy and happiness can come in any shape or size."

She sighed. Never had she needed to give a pep talk like that to her friends, but Ally's speech would be filed among the hundreds Mallory had received in her life. She was just…different. Her thin friends would never understand. "Thanks."

Ally sighed and her disappointment was evident. "Did you ever think about straight out asking him how he feels about you?"

Mallory made a rude noise. "Yeah. That's not going

to happen. He already lectures me about being too hard on myself. I am not sharing my horrid opinions with him."

"Why? Maybe he'd be able to get through to you."

Or maybe I'll convince him and he'll finally start looking at me the way the rest of the world does. It hurt to imagine him seeing through her cheery attitude, to imagine him crossing that fine line of support that becomes chastisement every time she slipped up. Part of her liked pretending Finn might see something pretty when he looked at her, even if it was all a polite lie. She didn't have the courage to confront him, not when it could validate everything she knew deep down. She wasn't good enough for him.

Quietly, she whispered, "I can't. I just want us to be friends. Friends are safe and it doesn't matter what I weigh."

She felt her friends scowl through the phone. "I gained forty pounds in the last year."

"You were pregnant!"

"It doesn't matter. That's my point. Love is blind, Mallory. When will you learn that?"

Whoa. No one was talking about love. "Trust me, Ally. He's just looking for filler. I don't want to be filler."

She sighed. "You're not filler, honey. I wish you could see what the rest of us do when we look at you."

She was sort of grateful she didn't. It was always jarring whenever Mallory saw a picture of herself. She always got that same sick feeling followed by the realization that the ugly person in the picture was really what her friends saw.

The baby started to squawk and she knew their call wouldn't last much longer. "When are you coming home?" Ally asked.

"Probably not until Thanksgiving."

They made plans to hang out the night she returned home and Mallory mentally tried to imagine a newer her, a thinner version. Would they see a difference? She'd shed seventeen pounds since moving, but, to her eyes, she still looked the same.

Will I ever like me?

After getting off the phone she gathered up her dirty clothes and detergent. She needed to do something productive and might as well get her errands done if she couldn't work out.

FINN SHIMMIED down the trunk of the oak and his boots landed with a thud. He rarely worked Saturdays, but he needed to get out. The rain was an irrelevant nuisance, only adding to his gloomy mood.

He unlatched his harness and turned when he heard a truck approaching behind him. His father parked several yards away and met his gaze. "Aren't gonna get much done in this weather, Finnegan."

He cut his line with a bowie knife and ignored the

wisdom in his father's voice. "These branches need to be hauled. Why wait until Monday to get it done?"

The soggy ground squished under his father's boots as he approached. Frank's hand pressed into the girth of the trunk and Finn eyed him curiously.

"You and Erin have a fight?"

Finn tugged his gloves up and bent to drag a limb over to the chipper. His father followed. "You could say that. We broke up."

"Wanna talk about it?"

He shrugged and hoisted the limb into the debris piled. "Nothing to say. It is what it is."

His father followed him back to the tree and removed a rough pair of leather gloves from his back pocket. Under the drizzle, they worked in silence lugging the branches to the chipper pile. The consistent tap of raindrops on the leaves made a soothing melody.

"I ever tell you about the woman I dated before your mother?"

"I thought you and Mom were together since you were teenagers. Wasn't that when Grandpop shot you?"

"He missed and that wasn't until we ran off and got married. But there was a girl before her. Her name was Elizabeth."

This was news to Finn. His parents often regaled them with stories of their scandalous affair and how his father had stolen his mother away against her father's wishes, but never had he heard him speak of any other woman.

They tossed a large branch and trekked back to the tree. "She was a beauty, different than your mother. There's no one quite like Maureen. We went to school together and I was shocked the day she sat with me for lunch. Elizabeth was a popular girl, always had the cutest scarves tied around her neck and her ankles done in those little lace socks girls wore back then."

"Did you go out with her?"

"A few times. Then I slept with her and she pretty much owned me. Kids are stupid once they start with the fornicating and groping."

Finn raised his brow and gave his dad a comical look, biting back a laugh. "Fornicating and groping? Really, Dad?"

His father rolled his eyes. "I can't keep up with you kids and your terms these days. Anyway, she gave me what I wanted and I gave her anything she asked for. But that was all there really was to us. I can't even remember the color of her eyes, son. I just remember that she was pretty and she let me get under her skirt."

"Why are you telling me this?" He stood from crouching and braced his hands on his hips.

"Because sometimes men think with the wrong brain, Finnegan. Don't be one of those idiots. Don't sentence yourself to less than you deserve. Marriage isn't about sex. God, after you start having babies you have to become a master of stealth to even get one of those little climbers off the teat."

"Dad!"

"It's true. What I'm trying to say is, maybe you and Erin breaking up is for the best. You two are always arguing and I never see you really get excited to go out with her anymore. I know you were planning on marrying her, but why? Why marry someone who can't even make you laugh? In the end, laughing is worth more than a little poontang."

Finn nearly spit. "It's better when you call it fornicating, Dad."

His father shrugged. "Call it whatever you want, so long as you understand what I'm trying to say."

"I get it. I've been thinking the same for a while now. I don't think Erin and I will ever see eye-to-eye. And, you know, I think I'm all right with that."

"So why are you out here on your day off working in the rain?"

Because he ran out of things to keep him busy and it was taking everything he had not to go annoy Mallory. "I don't know."

His father studied him for a long minute. "This have to do with that girl you brought to breakfast last week, the pretty, blue eyed one?"

He shifted uncomfortably. "Maybe."

"That's a yes. You like her?"

Heat rushed to the back of his neck. "It doesn't matter."

"Why's that?"

"She doesn't look at me that way."

His father dug his boot into the ground, dislodging a bit of moss. "Not all girls are easy, Finnegan. The good ones take the most work. No one expects you to be married by a certain date and starting a brood of your own. Sometimes slow is better. Savor it. She'll eventually come around."

He nodded. No point in telling his father how he messed up and kissed her. What was done was done. She didn't see him that way and he'd either have to suck it up and go back to pretending he saw her as just a friend or lose her completely, something he knew would kill him. "Thanks for the talk."

The heavy weight of his father's gloved palm landed on his shoulder. "That's what I'm here for. Now, come on home. This shit can wait until Monday."

THE RAIN DRIED up by that afternoon. Mallory was carrying her laundry back from the Laundromat when her breath caught at the sight of Finn's truck outside her apartment. She did a quick inventory of her appearance. The yoga pants and T-shirt weren't really working for her, but that was good. They needed to get back to basics and she didn't want to address the kiss situation again.

She turned the corner and there he was, leaning up against the railing of her steps, looking all mountain-y delicious. *Shit.*

"Hey," he greeted her, softly.

She shifted her basket on her hip. "Hey."

"I missed you."

Alert! Alert! Her heart did something totally inappropriate and seemed to flutter madly in her chest. "How was your week?"

"Long. How was yours?"

"The same."

They stood in awkward silence for a bit. This was what she feared. They wouldn't be able to get past the kiss.

He took a few steps toward her. "Here, I'll carry that up for you."

She was relieved of her basket and headed for the stairs. His steps echoed behind hers as her heartbeat did a drumroll in her ears. When they reached the small landing she reached for her keys, coming up short when she realized she didn't have pockets.

Turning, she said, "My keys are in the basket." Fumbling, she awkwardly fished out the keys. They were too close. The metal turned in the lock and she stilled when he spoke.

"I like those pants."

Change! "Th—thanks." The door slid open and she quickly dashed inside.

At the kitchen she busied herself, cursing that she'd done all the dishes that morning.

Finn dropped the basket on her couch and came to lean his hip into the counter as she pulled out a can of tuna. Tuna salad took a while. She'd make that. Her fingers twisted the can opener and stinky juice spattered on her hand when he startled her by asking, "Should we talk about it?"

Her shoulders tensed as she proceeded to drain the tuna. "I don't see why we should." She dumped the fish into a bowl and began forking the chunks apart.

"Mallory?" He was standing right beside her.

She continued to fork and sprinkled some pepper in the bowl.

"Mallory," he repeated. "Can you at least look at me?"

She shut her eyes and wished she were somewhere else.

"I'm sorry. I shouldn't have kissed you. I thought…it doesn't matter what I thought. I just want you to know I regret it and I'm sorry."

That sounded about right. She knew he would regret anything remotely sexual with her, thus why she didn't want to ever go there with him. "It's okay," she mumbled, skirting past him to grab some fat-free mayo and cottage cheese from the fridge.

He huffed. "You aren't acting like it's okay."

"It's fine, Finnegan. Let's move on."

He caught her elbow and she froze. Electricity zinged up her arm and her insides quivered. He sucked in an audible breath and released her. "I just want you to know it won't happen again."

Relief was quickly followed by a sense of disappointment. "Good. Did you want a tuna melt? I make them on mushrooms."

"Sure. Sounds delicious."

He abandoned the kitchen and she exhaled. The television clicked on and her mind focused on making their lunch. The weighted silence over the TV was tedious and she never forgot he was sitting only a few feet away. Was he watching her? She was too chicken shit to look.

When lunch was done, she popped it in the oven for twenty minutes and collected her basket. "I'm going to put these away. I'll be right back."

As she was slipping her panties into a drawer Finn's phone rang. Her hands stilled and she stopped breathing to listen.

"Hello? Hey. I don't know, probably." He sighed and sounded stressed. "Erin..."

Mallory's stomach knotted. Why was she calling him? Was that why he'd been MIA all week? Did they get back together? Was that the main reason he was sorry he kissed her?

"I'm not going through this again. I can give you a ride to drop off your car, but next time you need to—" His words cut off abruptly, then in a softer voice. "I know. Me too. Yeah."

The apartment was quiet and then the door to her bedroom squeaked. "I have to go," he said, standing in her doorway.

"Oh. Okay. Is everything all right?"

He nodded. "Yeah. I just have to give a friend a hand with something."

Friend? Don't lie to me, Finnegan McCullough. "All right."

She shut her drawer and he shifted. "Do you wanna go out tonight?"

She hesitated. "Where?"

His shoulder lifted and dropped. "Maybe catch a movie, grab something to eat. We can see if anyone's hanging out at O'Malley's."

"A movie sounds good. Nothing scary, though."

"Big baby."

She smiled. That was the first thing he said that made her feel like they were normal again. She could do sarcasm. She was a master at it.

"I'll pick you up around seven, how's that sound?" he asked.

"Good."

He left and the oven beeped. He never got to have lunch.

. . .

THAT NIGHT they went to the Cineplex and saw a raunchy war film with lots of bombs and explosions. Getting past the concession stand was no easy task, but she managed.

Finn held an enormous bucket of greasy popcorn that smelled orgasmic, but she was fully enjoying her bottle of water. "I have something for you," he whispered, the soft musk of his woodsy cologne tickled her nose and sent quivers to other parts.

"You do?"

He shifted in his seat, lifting his hips. Her eyes locked on the way his zipper curved outward over his jeans and she quickly darted her gaze to the screen.

"Here." He produced a yellow apple from his pocket.

It was just an apple. There was no call for trumpets and doves, but that's exactly what filled her mind. As though a magical light from heaven shone on that little piece of fruit as angels sang, she stared at the offering and wanted to cry. He'd thought of her and brought an apple, knowing her well enough to predict she wouldn't let herself snack on the junk they served at the theater.

His eyes moved under the thick dusting of lashes as he waited for her to take it. Her breath came in low pants as she simply stared at it. That stupid piece of fruit would be her undoing. He wasn't allowed to do nice things like that if they were to remain platonic.

"Thanks," she said, hoping her voice disguised how much the gift meant to her.

He smiled and faced the screen. As she bit into the juicy Golden Delicious, he sipped noisily from his Slurpee. On the screen, people died and tanks blew up, but nothing was as entertaining as the replay in her mind of him offering her an apple.

When the movie let out, they walked through the dark lot and found his truck. He opened her door and she frowned. He needed to stop doing nice things. Guys at home didn't open doors. Even Joe, Ally's husband, who doted on her whenever he had the chance, never opened Ally's door.

"Wanna grab some dinner?"

"Sure."

"What are you in the mood for?"

Your body. "Salad."

He shot her an exasperated look. "O'Malley's does a grilled chicken Caesar. Wanna go there?"

"Okay."

On the way to the bar they listened to the radio. Finn liked country and that seemed fitting. The lot was full when they parked and while she opened the passenger door of the truck, he held it, and shut it.

"Th—thanks."

The pub was busy. He directed her to a booth in the back and she tried hard not to tense as he placed his warm palm just above her butt. *Breathe and knock it off!*

Kelly waved and sent a waitress over. She was perky and everything Mallory was not. "Hey, Finn, what can I get you guys tonight?"

Yup, you're just one of the guys...

Finn ordered a burger for himself and a salad for her. "What to you want to drink, Philly?"

"I'll take a Cosmo."

The waitress raised a brow and jotted down their order on a little pad. What? Did people not do martinis around here?

When the waitress left, Finn reclined in his seat, his arm draped over the back. He had great, rugged hands, creased at the knuckles, and sort of permanently beaten up from work.

Oh my God, there is something wrong with you! Stop looking at his hands!

She pulled over the little rack filled with sugars and began shuffling and reorganizing them. The waitress returned and plopped down Finn's draft and her martini. Her fingers curled around the glass as she brought it to her lips for a sip. "Hoo! That's got a kick!"

Finn chuckled. "Should I be preparing for another evening in your bathroom?"

"Maybe. You know I'm an awesome toilet pow-wow talker."

He laughed. "Pretty much."

A man walked by with a large speaker and she frowned.

"There's a band tonight," Finn said, obviously catching her confusion.

"What kind of band?"

He arched his neck to read the chalkboard behind the bar. "Gridlock 64. They're great. They do a little bit of everything."

"Country?"

"More rock and stuff. This place will be a madhouse once they start."

She sipped her Cosmo. "Do you dance?"

He laughed. "I try not to."

"Not unless someone's chasing you?"

"No, when something's chasing me I run. I usually only dance if someone's shooting at my feet."

She grinned. "I'll get my gun."

Their food was delivered and by the time the band took the stage and opened with a familiar alternative rock ballad, they were finished eating and the crowd had doubled. The waitress refreshed their drinks and they watched as people began to fill the area where tables had been pushed back.

"Did you want to dance?" Finn shouted.

"I don't have my gun."

He grinned. "We'll call it a favor. You'll owe me one."

She eyed the stage and the crowd. The band was singing *Friends in Low Places*. "I don't know how to dance to this."

People passed as they watched the crowd. This was

the busiest O'Malley's had ever been since she'd started coming there. She wondered where all these young people hid throughout the workweek, because she didn't recognize half of them. The band must be great. Everyone seemed to have come out to hear them play.

The song ended and the crowd cheered. "How's everyone doing tonight?" the lead singer asked over the microphone. "How 'bout we start this night off with a social. If you got a drink, hold it up. If you don't, get one. Now lift it up and when I say drink, everyone drink. Drink!" The people cheered and the bass and guitar player folded into a rhythm. "Now let's have some fun, Center County. We're Gridlock 64 and we're here until one, so tip your bartenders and servers and come out and dance."

Blue lights transformed the stage as steam coiled through the dancers. They had a great sound, a nice, alternative twang. Finn stood. "Come on, Philly, let's see if you can dance in those shoes."

She'd worn her tangerine pumps with black pants and a plain, black shirt. They weren't the best for dancing, but she'd done her fair share of clubbing back in the day. She could hold her own.

The 'dance floor' was packed. Finn slipped behind her as they found a niche to claim. She moved to the beat and burst out laughing when she saw Finn's moves. They were from an era way before their time.

"What are you doing?" she shouted over the music. It was much louder this close to the stage.

"What? This is my signature move. How about this? I call this the lawn sprinkler."

He clamped his hand on the back of his head and extended his other arm outward, ticking it slowly in clockwise motion then drawing it back like a sprinkler.

She laughed. "You're going to have to stop doing that, right now."

He shrugged and went back to his horrible impersonation of she didn't know what. It was like Emilio Estevez dancing in *The Breakfast Club*, but on crack and mingled with parts of The Hustle. He was hysterical and made it tempting to stop caring what others thought and just let loose and have fun.

"How about this one," she said. "I call it the shopping cart." Her feet marched in place as one hand steered an invisible cart and the other arm reached for invisible items on a shelf, pretending to plop them in the cart.

His head tipped back as he laughed. "Awesome! Remember *Thriller?*" He went into full zombie lurch.

Invigorated, she jumped back, held out her hand as the other one swatted out several air spanks. Finn turned and did an Apache-like-booty dance. Even when he was acting like an ass, his ass looked great.

"I call this the SpongeBob." She started kicking her legs out like a little Russian soldier. They'd fallen into a full-blown dance off.

"This is the lawn mower," he yelled as he bent like he was repeatedly yanking a cord. Her face hurt from smiling.

She busted out her sweetest surfer moves and jerked to a halt when someone's hands were suddenly fondling her butt. Her gaze snapped behind her where some drunk guy was laughing. Finn's smile morphed into a death stare.

"Hey! Hands off!"

The guy held up his palms and thrust his hips. "Aw, come on, dude. She's got plenty to go around."

Mortification gutted her as she caught the asshole's words shouted over the band's music.

Finn took a deadly step forward. "What the fuck did you just say?"

"Finn," she said, used to those sorts of comments, but her voice was suddenly small and he didn't seem to hear her.

The guy said something back and Finn towered over him, pushing her behind his broad back. She pressed against him, trying to break them apart, but the band was killing it and the throng of dancers crowded her to the point she could barely move. No one seemed to notice what was happening.

"Apologize," Finn growled.

She tugged on his shirt. "Come on, Finnegan. Let's go back to the table." He ignored her.

"Yeah, go back to your table. You're probably hungry

from staring at her muffin top all day," the guy said and she flinched.

Finn looked back at her quickly and the pity she recognized mixing with panic in his eyes slayed her. She blinked back tears of humiliation and whispered, "Let's go."

His lips formed a thin line and he scowled, but thankfully nodded, and exhaled. Assholes were everywhere. She was used to it.

"Hey, tonight when you're tapping that, you might want to try some fantasy play. I highly recommend the Princess Leah in the gold bikini. She can be Jabba the Hut."

"Motherfucker," Finn hissed and turned. The next thing she knew people were screaming and the asshole was on the floor.

She panicked and turned to the bar just as Kelly was leaping over the counter. He pushed her aside and yanked his brother back. She couldn't take anymore. Everything erupted into absolute chaos and she forced her way through the dancers and rubberneckers to escape to the bathroom. Once in there she locked herself in a stall, dropped to the seat, and started to cry.

Her fingers struggled to pull a reasonable length of toilet paper out of the jammed dispenser, which only upset her more. The music stopped and all she could make out was the sound of people talking. Hopefully Kelly broke it up before anyone got hurt.

She glanced down at her feet. They were slightly swollen from dancing. The entire evening was a waste. Sometimes she hated being her. She'd been having so much fun, really enjoying the live music, and then some dickless ass-clown had to molest her and call her names.

The names she could take. No matter what he said, it didn't erase the fact that he'd had his hands all over her. He'd obviously seen her as an easy kill and was offended when she—the chubby girl on the dance floor —rejected him. But it wasn't what he said that hurt. It was the fact that he'd said those things in front of Finn.

She'd heard it all. Guys at school used to call her peanut butter because she was extra chunky. Once, at a party in college, some bitch sang Carole King's *I Feel the Earth Move* the moment Mallory walked in. People had beeped when she'd backed up, called her Fat Sajak, blubbers, and worse. She was immune.

The door opened and she sucked in a breath, trying to be invisible.

"Mallory?"

Her head snapped up. Finn? *Shh. Don't say anything. Make him think you left.*

He tapped on the stall door. "Hey, Mallory, you in there?" She remained silent. There was no way she was letting him catch her crying in some bathroom after what just happened. "I can see your feet."

Fuck.

"This is the ladies' room," she hissed.

"Are you okay?"

"I'm fine. Are you? You're the one who decided to go Old West and punch the guy."

"He deserved it." They were both silent for a moment. "He's gone now."

Great. Nothing like making the walk of shame back to her table after being the cause of a spectacle. "Okay."

The door jiggled and her spine stiffened. "Open the door."

"Finnegan! I'm in the bathroom."

"Are you peeing?"

Her face scrunched as she stared at the chipped paint on the stall in total shock. "No!"

A few seconds passed. Quietly, he asked, "Pooping?"

"Oh my God! *Get. Out!*"

He didn't sound bothered. "Will you come back to the table? I was having fun dancing with you."

Yeah, there'd be no more dancing for this girl for a while. "I'll be out in a few minutes."

"All right."

The door opened and closed. Sighing, she stood and pressed her foot into the flusher even though she hadn't used the toilet, she'd accumulated a glob of tear and makeup stained tissue. She unlatched the stall and gasped. Finn stood on the inside of the door waiting for her.

"You *were* crying."

She turned her face and quickly washed her hands. "No, I wasn't."

When she reached for a towel he was behind her, watching her in the mirror. His expression was a mixture of concern and regret. *Yeah, get used to it, Finnegan McCullough. That's what happens when you hang out with someone like me.*

"Why are you still here?" she snapped. Dear God, what if she actually *had* been using the bathroom.

He stepped closer and her breath stuttered in her lungs. "Nothing that guy said was true," he whispered.

Uh, yeah, it was. "He's a jerk. I'm used to it. I couldn't give two shits about what people like him think or say."

His brow lowered and he studied her as if weighing the sincerity of her words. "You're beautiful, Mallory. Don't let anyone tell you differently."

The same tightening she always got in her chest when a friend lied to her clamped down on her heart. "Thanks. Let's go back out there."

He caught her arm and she stilled. Her focus latched on those large fingers wrapped around her skin. Her gaze darted to his eyes. He shook his head and drew her back to the sinks. His hands caught her shoulders as he turned her toward the mirror. "Look at yourself. See what everyone else sees."

She scowled at her reflection, hating it. She *did* see what everyone else saw. That was the problem. Every time she caught her reflection in a store window or in a picture she hadn't known was taken, she broke a little bit more.

There was no missing the way her face was too round and her breasts were too big for any proper-fitting bra. Her stomach wasn't flat and her shirts didn't always hide the unsightly bulges. The only thing that made her happy with that mirror was the fact that it wasn't full length.

"I see it, Finnegan. Now let's go." She moved to turn and his grip tightened.

"No."

"Finnegan—"

"Really look, Mallory. Look at your eyes. They're the prettiest blue I've ever seen. And your lips are full and always the perfect shade of pink. You're hair is thick and always smells like flowers. Your skin is softer than silk. Yes, you're curvy, but who ever said that was a bad thing?"

"I'm not curvy. I'm fat."

"Stop calling yourself that!"

"It's what I am!"

"Why?" He jerked her shoulders. "Because some doctor showed you a chart? It's an ugly fucking word and I'm sick of hearing you use it to describe yourself. So what if you have some weight you want to lose? We all want to improve ourselves in some way."

"Yeah, well, I wasn't the one insulting myself tonight. It was that guy out there. There's always someone judging me, seeing the things you clearly don't."

"I see them, Mallory. I just…I don't see them as flaws. This is who you are."

No! It's not! In her dreams, she was always skinny. This was not how she imagined herself. It was like she was trapped in a body she hated. She desperately wanted to shed the mask. She was light and airy and easygoing. The outside package matched nothing on her inside.

"This may be who I am, but I won't be like this for long."

His eyes closed for a brief moment. "Did you ever think that maybe you're just built this way? I'm not saying you should give up on all your exercise, but what if you change your BMI and shed a few pounds? You aren't built like a little boy. Why is that a bad thing?"

She'd long ago gotten bikinis and short-shorts out of her head. Her expectations were realistic. She was aiming for one-seventy, not one-seventeen. Chances were, she'd always be of the rounded variety. "It doesn't matter. It makes no difference what you see, or I see, or what all the assholes out there see. I'm sick of being me and I'm done talking about this."

"Well, I'm glad you're you."

She narrowed her eyes. How could he be glad about something that made her so miserable? "Thanks," she said, none too nice.

He released her shoulders and stepped back. "Do you want to go somewhere else?"

She wanted to go home and hit the reset button on the day. "I think I'm ready to call it a night."

He nodded. She followed him back to the table and they squared up the bill after she threatened him when he wouldn't take her money. She left it on the table. It was either going to him or the waitress.

They drove home in silence. When he parked she just sat there, too tired to move. "Did you get hurt?" she asked, thinking she should have asked that an hour ago. It wasn't often—or ever—someone punched someone in her defense.

"No. He's seen better days, though."

She laughed without much humor. "There'll be others. You can't go around punching people every time someone insults me."

"Why not?"

"Um, because you'll go to jail."

"It'd be worth it."

"Finn—"

He shifted so he fully faced her. "Don't. I'm done with listening to you put yourself down and acting like you deserve less respect than everyone else. Done, Mallory. Do you understand? Done."

She swallowed. "Yes. Sorry." She faced the dark windshield. "Did you want to come in and watch some TV or something?"

"No."

His clipped reply cut her to the quick. "Okay." Her hand went to the door.

"I don't want to come in because I don't want to watch TV with you."

Her shoulders hunched as she tried to curl into herself, curl away from his rejection. Her fingers tightened on the latch as she breathed out some form of a reply and nodded.

"I want to kiss you and touch you, but you don't want that, and I'm not sure I can keep acting like I feel the same."

Her entire body froze. What did he just say? Ally's words played in her head and she battled to find some form of truth or motive.

"I like you, Mallory. I know you don't feel the same, but you're my friend and I can't lie to you. When we were dancing tonight all I wanted to do was kiss that smile off your face. It's getting difficult to stand upright when I'm around you."

She choked on her objection. "What?"

"I get that you just want to be friends, but I just thought you should know…it's how I feel."

Her neck twisted until she was facing him. There was no sarcasm in his expression. "If this is some method of getting over Erin—"

"It has nothing to do with Erin and everything to do with you."

"You're just horny."

He scowled at her. "Don't do that. Don't tell me what I'm feeling. I've been feeling this way for weeks and when I realized you didn't feel the same I tried to excuse it as something else. Trust me. It's not. It's you."

"Wh—why?"

He shrugged. "I just…want you."

He wants you. No one has ever said those words. Her breath came out in a slow, jagged release. "Finn, I…You see someone I don't know. The real me isn't that. We're friends. I couldn't bear losing our friendship because we let our feelings cloud our better judgment."

His gaze snapped to hers. "*Our* feelings?"

"Yours, mine, whatever. I'm just saying—"

"Are you attracted to me?" he interrupted.

She stuttered. "I…you're obviously handsome." The side of his mouth slowly curved, producing the cutest dimple she'd ever seen. "But that doesn't change the fact that we're better off as friends."

He picked up her hand and when she tried to pull it back to her lap his fingers tightened. Whatever she'd been about to say fled her mind as he scooted closer and tucked her hair behind her ear. "I want to kiss you, Mallory, and I'm going to. You give me one minute and then I'll decide if I believe your line of bullshit about us being better off as friends."

"Finn—"

"Shh…" His mouth lowered toward hers and she

stiffened. Gentle pulls of lips slowly had her body softening, but her conscience always crept back in to remind her that enjoying his touch was a mistake. She kept her mouth closed and her eyes open.

His head tilted and his hand gently landed over her eyes. "Clock doesn't start until you kiss me back, Philly," he whispered against her lips.

She made a soft sound of protest and shut her eyes against the weight of his palm then tilted her head. His hand slipped beneath her ear and around the back of her neck, drawing her in. His scent was all over her as he shifted closer.

When his tongue gently traced over the seam of her lips, she whimpered.

"Let me in," he rasped and she opened.

His mouth sealed over hers, opening and closing softly. She'd been kissed before and done a number of other things, but never could she recall ever being kissed like this. This was no prelude to fucking. This was an event in and of itself.

Finn's hand sifted through her hair and goose bumps chased down her arms. Warm, buttery sensations unfurled in her belly and she sighed. His tongue teased and tangled with hers and the next thing she knew she was practically reclining against the truck door. The handle dug into her back, but it didn't matter. Nothing mattered as long as he continued to kiss her that way.

"Jesus, Philly," he cursed and the kiss intensified. His weight pressed deliciously into her front as he leaned over her. Her fingers flexed over his broad shoulders and then his mouth left hers to kiss a trail of delicate smooches down her throat.

Could someone come from kissing? No, but she felt like she was about to. When he finally eased back, his cheeks were flushed under the foggy shadows of moonlight pouring through the glass. He licked his lips as though savoring her taste. She remained slumped over in her seat, speechless.

"You were saying?" he asked, a cocky grin on his face.

She blinked stupidly at him. "I…I don't think you know what you're asking for."

He grabbed her hand and pressed it to the denim bulge at his crotch. She gasped and he said in a husky voice, "Oh, I know exactly what I'm asking for."

She snatched back her fingers as if he'd burned her and cradled them in her other hand. Sex. He wanted sex. Before she could voice her objections, he said, "It's not about fucking, Philly. That's just the pot of gold at the end of the rainbow. I'm content with simply enjoying the ride. I can wait, so long as you know where I stand."

"I don't understand what you mean."

"Want me to kiss you again so you can find out?"

"No."

He laughed. "All right, but tomorrow I plan on doing that again. A little longer, a little slower, and soon you're gonna stop acting like we're just friends and own up to the chemistry we share."

Jesus Christ, no one had ever come onto her so blatantly. This couldn't be all an act. She had nothing to say. What could she say?

"Now, go ahead in, before I kiss you some more."

She quickly sat up and the door flung open. She scurried out of the truck in record time and slammed the door. His finger pressed into the foggy glass and squeaked as the calloused tip of his thumb wrote XO.

Danger whistles and warning bells clamored in her head. He was going to kiss her again, longer and slower. And then he'd probably get her clothes off, mostly because she wanted to get him out of his. And then, in short order, he'd rip out her heart and she'd never be the same again.

CHAPTER 8

Finn climbed the steps to Mallory's apartment and shifted the sack of food he carried in order to knock. He grinned when he heard her stumbling around. The door opened and she frowned up at him, her hair a rat's nest of wild waves and her eyes still puffy from sleep.

"What time is it?"

He glanced at his watch. "Eight-fifteen. I brought you breakfast."

She glanced at the bag as if it were a dead raccoon and stepped back. "Come in. I have to pee."

It amused him how she was so frank about such things. He dropped the bag on the table and began unloading containers. The toilet flushed and he heard her brushing her teeth. When she came back out, her hair was tied back in a lopsided knot. That, paired with her tiger print pajama pants, was probably the cutest vision he'd ever seen.

"Grab a plate. I have a bunch of greasy meat byproducts I know you're gonna want to tear into."

She frowned at him, but brought two plates and silverware over to the table. He popped the lid off the fruit salad and sighed. "What? This isn't bacon?" He opened the other little tin. "And who put this egg white omelet in here? Looks like they stuffed it with spinach and mushrooms. Well, I can't eat this."

When he glanced at her she was smiling. He passed her the container and she sniffed happily. "Very sweet, Finnegan McCullough. What's in the other container?"

"Oh, that…that's just some disgusting concoction. You eat that. I'll take one for the team and eat the other garbage."

He opened up his breakfast and dug in. The bacon was crisp, the pancakes were fluffy, and the eggs were slathered in cheese. He made sure to keep his plate discretely hidden, because he knew it would piss her off, but she didn't seem to mind. The sounds she made as she ate her own breakfast were almost sexual and his appetite switched to a completely different sort of hunger.

"Is your mom not making breakfast today?"

"She is, but that's later. First, they all go to church."

Her lips closed over a ripe berry speared on the end of her fork. "Don't you go to church?"

He shrugged. "Now and then. Me and God have a special understanding."

"Is your family very religious?"

"My brother was going to be a priest. What do you think?"

"Oh, right. I can't imagine Colin as a priest."

He laughed. It was still difficult to imagine his brother as anything else, but Colin was madly in love with Samantha and his daughter, so there was no doubting this was the path God had intended for him.

When his stomach was full he closed his container and carried it to the trash. She nibbled her fruit salad. "Thanks for breakfast. Everything was great."

He liked the way she didn't sit on the chair like a lady. No, not Philly. She kept one foot on the seat and her knee by her chest. She was perfectly relaxed at the moment and the way her skin still appeared soft from sleep made him want to rub up against her…maybe do some groping and fornicating…

"What are your plans for the day?" he asked, returning to his chair.

"I have to run. I didn't exercise yesterday."

He gasped in mock outrage. "Oh no! Whatever will we do?"

She chucked a berry at him and he caught it in his mouth. She giggled. "That means I have to do something extra today to make up for it."

He could give her some ideas. Maybe burn a few calories himself. "Are you running soon?"

She lifted her creamy shoulder. She had the nicest complexion. "Soon. If I wait too long I'll get tired and start making excuses."

"I know something we can do. What? I'm serious. Did you ever climb a tree?"

"When I was little."

"How would you like to climb a big tree?"

She grinned and looked at him challengingly. "How big?"

"How big do you want it?" Her cheeks flushed and she glanced away. "We have a hundred foot tree we use for training. You can go as high as you can manage."

"Is it dangerous?"

"I won't let you do anything dangerous. I've been logging since I was a teen. I know how to do it safely. It's a great workout."

"I bet. I'm mean, you're in terrible shape."

He grinned and flashed her a shot of his abs, shaking his head in mock disappointment. "Terrible," he agreed.

Her lips parted and she rasped, "Abysmal."

Dropping his shirt, he said, "What do you say? Wanna see what I do for a living?"

"Sure. What should I wear?"

"Do you have boots, like hiking boots?"

"No."

"Then sneakers, heavy jeans, and long sleeves. I have everything else at the site."

As Mallory changed, he cleaned up from breakfast. When she reappeared she looked rugged in the sexiest sense of the word. Her hips filled out a pair of dark denim jeans and she had on a thermal under a baggy T-shirt. "Ready?"

As they drove to the site, she complained about how logging wasn't sympathetic to the weather and worried about sweating. *Girls.* However, he'd never taken a girl climbing. She got cool points simply for agreeing to try it out.

He parked about a hundred yards from the tree they were going to scale. As soon as he climbed out of the truck he went to get her door. She got there first, but he cornered her before her feet had a chance to touch the ground.

Her scent crawled into him, all soft and flowery. He'd been breathing it in since she got in his truck. She stilled as he helped her down and proceeded to back her into the door.

"Finn," she said in warning.

He ignored her and smirked as he lowered his mouth to hers. Warm, soft lips greeted his and she sighed. There was no more reluctance once he pressed her mouth open and stole a taste. He gripped her hips and pulled her to his front. Her hands crawled slowly over his shoulders as their heads tilted.

There was something about kissing Mallory that was different from all the other women he'd kissed. She was tender and warm. He loved putting his hands on her. When he pulled back she blinked up at him, her cheeks a bit flushed and eyelids at half-mast. Even though he'd just kissed her, he wanted to do it again.

Grunting, he turned to get the equipment out of his toolbox in the back of his truck. When he thought she wasn't looking, he did a quick readjustment of his situation down below.

Grabbing some belts, harnesses, and two pairs of spikes, he tossed the equipment over his shoulder and led her to the tree they'd use. "Here it is."

She looked up and squinted into the sun. The tree had been trimmed just for climbing, so there weren't any branches. "There's no way I'm making it to the top."

"Bet you can get halfway there."

She snorted. "Yeah, right. You can climb this?"

"Sure. Want to see me do it first?"

She nodded. He dropped the equipment on the ground and sat on a stump. His foot slid into the spiked brace and he tightened the strap around his calf.

"What are they?"

"These are my spikes. They're essential. They need to be tight and sharp or else you could really mess yourself up."

She watched as he tightened the spikes and stepped into his harness. After lacing the rope through each clamp, he tugged to check that all his knots were secure.

"What's that?"

He lifted his rope. "This is your standard steel cord lanyard. It's a bit stiffer than rope, so it's easier to shimmy with." He latched it to his belt and faced the trunk. The lanyard swung around the girth of the tree and he caught it, locking the other end to his harness.

"So once you're all locked in, you lift it." The rope flipped up. "It's rigid, so it moves fairly easy."

She crept closer to see what he was doing. He dug his spikes into the tree and leaned away from the bark, trusting his harness to hold his weight.

"Is it hard to get your spikes to stick?" she asked.

"You gotta put some force into it, but you'll be able to do it. There are grooves from other climbers to guide you. You want to lean away from the tree. If you're too close it makes it difficult. Keep your legs straight and your spikes at an angle so they don't slip. Hand me that helmet."

She handed him a helmet and he latched it tight. His safety glasses covered his eyes and he tightened his gloves. "So basically, you flick your lanyard."

"The rope?"

"Right." He flicked it up a few feet. "Then you move up a few steps like this. Lean forward, flick, step." The spikes punctured the bark with a metal click at every step. "It's the same coming down as going up, but you want to take it slow, smaller steps."

"How high can you go?"

Squinting at the sky he said, "I've been to the top."

"Wow."

He climbed down about ten feet, showing her how it worked. "Wanna try?"

She nodded. He shimmied down the rest of the way. His boots landed in the dirt with a metal clank.

"Let's get you into your harness first, then I'll help you with your spurs."

She went over to the pile of equipment and folded her arms. "Which one's the harness? There are a lot of them."

He scooped up what she needed. "This part latches around your waist." He waited for her to make some snide, bullshit comment about her body, but when she didn't he was glad.

She stepped close as he buckled the belt around her. She was buried beneath the fabric of her shirt. "Your shirts too big. Here, come closer. You want it tight, but comfortable enough to breathe."

His fingers brushed over her clothing. Their breath mingled as he fit the harness around her. "Next we snap the leg harnesses." She passively stood as his adjusted the belts around her thighs. He had to tighten them quite a bit to fit her. "Sit down and I'll help you with your spurs."

She lowered herself to the stump and he laughed. She frowned. "What?"

"Nothing."

"It's obviously something. Am I doing something wrong?"

"No. I was laughing at your little feet." He fit her sneaker into the spurs and tightened the lock around her calf. "How's that feel?"

"Tight."

"Too tight?"

She wiggled her foot. "No. It sort of feels like I'm wearing skis."

He latched the other one and helped her up. "You ready?"

Glancing up at the sky, she sighed. "As I'll ever be."

"Good. Put these on." He tossed her a helmet, glasses, and gloves. She looked adorable. His type of woman. Without thinking, he reached into his pocket, and withdrew his phone.

"Did you just take my picture?"

"Maybe."

"Why?"

He shrugged. "You look all cute. Philly gone mountain. I dig it."

She growled. "I probably look like a trussed up—" she stopped when she caught his warning glance. "Whatever. I'll delete it when you're not looking."

He dropped the phone into his pants. "Gonna have to search me for it."

"Jerk."

"Come on." His hand slapped the top of her hardhat and he picked up the other lanyard. She faced the trunk and he latched it to her belt, double checking all the knots and clips. "Now swing this around and try to catch it in your other hand, just like I showed you."

Her arm cast the rope out and it clattered to the ground. She growled and pulled it back in. The second time she tossed it a little harder, but it went in the wrong direction. She pulled it in again. Her third try wasn't much better. She growled in frustration.

"Come on, really swing it."

She tried again and the cord whipped against the bark and fell to the ground. "I can't do it."

"Sure you can. You gotta really want it. Throw it again and this time put some stank on it."

She bared her teeth and swung. This time was much better, but her little arms couldn't seem to catch it. "I'm really climbing my ass off. This sucks," she said sarcastically.

SHE WANTED to climb the damn tree, but the stupid rope thing wouldn't work. She tried again and grit her teeth. This time when the lanyard came around the clip hit her in the knuckle. "Ouch!"

"Let me help you."

Her spine stiffened as the heat from Finn's body seeped into her back. His breath tickled her neck as his hand slid over hers and removed the clip from her grip.

The press of his hips was a huge distraction. Her skin was hot under her long sleeves and he only seemed to make her warmer.

"The trick is," he said, whispering in her ear and sending chills down her back. "To thrust hard and know exactly what angle will make it come."

What did he just say? Get your mind out of the gutter and focus. He cast out the lanyard and his body pressed firmly into hers as he caught it in his other hand. He chuckled and latched it to her belt with a tug.

"There."

She didn't breathe until he stepped away. Her hands curled over the rope, playing with its weight.

"Now dig your spike in over that root."

She lifted her leg and kicked her foot down. The spurs were heavy, but punctured the bark with more ease than she suspected they would. She did the same with her other foot. Finn was behind her once more, this time adjusting the slack in the rope.

"Lean into me. You won't fall."

As she eased back her legs stretched and her arms bore a great deal of her weight.

"Keep your legs straight, so you don't slip. Good. Now pull in and flick the rope up. Now step."

She followed his instructions and took her first step. It was a full body workout. Her arms remained tense and her legs rigid. Every step was an effort, as she had to pack enough force to puncture the trunk. After a few steps she was already shaking from exertion and getting tired. When she glanced down she was disappointed to see her body was only about six feet from the ground.

Her head tilted as she tried to see the top of the tree. No wonder he was ripped. This was insane.

"You giving up on me, Philly?"

"No." Her grip tightened as she gave the rope a flick. She traveled several more feet into the air and paused to catch her breath. Finn was shrinking with every flick and step. She was about twelve feet off the ground. Her belly swirled as she considered falling from that height. "Are these ropes going to hold?"

"You're fine. Do you want to come down?"

Every time he gave her the option of quitting she took another step. She could do this. Her gaze assessed the towering trunk and she grit her teeth. Flick, step, step. Flick, step, step.

Sweat trickled from her brow, as she found her rhythm. Her body trembled, as she held on tightly. Her thighs and calves throbbed the higher she went, and her arms were slowly growing weak. Even her core muscles were feeling it.

Finn whistled. "Hey, Philly, you're getting pretty

high. Don't forget you have to save some strength to get back down."

She peeked beneath her arm and cursed. She was really far from the ground. Her heart raced as a sort of paralysis set in. "How do I get down again?"

"Same as you got up, just smaller steps and shorter flicks."

Her lips blew out a tight breath. Tightening her grip, she flicked the rope downward. "Shit!" The slack put more pressure on her muscles and she shook, terrified she was going to fall. It was like pulling her leg from drying cement, forcing her foot to step down.

"You all right?" he yelled.

"Yeah," she shouted back. Then in a smaller voice she mumbled, "I hope."

The rope flicked again and down she stepped. Climbing was work, but at least it was fun work. This going down stuff was for the birds. It felt like days before she reached a height she was comfortable with. Once she knew she was a distance from the ground that wouldn't kill her if she fell, her steps became more confident.

When she finally reached the base of the tree Finn caught her hips. "You made it!"

She was out of breath and trembling. "Barely."

He laughed and pressed a kiss to her neck. She drew back, knowing sweat covered her skin. His fingers undid the clip and she stepped off the tree. "What do you think?"

"I think it's crazy that you do that every day. I'm not going to be able to move tomorrow."

"Told you it was a good workout."

She practically wept when he undid her spurs and harness. Collapsing back on the stump she let out a deep breath. Finn loaded up the gear in the truck and she could barely move.

"Uh-oh, we got a piper down."

She gave him the finger and even that took too much work. "How many calories does tree climbing burn?"

"I have no idea. Come on." He held out a hand and she gripped it weakly.

"You're worse than a personal trainer. Stop making me move," she whined, hoisting herself to her feet. Her knees jiggled like pudding.

"How you ever gonna run those Rocky steps with that sort of attitude, Philly? Where did my tough girl go?"

"You killed her."

He laughed and they walked back to the truck. "What do you want to do now?" he asked as he held her door.

"Nap. Some crazy Irish guy woke me up way too early and made me climb trees all morning."

"Can I come?"

She stilled. Where? To nap with her? "Um…I need a shower." The side of his mouth kicked up and she snapped, "You aren't invited to shower. A nap, I can tolerate."

He kissed her, a quick peck on the lips. "You're no fun."

CHAPTER 9

There was something wrong with her lungs. They needed more air than usual and Mallory couldn't seem to draw in a full breath. The entire ride home she stared out the window, afraid to look to her left. The truck filled with their mixed scents, the autumn breeze laced with fresh air, and the fragrance of exertion. The only way to describe it was heady.

When they returned to her place, Finn plopped on the couch as usual and she stumbled into the kitchen, mumbling some excuse, as she fled to the bathroom. Currently, she stood under the warm flow of rushing water doing nothing.

Her vision kept returning to her razor, each time zooming in with rapid succession like some horror flick. She should shave, but if she shaved she wouldn't have an excuse to stop him. If she left her legs prickly that would be the brake light she needed.

Her gaze did the crazy zoom thing on the razor again. This time she swore she heard some Beethoven type build in her head too. "Crap."

She grabbed the razor and lathered her legs with her peach scented shaving gel. Ten minutes later, the water had dwindled from steaming hot to tepid and she'd managed to shave places she'd never shaved before. For some strange reason she associated Finn with smooth skin. Well, she had a lot of skin. Maybe if it were super smooth he wouldn't notice the way it rolled and sagged in all the wrong places.

Frustrated, she flung the razor into the corner and rinsed off. After shutting the water off, she grabbed her towel and stood before the fogged up mirror. She didn't need a reflection to know what she looked like, but as she saw herself her mood fell to devastatingly low places that she usually tried not to venture.

What was she doing? She was smarter than this. If she continued to let Finn kiss her he'd eventually want to touch her beneath her clothes. And then there would be that awful moment when he paused, only for a split second, but it would be enough for her to know he stumbled across the disgusting reality that was her body.

Her lips thinned as her throat pinched with the need to cry. She wouldn't cry, however, because crying over skin was stupid. All of her life she'd dieted and all of her life she'd continued to gain weight. It wasn't fair that six months of denying herself would result in a loss of fifteen pounds, but two months of falling off the wagon would pack on twenty. That was her track record, down ten, up fifteen, down twenty, up thirty.

Sometimes she wondered if she would choose contentment with her physique over actual skinniness. She was so screwed up. She knew she was pretty, but society had done such a number on her she felt permanently broken inside. If she lost all the weight that burdened her, would she just be one of those thin people who still hated themselves?

Very aware that she was entering a dark place of self-loathing with Finn sitting on the other side of the door waiting, she tried to pick herself up. She hadn't gotten this way in a day, a month, or a year. It was unrealistic to think she could get herself back to a healthy weight in such short increments of time as well.

The horrible thing was, no matter how healthy her body became, her mind was not healthy at all. She wished, just for a day, she could know what if felt like to exist without the pain of low self-esteem.

Her hand squeaked over the glass as she wiped down the mirror. Her eyes darted to the lock on the bathroom door. She sucked in a breath and dropped the towel.

Her brow crumpled and her shoulders sagged. She

hated her reflection. Her breasts hung heavy. Her stomach made a pouch of flab. There was probably a six-pack under there somewhere from all the sit-ups she'd been doing, but who would ever know? Her hips were thick and her thighs were way too full. Dimples showed where smoothness should have been. Then there were those horrid little jagged white scars, marks from her skin stretching.

Shutting her eyes, she tried to block out the image, but it was no use. She knew it by heart. She thought about Finn. He was so tall and broad and tan. He had cut arms and those hands…he probably looked like a chiseled statue of a Greek god naked, while she was built like a dowdy milkmaid.

Everything seemed so suddenly hopeless she wanted to sneak out of the apartment and go stuff her face with ice cream until the pain faded.

The steam in the bathroom dissipated and her hair started to kink and air dry. She'd been in there a long time, probably almost an hour. Taking a courageous breath that was mostly hot air, she tied her robe and unlocked the door. Shaved or not, he wasn't touching her.

The bathroom door creaked quietly and she crept out. Finn was slouched on the couch, sound asleep. She tiptoed past him and shut herself in her room where she dressed in cotton pants and an old T-shirt.

Emotionally whipped, she climbed into bed and

shut her eyes. No tears would fall, because self-pity was worthless. Maybe when she woke up he'd be gone.

Her self-deprecating thoughts slowed and her mind drifted in and out of dreams. She was in that foggy place where the brain was still awake, but the body was starting to fall asleep when she heard him enter the room.

Pretend you're still asleep.

She barely breathed, as she waited for him to say something. Completely aware that he was watching, she mentally curled into a ball, but her physical body didn't move a muscle. When the bed dipped she stopped breathing completely.

Covers were lifted and his body suddenly warmed her back, as he curled behind her into the bed. He must have thought she was asleep, because he didn't say a word. Something in her softened as he filled the space at her back.

He was warm and strong and so much better than her. She'd never measure up. It was only a matter of time before he realized the truth and she was out a good friend.

The weight of his palm settled on her hip and she prayed he didn't move. At least her hip had a bone to keep it semi-firm. Two inches up and he'd hit the land of blubber. Two inches down and he'd find himself in Beyoncé's nightmare.

A soft sigh filled the room. It was a masculine sound

of contentment and she blinked into the dim shadows. How did he sound so content? Didn't he see and feel what he was touching?

Her body grew stiff the longer she lay there. Finn likely drifted off to sleep, but she wasn't sure. A piece of hair kept tickling her nose and she wanted to bat it away, but was too terrified of moving and waking him. She'd wait ten more minutes then slip out of bed and find something else to do.

Five minutes later her eyes were growing heavy. Finn's arm weighed over her side and, although they hadn't moved, he seemed to be holding her tighter. If she could forget about the shape of her body, she could almost fall asleep.

Wake up!

Her lashes fluttered open only to droop once more. *Don't go to sleep!*

No matter how much she commanded her body to remain awake she was losing the battle. She must have made it about eight minutes before she surrendered and let go. Her thoughts fell away and she sagged into the mattress, into Finn's hold. Cozy peace carried her away to a land of slumber and she slept like she had as a child.

Finn awoke and it took him a split second to remember where he was. Mallory's bed. He grinned in the dimly shadowed room and snuggled into her soft-ness. She was so damn cozy. And she smelled incredi-ble, like peaches or apricots or some other girly shit.

Her hair was a wild mess and tickled his nose as he nestled into the back of her shoulder. He didn't want to wake her, but at the same time, he did. He wanted to glide his hand up a little higher and explore her curves, feel the weight of her unbound breasts in his hands.

Settle down, McCullough.

Very aware that he was packing some wood, he resisted the urge to flex his hips into hers. Shit. It was growing. He tried to wiggle back some, but Mallory made the most adorable snuffle sound and stiffened. She was awake.

They must have been sleeping there for at least an hour. "You awake?"

She whined something between a yes and a sound of distress. He gently massaged her hip and snuggled closer. No point trying to hide what he couldn't.

"Finn?"

"Yeah?"

"What are you doing?"

"Cuddling."

"Oh."

They were silent for over a minute. Then she said, "I should get up."

He tightened his fingers over her hip. "Not yet."

She sure woke up tense. The tips of his fingers

fanned over her hip and found a pocket of warmth when he reached soft skin. Her hand snapped down over his. "Don't."

He stilled, not sure what to do. He was only touching her side. There really wasn't anything sexual about it—sort of. "Okay," he said in a measured, calm voice.

She lifted her hand from his and he moved his palm to her outer thigh—nothing but cotton there. It wasn't as nice, but he was still touching her. He couldn't seem to make himself *not* touch her.

"I need to get up," she said.

His hand abandoned her thigh and went to the tangled mess of hair lying over the pillow. Gathering the stands and pulling them out of the way, he kissed the back of her soft neck. "Wait. Lay here with me a little longer."

She didn't argue, but her body didn't relax. Pressing soft kisses into the curve of her neck and shoulder, he rubbed her arm and tried to ease her. "I like kissing you."

"Well, I just woke up and I need to brush my teeth."

Ignoring her, he tugged the collar of her shirt back and kissed over the soft skin above her shoulder blade. "You have a freckle here." He licked over the soft brown mark.

Her shoulders shifted. He wasn't sure if she was trying to nudge him off or if he was giving her the chills. He continued to place slow, gentle kisses over her shoulders, neck, and back.

She drew in a shaky breath and he sensed he was breaking down her walls. Giving her shoulder a gentle tug, he rasped, "Come here."

When she resisted, he applied a bit of pressure, and eased her onto her back. Her expression was blank as she blinked up at him. He fit his body over hers, careful not to crush her. Her unsupported breasts filled her T-shirt and there was no mistaking the press of her nipples against the worn fabric.

His lips sealed to her neck as he tickled his tongue up to her ear. She sighed, but her body still remained stiff. When he closed his lips over the tender lobe of her ear she gasped and arched. Trumpets of victory hummed in his head as he caught a glimpse of the passion she kept so bottled up. He sucked her lobe and teased the shell of her ear with his tongue. Her breath was raspy and coming faster. Taking a risk he ground his pelvis into hers and she made the softest gasp.

She was so fucking hot. His hands sifted through her tangled hair and cupped her head. His mouth made a slow journey to hers. When his lips touched the corner of hers she turned away.

"Hey," he whispered softly. "Let me kiss you."

"I just woke up," she said in a pleading voice. Her eyes blinked up at him so innocently it only fueled the fire building inside of him. He would never rush her into anything. He could wait for the bigger stuff, but he needed to kiss her.

"I don't care."

"Finn—"

"Are you turned on right now, Mallory? Be honest. Please."

She was quiet for several beats and then she quietly said, "Extremely."

Finally! "Then let me kiss you," he said just as his lips closed over hers.

She was stubborn, keeping her mouth sealed tight. But he wanted in. He pressed his tongue over the seam of her lips until she finally opened. Sweeping his tongue deeply, he kissed her with all the passion he held.

She slowly softened until her efforts to not give over were futile. When he felt her small hands curl over his shoulders he felt like his team just won the Super Bowl with all his money riding on it. He growled and deepened the kiss, pulling her tightly to him.

Her knees tightened on his hips as he ground into her sex. Jesus, he hadn't made out like this in years. Hands pulled, heads dipped, and backs arched. It was already qualifying as one of the hottest sexual experiences he'd had since being a kid.

When things got a bit too intense, he pulled away, and pressed his head into her shoulder to catch his breath. "Jesus, Mallory. Kissing you is like…I don't even know what. Give me a second."

He shouldn't have stopped. Once he gave her a moment to clear her head, the walls resurrected. He could almost hear the echo of brick slamming down around her. Pressing his lips to the soft skin below her ear—*magic spot*—he said, "You're so hot."

Wrong thing to say. Her body grew as tense as a corpse and she nudged him to get off. "I can't breathe," she muttered.

He eased back and she maneuvered out from under him. In a matter of seconds she was standing, adjusting her clothes, and looking anywhere but at the bed.

"You okay?"

"Fine." The answer was too high pitched and quick to be true.

"Did I say something wrong?"

"No. I'll be back." She left the room like her bed was on fire.

He stood and adjusted the blue Smurf village setting up camp in his pants. Well, maybe Smurf wasn't the best way to describe his body at that moment. There was definitely a code blue in play, but there was nothing small about it.

When she didn't return, he headed out to the living room and found her at the kitchen counter drinking a bottle of water. "You okay?"

"Mm—hmm." She was lying.

She chugged the water and proceeded to dig around in the fridge. He crept up behind her and wrapped his arms around her waist. She jumped and slammed the top of her head into the freezer door causing all the jars in the fridge rattled.

"Jesus, Philly, are you all right?"

She stood and rubbed her head. "I'm fine. Stop asking if I'm okay. I'm fine. Fine."

He held up his hands. "All right. But you just whacked your head pretty hard. Do you want some ice?"

Her eyes were wild and then abruptly they glazed with tears. He stepped closer to comfort her, but she held up a hand. "Don't. I'm fine."

Frustrated, he said, "You're obviously *not* fine. You look ready to cry."

Her lashes fluttered so rapidly he knew she was trying to hide it. Unfortunately, one lone tear slipped past and landed on her breast, turning the cotton of her shirt dark gray.

"I think you should go." He wasn't expecting that.

Feeling the returning sting of her rejection, he stepped back. "What? Why?"

"Because…I just think you should go."

Fuck that.

He stepped closer and caught the hand trying to hold him at bay. Her other hand continued to rub her head where an egg was likely forming. "I don't want to go," he said, replacing the hand on her head with his own. Yup, there was a lump.

He kissed her hair and pulled her into a hug. She was tense and he wasn't sure why. "Mallory, if I did something wrong, tell me. I mean, aside for startling you and making you whack your head."

Her shoulders lifted as she let out a long breath. She breathed in and he had the suspicion she was sniffing his shirt. "You didn't do anything wrong," she mumbled into his armpit. "It's me. I'm crazy."

He laughed and rubbed a hand down her back. "I know, but I like you that way."

She pushed him away and took a step back. Looking at the ground, she frowned and wrung her hands. "I…I don't know how to do this with you."

"Do what?"

She waved her hand in the air as if that explained things. "The…kissing…and stuff."

"Seemed to me you know how to kiss just fine."

Her lips twisted and she shot him a sardonic look. "You know what I mean."

"No, I don't. Explain it to me."

She sighed. "We're friends, Finn. If we cross that line there's no uncrossing it."

"So?"

"So aren't you worried we'll wreck our friendship?"

Well, yes, he'd thought of that, but…he wanted her. He wanted her badly. Not just once, either. He needed to have her. He didn't have friends like Mallory. She was special. His instincts told him that the two of them as a couple would be incredible. Once in his head, he couldn't convince himself to back down. This was right. "I won't let that happen."

"You can't promise it won't," she argued.

"I'm not a jerk, Mallory. I'd never stop being your friend. I'm just not that type of guy."

"Well, I don't know if I'm the type of girl who can have sex with someone and then go back to being friends."

He held up his hands. "Whoa! Who's having sex?"

Her mouth opened and closed. "Well...I thought..." She covered her face with her palms. "Oh, God, never mind. I'm such an idiot."

He had to laugh. She was adorably confused. He grabbed her forearm and pulled her to the couch.

When he sat down beside her, he said, "Mallory, *if* we eventually have sex, that's something we will deal with then. Right now, I promise you, we aren't. You can trust me. Let down your guard. I'd never rush into sex with you until we discussed it—not when we're all wrapped up in each other's bodies and incapable of thinking clearly. I mean we'll discuss it like two mature adults considering taking their relationship to the next level. You would know when I planned on sleeping with you, because I would have to know you planned the same. Consensual."

"But people get carried away—"

"I don't. It's difficult. I'll admit I was pretty turned

on in bed with you, but I had it under control. I know when to stop."

She looked at her lap and mumbled, "Sometimes there are things more intimate than actual sex. When we were kissing…I don't think I've ever been kissed like that. It was…different."

Thank God!

"I felt that too. It's us. That's what I'm talking about. We're attracted to each other—really attracted. If we try to ignore it, that may be what ruins our friendship. I'm not asking you for anything you aren't willing to give. You say stop and I stop. But I don't know if I can go too long without being able to touch you. I loved napping with you and waking up with you in my arms."

She twisted her lips. "Yeah, well, I'm not used to being touched."

"I noticed. Why is that? You had to have had boyfriends back in Philly."

She shrugged. "I guess."

"You guess?"

"I mean I had friends that were guys. I'm not a virgin, but…I've never slept with a guy."

"You're not a virgin, but you've never slept with a guy?"

"I've had sex. Several times. I'm not a whore or anything. I've been with three men. Well, the first time I was seventeen, so actually, he was a kid. But as an adult there were two others."

"Okay." This was good to know. "Do you want to know how many people I've been with?"

"Oh, God. No thanks. You probably have a list of beauties. Knowing will only make me more self-conscious."

"One."

Her head kicked up and her eyes bore into his. "*One?*"

He grinned and nodded. "One. I lost my virginity to Erin senior year after the homecoming game and I've never been with anyone else."

"How is that possible? Have you seen you?"

He chuckled. She saw him as something he wasn't. He was just an average guy. Of all the McCullough siblings, he was probably the least interesting.

"It's not about looks. Sleeping with someone is about sharing that intimate connection, feeling like you're home when you're in their arms. I mean, sure, it can be exciting and great, but without that emotional link, I'd rather pass."

She stared at him, slack-jawed, for several seconds. "Are you for real?"

"Yeah. Why?"

Shaking her head, she said, "Where I'm from, guys don't think like that, at least not the guys I know."

"Maybe that's why you haven't found the right guy yet."

"Or maybe it's me."

He grabbed her chin and forced her to meet his gaze. "Hey, I can assure you it's not you. You're beautiful, sexy, smart, and funny. Those guys were assholes if they didn't see you for who you are, but I'm sort of glad they didn't. If they did, you might not be here with me."

When she smiled he felt like he may have gotten through to her on some level. It wasn't right, how hard she was on herself. So what if she wasn't a size two? Most women weren't. After marriage people had families and all that superficial stuff went out the window anyway. She needed to stop beating herself up. He put a stop to the image put-downs, but sensing she might still think she wasn't good enough really pissed him off.

"I'm sort of glad, too," she admitted quietly. "Next to all the guys back home, none of them can even compare to you."

His chest tightened at the compliment. He wasn't used to hearing things like that about himself. It felt nice. He pulled her into a hug and kissed the top of her head. "Thank you. That was really nice."

"It's true."

He settled back into the couch with her, refusing to let her go. "You know what this means now, don't you?"

"What?"

"It means you're my girlfriend."

He flinched as she poked him in the stomach. "No, I'm not. You have to ask."

He sighed dramatically. "Will you be my girlfriend?"

"Maybe you should have one of your friends pass me a note so I can circle yes or no if I like *like* you."

"Are you making fun of me?"

"Yes."

He bit her shoulder and she squeaked. When he faced her, he said, "Philly, I like *like* you. Will you go steady with me and wear my pin?"

She held out her hand and smiled.

He stared at her open palm. "What?"

"Where's the pin?"

"Oh. I don't have one. But I'll get you one."

She rolled her eyes. "That's so anti-climactic."

"Does that mean yes?" he asked.

She pulled out of his grip, grabbed the notepad on the table, and scribbled something. When she flashed it at him it said 'yes' with the word circled.

A shit-eating grin spread over his face. "You know what this means now, don't you?"

"What?"

"I get to kiss you whenever I want." He lunged at her and she squealed, but soon he silenced her with his lips.

The following week was fantastic. The sky was a little bluer. The changing autumn leaves seemed more radiant. The chatter of children playing outside her office window at recess sounded more harmonized. And she breathed a little easier. Why? *Because she had a boyfriend!*

Only because it was completely inappropriate to doodle hearts with her and Finn's initials all over the attendance sheets, did she resist the urge. But the temptation was definitively there. All week long she had a proud version of her own voice cheering in her head, which kept a smile pasted on her face.

Who's that sexy mountain man?
My boyfriend!
Which McCullough is the cutest?
My boyfriend!

Where were you last night?
Out with my boyfriend!
Did you kiss him?
Oh yeah! I kissed him! I kissed him up real nice!

She'd regressed to the age of fifteen, but was doing a good impression of a woman in her thirties. How the hell had she gone thirty years and not once known what it was to have a real boyfriend? She was walking around like she defined awesomeness and there was nothing that could hinder her mood.

Student sent to the office for putting gum in Tiffany's hair—no problem. She smiled at him and gave him a piece of candy from the jar on her desk, convincing herself he probably did it because he like *liked* her. She saw everything differently. Gone was the cynic and in came the optimist.

The craziest realization was that she—for the first time ever—started to consider that she might actually be sexy. Maybe. Finn thought she was.

They'd exchanged phone numbers and he had made a point to text her regularly. Mostly little things, like 'How's your day going?' or 'Thinking of you.' Or—her personal favorite—'Can't wait to see you and kiss that soft spot by your ear.'

She was a goner, but she didn't care. Finn was probably the nicest guy she'd ever met. And the sexiest. And the best kisser. And he was hers! She really needed to get that pin he'd talked about, so others knew it.

At night, she'd stare up at her ceiling. Daydreams of kissing and hanging out with Finn turned into night dreams that entailed a whole lot more. She could fantasize about naked stuff in her dreams, because when she slept, she saw herself differently. It was as though her soul shaped her body and she liked who she was.

She'd started running an extra mile that week. Knowing Finn wanted her—*her*—motivated her to be the woman he deserved. She was down a total of twenty-one pounds. Less than nine away from her first major benchmark. Every time she felt like quitting, she told herself if she hadn't gotten this far a man like Finn might have never noticed her in the first place.

It was strange. Suddenly, when she measured her value in accordance with the shape of her body, things stopped adding up. That was shaky ground. It only made sense to believe Finn was attracted to the *new* her. The old her was gross. But there wasn't much of a difference, was there?

She was her hardest critic. Some rational side of her commonsense stood up for her battered self-esteem and seemed to be speaking up more and more, telling her it didn't matter if she was thirty pounds lighter or a hundred pounds heavier. He liked her for her. She didn't trust this new theory and it scared her. All his compliments were starting to confuse what she always believed to be true.

Her clothes were falling off her hips and she took

great pride in bagging things up for charity. Tonight she was going to the mall to buy herself a new outfit. She wouldn't go nuts, because she wasn't stopping her progress, and would soon need to buy new clothes again. But she wanted something pretty to wear if Finn asked her out that weekend.

After work she did her run, showered, went to the bank, and then headed to the mall. When she lived in the city her pants had been anywhere between a size twenty-two and twenty-six. There were no words to describe what it felt like to walk out of the store carrying size eighteen jeans. *Eighteen!*

On the ride home her phone was buzzing like crazy, all texts from Finn. She couldn't answer, because she was driving, but the rush of being in such high demand was euphoric.

When she pulled up at her place it was dark, but there was no missing the reflection of her headlights in the taillights of his truck. Adrenaline pumped through her as she climbed out of the car and walked around the corner of the building.

She hadn't seen him for a few days and her heart raced with anticipation. There he was. Beautiful. *Her* boyfriend.

He smiled and stood from where he was lounging on the bottom three steps. "Hey, beautiful."

That was her name for him, but he could borrow it. He made her feel beautiful. "Hey."

His gaze traveled to the bags in her hands. "Go shopping?"

"Yes."

He approached and she watched mesmerized. Only cowboys could get away with that sort of swagger—cowboys and McCulloughs. He relieved her of her bags and kissed her lightly on the lips. It took all of her might not to swoon or rape him on the spot.

He followed her up the stairs and with each step something potent tightened inside of her. He was finally there. Her hands shook as she unlocked the door. The moment she stepped inside he dropped the bags and gripped her shoulders. Her back hit the wall and his mouth was on her.

Deep, hard, thrusts of his tongue expressed how much he'd missed her. She sifted her fingers through his soft hair and fisted, loving the soft weight between her knuckles. His growl was swallowed by their kiss as he proceeded to take over, claiming her mouth, sending shivers up her spine.

Something hot and molten unfurled inside of her. She shaved that morning and wanted him to touch her. Not get fully naked, but she really wanted to feel his rough palm chasing chills over her flesh.

Then there was his flesh. She could touch him too. Her hands bunched up the soft cotton of his shirt and landed on hot, firm skin. She gripped his hip, peeking out just above the thick leather belt at his waist, and he moaned.

Her senses were getting carried away and she was about to do something incredibly stupid when he backed away. His thumb pressed over her kiss-swollen lips and he whispered, "I missed you, Philly."

"I missed you too. I couldn't answer your texts because I was driving."

"I figured. Did you eat?"

"I haven't had dinner yet. Do you want me to cook something?"

His smile turned into something spectacular. She wanted to know what he was thinking. "What?"

"I like that you cook. Not that it's a requirement, but I just…like it. My mom always cooked for my dad and all of us kids. Nowadays it isn't easy to find a woman willing to take up that role."

"Settle down. I meant I'd cook you a meal, not change my life and turn into Donna Reed." She turned and started pulling out pans and items from the cabinets.

Truth be told, she didn't mind cooking, especially for a guy like Finn who enjoyed eating so much. She understood what he meant. There was something to be said for a woman willing to take care of her man and family. Finn was an old fashioned kind of guy so she could understand why he found that attractive. "Did Erin cook for you?"

Before she could pull the words back they were out.

He cleared his throat. "Not really. She liked to eat out a lot. What are you making?"

She unfolded the butcher paper and showed him. "I picked up Tilapia. I was going to make it with some lemon and herbs."

He came around the counter and wrapped his arms over her waist. She sucked in as he kissed her shoulder. "You take good care of me. Can I help?"

"Uh, sure." She rolled her shoulder causing him to step back. She needed to think when she cooked and she couldn't think when he touched her. "I was also going to make broccoli. You can wash it off."

They worked around each other in the small kitchen. Finn asked questions and was very helpful. However, he did steal food right off the pan. When they sat down she opened a bottle of wine and they feasted.

"This is amazing," he said over a mouthful of fish.

"Thanks. It's one of my favorites. Tilapia tastes good with anything."

They finished eating and sipped their wine, making small talk. The sexual tension worked like static electricity, tripping over every nerve she had. She wondered if it was one-sided or if he was feeling it too.

There was a very naughty side to her that wanted to do very bad things to him, but her self-image always seemed to intervene just in time. The pull to explore his body was becoming more difficult to ignore by the minute.

Finn set his glass down with a hard click and her gaze jerked to his. Tight breaths filled her lungs as they stared at each other in silence. What was he looking at? Did she have food on her face? She self-consciously wiped her cheek. When he stood, the motion was abrupt and he jostled the table. A heartbeat later he was in front of her and she knew he was going to kiss her.

Staring up at him, she waited, but he didn't lean in. His hand slowly lifted to her face and her stomach sunk. Crap, she probably did have something on her face. His hand cupped her jaw, not to wipe away food, but to simply caress her. Rough, calloused fingers tripped over her soft skin. Her lashes lowered and she leaned into his warm palm and moaned.

"Shit, Philly, I may not be able to stay long tonight."

Her eyes shot open. "Why?" She didn't want him to go.

"Because I can't think straight around you. I want…" He shook his head as though he was waging some internal war. "You."

Her breath caught. Oh, the naughty Mallory was coming out. She placed her napkin on the table and slowly stood. Taking his hand she led him to her room and shut the door. They stood at the foot of the bed and his chest rose and fell with deep breaths. Never before in her life had she felt such a potent pull to a man.

You cannot have sex with him!

I know!

Leaning up on her toes, she pressed her lips to his, and the core of the earth seemed to crack open and swallow them whole. His hands tightened on her as they fell onto the bed. Mouths, lips, and teeth clashed together as they kissed passionately.

Her fingers worked the buttons of his shirt and she found utopia. Sculpted muscles curved his chest. His abs showed like Jacob's ladder. Tanned skin met her fingertips as she explored him. He was utterly perfect. Her mouth kissed over his Gaelic tattoo and he cupped the back of her head as he stretched out beneath her touch.

She nipped and kissed at his belly smiling when she found his ticklish spot, taking an extra moment to tease him. When she tormented him past his limit, he rolled, and flipped her onto her back. His lips set in an evil grin as he lowered his mouth and kissed her slowly.

With drowsy eyes, he gazed down at her and tugged at the collar of her shirt. "Can I take this off?"

Her heart clamored against her ribs. She swallowed. "Sure. Shut off the light."

His brow creased. "Then I won't be able to see you."

"Exactly." She leaned over to hit the bedside lamp and he caught her hand.

"I want to see you, Mallory."

She gave him a pleading look. "No, you don't."

"Uh, yeah…I do."

"Finn—"

"Let me see you." He kissed her softly, persuasively.

"No."

"Are we going too fast?"

"No."

"Then…" The question fell away. "I see what this is." He shook his head and it was obvious she'd upset him.

Quickly trying to explain, she said, "I'm just not comfortable being naked."

"Do you think anyone is? We all have insecurities. They shouldn't exist between lovers."

"But we aren't lovers. At least, not yet."

"And when we are, will we only do it under the covers with the lights off? Because I got to tell you, Mallory, I'm not about that."

Weight settled on her chest. She wasn't trying to be ridiculous. It was like paralysis. She simply couldn't abide him seeing her naked. Every time she'd ever had sex her shirt had remained on and it was always in the dark. Her breasts were big and awkward and she could never relax enough to enjoy them being touched.

In a desperate act to distract him from her flaws, her hand went to the buckle of his belt. "We can do something else with the lights on." He caught her arm, his eyes set in disbelief, and her desperation morphed into shame.

"No. I don't want that from you. Especially not

when you're using it to divert my attention, Mallory. Sex in any form of manipulation is a turn off to me."

Swallowing tightly, she nodded, and withdrew her hand from his zipper. She usually experienced that self-deprecating sense of regret the morning after, but with Finn it was smack dab in the middle of what they were doing. Why did she just do that? She felt dirty and not in a good way. "I'm sorry."

"Hey," he snapped. "What happened? We were enjoying ourselves and everything just went wrong." He shook his head. "Let's rewind for a second. Come here."

He tried to pull her close, but she tilted her head away like a disgraced dog.

"Mallory, look at me."

She blinked at him with glazed eyes. "I'm sorry."

"Stop saying that! If you're too in your head while I'm touching you then *I'm* the one doing something wrong."

She gasped. "What? You didn't do anything wrong! It's me."

"And what did you do? Tell me what you did, because I see it in your eyes, and I know you're punishing yourself right now."

She nearly choked. "I don't know," she mumbled lamely, knowing exactly what was in her head but not having the right words to express it. Disgust. Self-loathing. Insecurity. Fat! It had absolutely nothing to do with him.

"Mallory, talk to me. It's just us. You can say whatever you're thinking."

She shook her head. No she couldn't.

He cupped her cheeks and she realized tears had started to fall. She was ruining everything. "Talk to me, Philly," he whispered and she had the urge to run away.

"I just wanted to please you."

"You *do* please me," he said emphatically.

"I don't want to see disappointment in your eyes when…I thought if I could distract you…"

He made a sound between a gasp and hurt, perhaps there was a tinge of disbelief as well.

She lowered her eyes. "I don't know why I'm like this. I've never been comfortable in my own skin."

His expression showed sympathy, but he didn't comment. She went on. "I'm…" Crap, she was really going to admit this. "I'm afraid if you see me naked you'll leave a Finn shaped hole in the door."

He laughed. "That's crazy talk. I see you all the time and I haven't run yet. Besides…unless something's chasing me…" He shrugged and she chucked. "I know what you look like, Mallory. Everything I've seen has only made me want to get closer to you. I'm not going anywhere."

Her breath was staggered as she glanced up at him. There was nothing but sincerity in his eyes. Why was this so hard for her?

Realizing there was no postponing the inevitable,

she stood. Taking a deep breath, she caught the hem of her shirt and slowly lifted it over her head. Her eyes sealed shut as the material hit the floor. The bed squeaked and she imagined herself standing in her white lace bra and him gathering his shoes and quietly leaving.

She flinched when his fingers grazed the exposed skin of her shoulders. "You're beautiful," he whispered and her expression tightened. For some reason those words caused a physical ache inside of her.

It felt like a lie, but sounded like truth, which made it cut a thousand times deeper. She couldn't abide Finn's pity and the chance that he was lying to her, because he somehow felt responsible for her inner turmoil, slayed her. Her head started to shake in denial, but he caught her chin in a firm grip.

"Yes," he said sternly. "*Beautiful.*"

When she opened her eyes his gaze was searching hers. He wasn't even looking at her belly or her breasts. He was looking into her soul. It was then that she realized he was telling the truth. He saw her as beautiful. The dose of honesty wasn't too hard to swallow, because it was quickly followed with her private admission.

I love him.

Stretching her arms behind her back, she undid the clasp of her bra and dragged the straps down her arms, letting it fall to the floor. Finn never took his eyes off of hers. His hand slowly slid down her arm to her fingertips. A soft caress whispered up her side and her flesh was suddenly engulfed in the warmth of his palm.

She sighed as his thumb slowly traced over her turgid nipple. His lips found hers and he kissed her slowly. Her passion had been banked to make room for something so much more.

Her body quivered as he touched her with gentle hands and soft lips. He pulled her to the bed and slowly eased her to her back. His hands trailed over her arms as he settled on top of her. She was grateful his body offered some sort of shelter.

"Kiss me, Mallory."

Her lips met his with barely restrained esteem. Only he could do this to her, push her to face her demons and loan her courage to carry on. At the press of his erection through the barrier of both of their pants, she realized he was aroused and it wasn't an act.

As if heaven opened up, assurance washed over her and she gripped his shoulders. The kiss deepened as his hands did amazing things to her breasts. She arched and moaned as his mouth captured her nipple. Every caress, every touch, liberated her a little bit more. Then something incredible happened.

Tightness coiled in her lower abdomen. Nothing like the rapid twitch she felt when she got herself off. This was molten and languid and oh so decadent. He suckled her breasts and the pulling continued. Like slow waves, it built and built until her legs were trembling and she was crying out.

His arms wrapped around her back and he held her as she came apart. Thirty years old and she'd just experienced her first orgasm from a man.

The scruff of his jaw rubbed over her shoulder as he kissed her throat. "You're so responsive," he whispered. "That was beautiful."

She was speechless. Nothing like that had ever happened to her before. He reached for the covers, pulled them up to their shoulders, and curled her into his side.

She should probably do or say something, but she had no idea what. Didn't he need to come? Men usually got grumpy when they didn't come.

His fingers combed through her hair and as much as she wanted to resolve the unattended issues, her body wanted to sleep. She shut her eyes, there in her boyfriend's arm with nothing but pants on, and let her mind rest.

"Finnegan McCullough, you had better have some good answers for why it's dawn and I'm just settin' eyes on your face now! Nothin' but trouble's open after two, and I want some answers!"

Finn winced as his mother scared the hell out of him as he crept in the front door. Jesus, was that the wooden spoon in her hand? "Christ, Ma, I'm twenty-eight years old! Are you gonna beat me with that spoon?"

"If I like. Where were you?"

"Out."

"Don't feed me that rubbish. Who were you with?"

"Friends."

"What friends? Kelly said he hadn't seen you last night. Were you with Erin?"

His gaze jerked back to the living room where he was almost free. "No. I wasn't with Erin. We broke up a few weeks ago and we won't be getting back together."

Her gaze studied him. "The city girl?"

"Her name is Mallory, and yes, I was with her."

This seemed to please his mother greatly, but her wide smile suddenly turned into a scowl. "Finnegan, love, I sure hope you didn't do anything stupid. A good girl deserves respect. I didn't raise my boys to run around fornicating all hours of the night."

He threw up his hands. "Jesus, Ma! I wasn't fornicating and I wish you and Dad would stop using that word."

"What were you doing then?"

"Sleeping. I didn't mean to stay this late, but we fell asleep after dinner. I'm still tired, so I'm going to bed now. Please put the spoon away."

He turned and his mother mumbled something about her sons being sluts. If only she knew how unslutty he had been last night. His shit still hurt. Rather than heading to his room, he hooked a left at the top of the steps and headed to the bathroom. He needed some relief.

After his shower, he fell into bed, but couldn't sleep. His mind filled with visions of Mallory. He understood why she was self-conscious. She wasn't built like the women plastered all over the media, but in his mind she was built better. It was amazing touching a woman who actually had breasts.

She was soft and curvy and he still could not believe he made her come without penetration. He would have accused her of faking it, but the shock that registered in her eyes showed she was as surprised as him.

He hadn't wanted to leave. When he woke up with her partially naked and warm in his arms, he'd wanted to stay there and touch her some more, but he knew his mother would be worried since he hadn't told anyone where he was going.

Sighing, he rolled to his back and stared up at the ceiling. The tightness in his cheeks told him he hadn't stopped smiling the whole ride home. Part of him, after spending time with Mallory, wondered why he'd been so stupid to stay with Erin all those years. They shared none of the chemistry he and Mallory shared. However, as he was grateful Mallory's experiences led her here, he supposed he had to be equally grateful Erin had kept him off the market.

They were so different. He'd thought Erin was the best he could do. He thought their sex was pretty good. Every foundation he'd assumed was wrecked after one night with Mallory and they hadn't even had sex. Being with Mallory topped every experience he'd ever shared with Erin. Their chemistry was simply off the charts, but it was so much more than that.

Mallory was real. She had feelings and emotions and struggled to communicate them as best she could. Erin never did anything but complain. Mallory always asked about his family and took them into consideration, but Erin…they were polar opposites.

All morning, as he contemplated his new relationship and newfound happiness, he kept stumbling over the same conclusion and tossing it away. He'd spent ten years with Erin and although they'd said they loved each other in high school and here and there, it held the same sentiment for him as it did when he told his friends.

Now those words, like everything else, took new meaning. He wanted to say them to Mallory, but feared he'd scare her. Was it possible to fall in love so fast? He wasn't thinking about marriage…well, maybe a little. It was just so easy to see Mallory in a home that wasn't built yet, smiling as she made dinner, and chased the kids out of the way.

"Fuck."

He rubbed his palms over his face. His brain was moving way too fast. Maybe he needed to put a little space between them, get a grip on his emotions. That's what he would do. Although, whenever he tried to stay away from her, his desire for her only became so much more intense.

"Shit."

Should he blow her off tonight and go out with friends? He grimaced. He didn't want to hang out with anyone but her. He also didn't want to smother her. If other people were around, that would be fine, so long as she was there. He wanted to gorge himself on her. Would he get tired of her then? Maybe he should be more worried about her getting sick of him.

Finn made it to three o'clock that afternoon before texting Mallory.

Hey, Philly. What are you up to?
    ~F.

Just got back from my run. About to shower. Are we going out
    tonight?
    ~M.

Yes. Where would you like to go?
    ~F.

· · ·

THE PUB? IDK. You choose.

   ~M.

AT SEVEN HE headed to her place to pick her up. The entire ride to Mallory's apartment, he gave himself a pep talk about keeping it in his pants and not letting his words get away from him. He felt pretty secure in his plan until Mallory opened the door and he saw what she was wearing.

Her legs were encased in tight black jeans and boots that went up to her knee. Not boots like those ugly wooly things girls wore. No. These were black, sexy as hell, Wonder Woman boots.

Her shirt was some flouncy pink thing that showed just the right amount of cleavage to make his jaw unhinge. And her hair was pulled up in some fancy twist thing with little sexy wisps falling down here and there. He was done for.

"Hi," she said as he stepped into her apartment.

He leaned in to offer a chaste kiss. "Hi." He cleared the gravel out of his throat. "You look pretty."

"Thanks."

He was amazed she didn't argue with him or show any signs of disagreement. The thought that she might *feel* pretty was very satisfying. He liked to think that maybe his honesty with her and constant reminders that she was beautiful might have helped her see herself as she really was.

"I thought we could go to that Mexican place for dinner. Then, if you're up for it, we could swing by O'Malley's and see what everyone's up to." He needed to prolong returning to her apartment. All he could picture was Mallory in those boots and nothing else.

"Okay. Let me get my jacket. It got cold today."

He turned and faced the door because his stupid boot fantasy was making him hard. "Yeah. Winters are pretty brutal here. I hope you have a good coat."

"Got a good man," she said, sneaking up beside him and pressing a kiss on his cheek. "He keeps me warm."

She perched up on her toes and traced her lips over his, teasing him with her tongue. He cleared his throat and put his hands on her shoulders. "If you want dinner, we better go."

She frowned, but nodded.

The ride to the restaurant was quiet. She asked about his day, but he had nothing exciting to report. She asked if they could go climbing again and he said sure. Other than that he was lost in his head. Terms of endearment and love cluttered his mouth to the point he was afraid to speak. Mentally he was a mess and physically he was even worse.

Just tell her.

He couldn't say he loved her. It was too soon and he didn't have the confidence to believe she could love him back so soon. He didn't want to cloud their relationship with lies and couldn't bare her saying it back out of a sense of obligation. He wasn't being honest, but he also wasn't lying. He'd just keep his mouth closed so he didn't screw up the first good thing he had.

As he held her door and she climbed down from the truck cab he noticed her boots again. "Are they new shoes?"

"Yup. This is the outfit I bought Friday. Do you like it?"

"Yeah, it's nice," he said, shutting the door and quickly turning away so as not to give away how much he liked it. He was hard as a rock.

When he took her hand and started walking she tugged him back. "Finn, what's wrong?"

He looked away and rubbed his neck with his free hand. "What? Nothing. Come on, let's eat. I'm starving."

As the waiter took their order, Mallory was quiet. She didn't have the smile she had earlier in the evening and he sort of felt responsible. Reaching across the table he took her hand. "You okay?"

She nodded unconvincingly.

Their food came and he devoured his steak fajitas while she seemed to enjoy her grilled bass. After dinner she had a glass of wine while he had a beer and the silence was getting to him. When she excused herself to use the bathroom, he flagged down the waiter and asked for the check. They needed to be around more people.

When she returned from the bathroom, he stood and handed over her purse. She frowned and glanced at her glass of wine. Shit. It wasn't even half empty. She could get another one at the bar.

He held her door as she got into the truck and when he started the engine he said, "O'Malley's?"

"Maybe you should just take me home."

His gaze jerked to her as heavy sadness filled him. "Why?"

She shrugged. "You don't seem like you're having much fun."

"Mallory…I'm having fun. I just…" He shook his head and swallowed. "I'm sorry. I'm being weird tonight. I didn't want to come on too strong, that's all."

She laughed without humor. "You have a funny way of showing it, McCullough."

He took her hand and squeezed gently. "I swear, the last thing I want to do is take you home."

She coughed. "Wow. Okay."

"No! That's not what I meant. I just mean…Fuck. I'm saying everything wrong. I want to take you home, but I don't want to do anything you aren't ready for. I wanted to take you out and show you a good time first —not first—just show you a good time period. Nothing else has to happen. I'm not expecting anything."

She scowled at him. "What are you saying,

Finnegan? You aren't indebted to me. If you want to drop me off, drop me off. I'm not going to attack you."

Why was everything he said coming out wrong? "I don't want to drop you off."

"Then why are you acting different? Look, I know we…messed around last night, but if you've had a change of heart, just tell me."

He did have a change of heart, just not the way she suspected. "Mallory, nothing's changed. I'm just having some issues."

"Issues with what?"

He pinched the bridge of his nose. "I'm afraid if we go back to your place I won't be able to walk away this time."

When she didn't say anything he glanced over his hand at her. Her mouth was agape and her eyes were wide. "What?" she rasped.

He shifted uncomfortably. He'd been hard for over twenty-four hours. It was getting to the point that he thought someone slipped him a pill. "I'm saying I want you. I want you bad and then I show up and you're wearing that sexy fucking outfit and those Wonder Woman boots and—"

"Wonder Woman wore red boots."

"You know what I mean. You look incredible. I'm afraid to be alone with you, because I don't know how in control I am right now."

She laughed. "You're afraid to be alone with me, because you're afraid we might have sex?"

"Yes. But it's more than that. I don't want you to get the wrong idea."

Her scowl returned. "What idea is that?"

"This is going to sound cliché, but the idea that I might just be using you, because I'm not."

When she was quiet he knew it was because she'd already considered that and it pissed him off. He was fucking head-over-heels for her and she thought there was a chance it was all bullshit. That was exactly why he couldn't sleep with her yet.

"I see," she said quietly, crossing her arms over her chest and facing the windshield. "So what happens now?"

"I figured we could go to the pub and have a few drinks."

"Because intoxication detours lust? I'm sorry, in my opinion, it has the opposite effect."

"I won't come in when I drop you off. I mean I'll walk you to the door, but that's it."

Her head lowered and she suddenly looked sad. "Okay."

He turned her chin and stared into her eyes. "Make no mistake, Mallory. I want you. This has nothing to do with the opposite and everything to do with me trying to be a gentleman."

She offered a half-smile. "Maybe I don't want you to be a gentleman."

"Don't say things like that," he rasped. "Unless you mean it. I'm holding on by a thread here."

MALLORY WEIGHED the sincerity in his eyes. He actually looked sort of desperate, like he was about to lose it. At first she thought her outfit was too much. It took a lot of guts for her to wear fitting clothes and when he didn't go overboard with compliments she began second-guessing everything, as usual. Now she realized she'd been way off. Maybe.

Crap. She didn't know what to believe.

There were two possibilities here. One, he was lying and making up all this crap so that he could avoid going home with her—a very not nice scenario. Or, two, he really did want her that much that he was in borderline pain trying to be a gentleman.

She glanced at his crotch. The truck was dark, but there was a bulge there. Finn wasn't a small guy, though. She'd never seen him naked. Maybe that's just how he always was. The thought gave her chills.

"Are you hard?" She gasped and covered her mouth as the words fell out.

He choked and even in the dark she saw his face flush. "Philly, I've been in pain for over twenty-four hours. I passed hard yesterday."

Her thighs clenched as a soft rhythm throbbed in her sex. She cleared her throat again. "Then, maybe you better take me home after all."

He sighed, and the sound was laced with defeat.

She stared out the front window and said with all the courage she could muster, "But maybe you better stop at the store first."

"Do you need something?"

"You need condoms."

The door slammed shut and Finn slid behind the wheel, a tiny, black bag in his hand. He wouldn't look at her.

"Are you sure about this?" he asked, shoulders tense as he gripped the wheel and stared straight ahead.

Was she sure? No. Yes. No. Maybe. Absolutely. While he ran in the store, she'd compiled a fairly reasonable list of reason why she *should* sleep with Finnegan McCullough.

One, he was the hottest man she'd ever set eyes on. Two, he apparently wanted to have sex with her. Three, she would do it eventually anyway. Four, he gave her butterflies that tickled her insides more than anything she'd ever felt. Five, she was in love with him—a dangerous truth, but true all the same.

The list went on and on. Reason thirty-six, he had

abs like a Greek god. Reason fifty-seven, he smelled like bottled heaven. Reason one hundred and one, that sexy dimple he got when he smiled.

It was a very convincing list, but her list of fears and reasons to run for the hills was also quite convincing. One, he could obliterate her heart. That was basically it on the con-list, but it was a big one.

They both seemed to be breathing loudly. She stared unblinking at the dashboard and said, "Yes."

They each appeared incapable of eye contact. It was a surprise when she felt his hand wrap around her fingers resting on the seat and give her a little squeeze. She turned and stared at him. Slowly, he faced her in his seat.

There was no cocky, player glint in his eyes, no pre-assumed edge of victory. It was then she understood this was big to him, possibly as monumental as it was for her.

He'd only ever slept with his high school sweetheart and she'd only ever had quickies in the dark with meaningless acquaintances she'd hoped to never see again. Those rules wouldn't apply to Finn. She was growing addicted to his presence in her life and she'd have to face him in the morning.

He would understand, once and for all, she was nothing like Erin or any other girl. He'd finally get to experience her, all of her.

He slowly backed out of the store parking lot and

they drove in silence. When he parked outside of her place the truck shut off and the only sound was the quiet pinging of the engine cooling. Dear God, what if she sucked at sex?

Panic had her heart racing. What if she was slow and awkward when he wanted fast and hard? What if she didn't make the right sounds or was too loud? What if she got sweaty or if he—

Stop it!

Her hands fisted on her lap. She jumped as he opened the passenger door. He seemed nervous. Maybe he was having second thoughts.

His gaze was lowered, lashes forming purple crescent shadows on his cheeks under the streetlight.

"We don't have to do this if you changed your mind," he said quietly. "I mean, I want to. I want you more than I think I've ever wanted a woman, but I don't want you with reservations. It'll keep, Philly. What I feel for you won't diminish if we say goodnight right here, right now and decide to hold off a while."

It was becoming harder and harder to breathe. Where did he come up with such perfect words? No one had ever made her feel so…wanted, right, worthwhile.

As she slowly faced him, she saw not the strong, sexy mountain man she'd bumped into in the woods several weeks back, but the stunning man inside. The one not everyone knew. She knew him. She got a side of Finnegan McCullough others often overlooked. He thought he was ordinary, but he was so perfectly simple, so perfectly sweet, he was everything a girl needed. She needed him.

"Just…be patient with me," she whispered, showing him with her eyes how much she wanted this, but that she still had vulnerabilities that could throw her.

Leaning in, he tenderly pressed his lips to hers, and all fear subsided. There was no way a man could fake such affection. It was surreal, believing he truly wanted *her*.

They held hands and took the steps slowly side-by-side. He relieved her of the keys and unlocked the door. Where had her voice gone?

She removed her jacket and placed it on the back of a kitchen chair. Clearing her throat in the silent apartment, she said, "Just give me a minute in the bathroom, okay?"

He nodded.

She went to the bathroom and stared in the mirror. She looked slightly different from the girl she left behind in Philly. Her jaw had narrowed and her cheeks were more defined. Her hair had grown in a bit. She undid her bun and let her hair fall over her shoulders.

Shaky fingers unzipped her boots and she stepped out of them, shrinking three inches. She undid her jeans and slid them off her legs. Taking a deep breath, she removed her shirt and folded it on the corner of the sink.

It wasn't easy to face her reflection, but with a slow turn she pivoted. Opening her eyes she tried to see herself, truly see her, the way Finn would see her. Her breasts were displayed in a satin, black bra, supported in a way they didn't naturally sit. Her stomach curved in wrong places and her belly button was a crease rather than the petite hole that a super model might show off.

The black lace of her boy shorts scalloped the pouch of her stomach, making her, again, appear more feminine than she actually was. She would not start berating herself, not now when this was going to happen.

Her fingers unclasped her bra and away went the support and down fell her breasts. Her nipples darkened and tightened in the cool air. She had nice nipples, not to big and not too small. Not too dark and not too pink.

Her gaze landed on the jagged white scars stretching over her breast. She'd started getting stretch marks when she was a teenager. No amount of lotion or magic cream took them away and she, for the most part, tried to ignore them. Maybe he would ignore them too.

Her head bowed as she slid off her panties. There she was, as naked as the day she was born. Wide hips creased by gravity made it difficult to notice the small patch of soft, brown curls at her apex.

Her gaze flowed over her reflection and took note of her better qualities. Her nails were painted and filed neatly. Her makeup was subtle, but nice. Her hair was long and natural in color. For some reason, it became important for her to show him exactly who she was. There would be no veils or facades, not tricks of beauty or accessories to distract the eye. It was all or nothing. If he wanted *her,* that was exactly who he was going to get.

She emerged from the bathroom wearing only her robe. Her breath caught when she saw him sitting on the bed in only his jeans, his bare chest showing in the soft lamplight from the nightstand. He was stunning.

A fine trail of golden, brown hair ran over his abs, disappearing behind the unbuttoned snap of his jeans. On the nightstand she spotted the infamous box of condoms. Funny, not until that moment did it actually register that she was going to have sex. The physical act was second hand to all the emotional repercussions.

She hadn't had sex in years. She almost forgot what it felt like. Chills skated up her spine as she drew the slow epiphany that whatever he was hiding in those jeans was going to be inside of her very soon.

She smiled and he reciprocated the gesture. With slow steps she walked into the bedroom. Taking one last look at the beautiful man sitting on her bed, her fingers went to the switch on the wall and extinguished the light.

Darkness settled on the room for only a second and then a soft click came from the bed as Finn leaned over and turned on the nightstand lamp. He slowly shook his head, telling her there would be no hiding.

Having her body displayed in light where unfavorable shadows could be cast was not a comforting thought. But the look in his eyes told her the idea of seeing her without shields was very favorable to him. She nodded in acceptance and he whispered, "Thank you."

Her feet carried her slowly to the bed. Standing at the foot, she struggled with the tie of her robe. He stood and met her at the foot of the bed, touching her hands softly, stilling her motions.

She let out a shaky breath as he took over the knot and whispered, "Let me."

Shutting her eyes, she nodded as the terrycloth lapels were drawn apart. He sucked in an audible breath and said, "Gorgeous."

She bit her tongue so as to not object to the compliment and gentle fingers tipped up her chin. Soft lips pressed into hers and she shivered. The heat of his body covered her front as he stepped even closer. Tender lips coaxed her mouth open as he kissed her softly. Their heads tilted and her body warmed.

Strong hands cupped her breasts as his thumb dragged over her nipples. Her body tightened as he deepened the kiss.

The backs of his knuckles caressed her stomach causing her to slightly suck in a breath. He teased at the soft curls at her apex and she whimpered.

"I love your body," he said against her lips.

His hand pressed into the base of her spine, drawing her closer. Every part of her shook. His mouth caressed the corner of her lips, and then trailed over her jaw and down to her throat. He nibbled at her ear and she nearly collapsed. There was something so magnificent about Finn's mouth on her ear. It made her insane.

Her sex clenched with rapid little flutters as moisture gathered at her folds. His fingers teased at the edge of her robe, up and down, over her breasts, and then the weight of the soft fabric fell away.

Blanketed in the cold of the room, she shivered. Her shoulders now exposed, he kissed them gently. His touch was so delicate. He made ever patch of flesh, every nerve, come to life.

He nudged her toward the bed and eased her down. Self-consciousness reared its ugly head as she sat. Quickly adjusting her pose in the skinniest fashion she could manage, she leaned all the way back on the cool bedding and extended her arms above her head.

Watching him, he breathed hard, his chest rising and falling with each pant. "I wish you could see yourself now," he said in a gravelly voice. "All soft curves and feminine perfection."

She nearly scoffed, but held back. Her cheeks heated

as he slowly undid the zipper of his jeans and eased them down. When his body unfolded and he was standing before her in all of his glory, her jaw unhinged. "Holy mother of penis."

He laughed. She hadn't meant to say the words out loud, but dear God that was a lot of man.

The side of his mouth kicked up in a half-smile and her heart fluttered as his dimple came into view. The bed dipped as he climbed over her. The heat of his body scorched her skin. His erection rested heavily over her hip as his mouth found hers.

She was suddenly a teenage girl with no clue what she was doing. Her hands traveled from his shoulders to his back to his hip, never quite sure of the best place to touch. It was all so perfect, so manly.

His mouth distracted her to the extreme as those soft lips closed over her nipple. She arched and reveled at the sense of being blanketed by him. Finn was so encompassing, when he held her she somehow felt small and delicate. It was a freeing sensation she'd never experienced before. It made her bold.

Her knees tightened on his hips and his arousal nudged her sex, causing her to gasp. He breathed into her shoulder and whispered words of sweetness, but she was beyond the point of comprehension. She wanted him *now!*

"Finn. Finnegan, please."

"Shh. Patience, Philly."

He kissed over her shoulder and found her breasts. It was so novel to have someone freely touch and taste her there. For as much as she wasn't a virgin, she never really allowed herself to fully experience sex. Foreplay was amazing and, up until then, she'd been missing out.

His tongue flicked and teased at her tip. His hands cupped and massaged. She couldn't seem to keep still. Very aware of his arousal nudging her sex, she dared to reach down and touch him. As her hand engulfed him he sucked a harsh breath through his teeth and cursed. She squeezed and ran her hand up and down his length slowly.

His flesh was taut, but smooth. His hips drew back as he glanced down at her hand on him. She looked down as well and reality split her in two. The sight of her naked flesh crashed over her arousal, piercing her confidence and her motions faltered.

His strong fingers wrapped over hers and he squeezed. She tried to get back to the place she was, but it proved elusive. Frustration hammered down on her as she screwed her eyes shut.

Finn's body lifted and he gently tugged her hand away. His mouth teased the spot beneath her ear. That was definitely the money spot. Every time he touched her there she melted.

Kisses trailed over her chest and down to her hips. Again, she was trembling. This time she would just keep her eyes closed. His hands teased over her hips and thighs. Her body stretched as his broad shoulders scooted lower.

Oh no!

"Finn, wait…" Her knees tightened. His fingers brushed over the dewy curls at the apex of her thighs.

It felt so good. She spread her legs only slightly, just enough for him to fit a finger. His digit probed gently and as he found his way into her slick core with his finger, she gasped. Slow, measured thrusts had her relaxing and opening for him.

He teased the bud of her sex and she began to moan. His mouth kissed her hip and then there was the softest flick of his tongue at the peek of her sex. She nearly sprung off the bed. She didn't do that. Ever.

"Finn…" She needed to stop him, but his tongue kept teasing that spot. Sensations she'd never before experienced crested through her body. She tightened and her heart began to beat in places outside of her chest.

"Open for me, Mallory."

Refusal played in her mind, but with only the slightest pressure, he parted her thighs. His mouth settled over her sex and his fingers continued to probe. She was breathing hard.

"Oh my God…Oh my God…"

He doubled his pace and kissed her sex. Sucking, licking, touching her like no man ever had, until she fell to pieces. Her legs trembled as a waterfall of color exploded behind her eyes. It was too much, but she never wanted it to stop.

Her voice echoed off the walls. Her heart raced. Finn kissed her thighs, her knees, her hips, and even her belly. She was beyond caring.

His weight lifted and he returned to her, his mouth again settling over hers. His lips tasted of what she assumed was her. Perhaps she should have minded, but she didn't. It was the most erotic kiss of her life.

His arousal pressed at her sex, the barrier of latex slightly altering the sensation. Her thighs opened.

"Look at me, Mallory."

Slowly, her lashes fluttered open. She stared into the depths of his blue eyes. They were wild and as dark as wet denim.

He placed a chaste kiss on her lips and whispered, "I love you."

His thickness stretched her and she gasped. Her body was beyond ready for the fullness that followed his startling announcement. She moaned, shocked in so many ways, shocked at his size, how right he felt, but mostly at what he said the second before he entered her.

Her mind spiraled, landing somewhere outside of her body. *What?* Overwhelmed by his words, she'd somehow missed the initial connection. He filled her and withdrew, thrusting deeply, over and over.

He loved her? Since when? How? *Why?*

Her cruel, cynical mind ached as she worried he said the words out of obligation. She didn't need the words. She was here of her own freewill. Yet, she couldn't quite wrap her brain around the action, because her emotions were suddenly all over the map.

Her body's autopilot took over. Sensations of fulfillment pushed responses from her vocal cords, her limbs, and her lungs. She was having sex with Finnegan McCullough and he'd said he loved her.

The sharp sting of tears prickled her eyes. No. He wasn't supposed to love her. If he put it out there, she wouldn't be able to hold her words back and if she admitted that she loved him, too, she'd love him too fiercely, too hard, and she'd break this incredible, delicate thing they'd created. Maybe he loved her as a friend. Mallory loved him as…there was no way to describe it. He was beautiful. He was the first boy to ever be nice to her. No one had ever made her feel the things Finnegan made her feel, and she feared her love was simply too potent to summarize in one four letter word.

He thrust deep and every thought skittered away. Holy God, he was in her soul. Something pinched warm and sweet in her womb as he rolled his hips. The physical act became too intense to ignore. It consumed her.

She arched in his hold and he thrust. Her sex contracted. She was actually going to have an orgasm this way. There was no fighting it. He thrust again and suddenly she was falling into a place of such acute pleasure she had no control over her words, her tears, or her actions.

Her fingers bit into his back as his pace quickened. Starbursts of pleasure rained over her. Her spine tingled and her voice rasped over his rugged breathing. "I love you too. I love you so much. I've never known anyone like you. Please don't hurt me. Just love me and I'll try my best not to ever let you down."

She couldn't stop the words. The sound of her raw pleas made her cry more. She was embarrassing herself. Thoughts of damage control flashed in her mind, but quickly skittered away as Finn's body tightened.

He buried himself in her and she felt his length pulse at her core. "Never. You could never let me down. I only want you, Mallory. You. No one else."

At the peak of their climaxes she blanked out. Never had she been so overwhelmed by another person, so laid bare, so exposed. His weight blanketed her and she came back to the present, recognizing the sound of his deep breathing and the press of his lips to her neck. Her pulse was fluttering like crazy. This was far better than any run she'd ever had.

He sighed. "I don't want to pull out. You're so warm."

Their bodies pressed together, sealing with the dew of perspiration. She likely looked a mess. Finn seemed to settle into her more as he turned and pulled them to their sides.

Her eyes opened and she stared at him. He smiled. Their faces were close and she could see the golden brown stubble covering his jaw. "Hi," she said softly.

"Hi." There was that dimple again. "How are we doing?"

"Oh, I'd say we're doing pretty good."

He chuckled. "You're incredible."

Her skin heated. No, she wasn't. She hadn't really done anything, but he was. "*You* are incredible."

His expression sobered. "I meant what I said, Mallory. I love you."

Her mood shifted. *Don't do this.* "You don't have to say it. I don't expect—"

"It isn't about what you expect. It's about what I feel. If I didn't love you, I wouldn't have agreed to do this tonight."

She loved him too, but she would have done this even if she didn't. The odd thing was, maybe she suspected he loved her all along. She'd decided to sleep with him simply because she owed it to women everywhere not to let the opportunity pass. But something had calmed her trepidation of showing him all of her. Was it her subconscious telling her he loved her enough to be gentle with her? No matter how much she wanted him, she wouldn't have slept with him had she not trusted him. Maybe she knew all along.

"You don't have to say it back just to say it, either. It's okay," he said.

She was always taken aback when he showed his own vulnerabilities. She cupped his face, amazed that *she* had the ability to assure this incredible man. "I meant what I said. All of it."

He kissed her.

CHAPTER 13

Finn sat on the edge of the bed and tied his boots. He looked longingly over at Mallory's body tucked beneath the covers. Glancing at his watch, he noted it was almost two in the morning. Sighing, he ran a hand over her shoulder.

She moaned and her soft lashes fluttered open. "Hey, what time is it?"

"Almost two. I have to go."

She sat up a little, pulling the sheet over her bare breasts. His mouth kicked up at her show of modesty. There was no point in hiding herself now. He saw all of her, tasted every inch, and planned on doing it again very soon.

"You don't have to leave," she said, tucking her hair behind her ear. "You could stay. I mean, if you want to."

He smiled and touched a strand of her soft brown

hair. "I want to, but I can't. My mum worries if I'm not home at a reasonable hour. It's a respect thing."

Her lashes lowered. "Okay."

He pinched her chin, tipping her face until her gaze met his again. "Hey, it isn't easy for me to leave. If I could, I'd stay."

She nodded, seeming to accept his words as truth. He kissed her softly and said, "I'll be back first thing in the morning. We'll go to breakfast and then I'll run with you if you want. Or we can climb. You let me know how you feel."

"Okay." She looked so soft. Forcing his legs to stand was like ripping off a layer of flesh.

"Thank you for tonight." He kissed her hair. "I'll lock the door behind me."

As he left, he locked the door. When he reached his truck he turned over the key and took a moment to simply be. Removing his phone from his pocket, he quickly punched out a text.

Love you.

   ~F.

It took only a minute for her response to come over.

. . .

Love u2.

~M.

HE SMILED in the dark and flipped on his headlights. "I'm gonna marry her," he said to himself as he put the truck in drive. He smiled the entire way home.

THE FOLLOWING MORNING, when Finn got to Mallory's, she was already showered and dressed for her run. She said she wanted to climb, but then claimed her body was a little sore. He felt a pinch of guilt for maybe being too rough, but she assured him it was simply because she was out of practice.

They ate at the diner and ran into a few of his friends. Mallory seemed shy around new people, but she was never rude. After breakfast they ran the field and he couldn't seem to take his eyes off of her.

As they sipped their water bottles his phone buzzed. Finn slid his thumb over the screen and cursed. "Shit."

"Something wrong?" Mallory asked, wiping her brow and squinting into the sun.

"I have to swing by my house. My grandmother fell. Do you mind?"

She was already walking to the truck. "Of course not. Come on."

He took the fastest route to the house, grateful they

were already on the property. His father had run out of town that morning to price a new chipper for the business and his mother was likely frantic.

When he pulled the truck along the front steps, gravel kicked out beneath the wheels. Taking the steps two at a time, he held open the door for Mallory who was right on his heels. "Mum?"

"In here." He turned and found his mother on her knees in the living room. His grandmother was also sitting on the floor propped against the base of the sofa. He winced when he saw the bruise already forming on her nearly translucent cheek.

He rushed to her side. "What happened?"

"I don't know. I was sitting with her all morning. I went in the kitchen to get a glass of water and then I heard a crash. I don't know what possessed her to get up without asking for help first." His mother was clearly frantic.

He took his grandmother's hand, which was also turning a dark shade of purple. She was on blood thinners and bruises were often a result of taking such medicines. "Morai, do you remember what happened?"

His grandmother glanced at him with a look of innocence that only a child should exhibit. Over the last year, he'd watch her change from the fiery spirit she'd always been to a quiet old woman who sometimes forgot his name.

"I...I don't know. I was up and then I was down."

It was clear that she was upset. He hated the way dementia could make a person who hadn't answered to anyone in years, suddenly appear frightened as if they would be chastised for things beyond their control.

"It's okay," he comforted. "Do you think you think you could stand up if I help you?"

"Oh, I don't know. The doctor told me to stay here."

He frowned and glanced at his mother. She shook her head telling him there had been no doctor. "Does anything hurt?"

"My side," she said, indicating her ribs.

His lips thinned. "Did you call 911, Mum?"

"I called you. I didn't know what to do. Thank you for coming so quickly, always my angel I can count on." His mother rubbed his head like he was four and he flushed, subconsciously glancing back at Mallory who was still waiting by the door.

"Let's get an ambulance here. They can at least look her over before we move her and then if she needs a doctor we can take her to the hospital. If she broke something I don't want to make it worse."

His mother nodded and started to stand. "My phone's in the kitchen."

"I've got it," Mallory said, already dialing.

For the first time his mother noticed he hadn't come alone. As Mallory placed the call to the dispatch operator his mother gripped his hand and whispered. "I hadn't meant to interrupt your day, Finnegan. I'm sorry."

"Don't be silly, Mum. You know I'm always here when you need me."

She smiled tightly, her copper lashes blinking. "I know you are, dearie."

By the time the EMTs left, his father had returned. The day had come and gone. His grandmother needed to take a trip to the hospital for some tests, which he knew would likely happen. His mother and father took the truck to follow the ambulance and he and Mallory were alone. It was rare that the big house was ever empty or quiet.

"I'm sorry about all this," he said, as he poured her a glass of water and carried a bowl of strawberries to the table.

"I don't mind at all. It's your family. What else could you have done, but be there when they needed you?"

He smiled at her as he tossed a berry into his mouth. She was so understanding. "Do you miss your family?"

She nibbled a berry, the juice staining her lips pink. "Yes. I'm used to not seeing my sister, but I miss my mom and dad. They lived in the city, too, and we usually saw each other once a week."

"Why don't you go home to visit?"

She glanced at the table, her fingertips ruffling the pile of soft green stems they'd collected on the plate. "I'm not ready to go back yet."

"Did something happen?"

"No. I just have this silly idea in my head that when I go back they'll see a difference. I think, in my own screwed up head, if I look better than I did when I left, they'll assume I'm happy here and not bug me to come home. It's hard telling them no."

He made no comment about her opinions and thoughts of looking better. She looked great. Sooner or later he'd get her to understand that. "Yeah, it's not always easy to go against your family's wishes. So when do you think you'll go back?"

"Probably Thanksgiving. The school's closed for two days, so I'll have a long weekend."

He swallowed. There was a part of him that feared what he didn't know. City life was exciting. A place like Philadelphia had so much more to offer than their small town here in Center County. "Can I come with you?"

Her gaze met his and her face split with a smile. "Would you want to?"

"Meet your family? Of course."

"Okay. The idea of you being there actually makes it a whole lot less intimidating. My parents will be shocked to see I have a real life, flesh and blood boyfriend."

"Stop."

"I'm serious. I've never brought a guy home. The only date they saw me go on was my senior prom and for that I took my cousin." She sighed. "My life is such a sad cliché."

He reached for her hand and said, "I didn't go to my prom. Erin and I had broken up for some stupid reason or another. My mom wanted me to take my cousin, but I said no. I don't much care for dancing."

She laughed. "Oh, but I've seen your moves. There's a disco queen hiding somewhere under all that flannel."

He put his finger to his lips. "Shh. No one's supposed to know about that. That was all part of my sexy plan of attack. I'm like a deranged bird trying to show off for its mate."

She giggled. "Well, you got me."

Warmth spread in his chest. Yeah, he got her. "I'd like to have you again."

Her mouth opened and her cheeks flushed. She looked around and whispered, "We're at your parents' house."

"No one's here. Wanna see my room?"

She smirked. "I feel like we're in high school."

"Well, we are going steady." He coughed. "I think that pin I wanted to give you is up there. Why don't you come help me find it?"

"Finnegan, what if we get caught?"

His lips twitched as he tried to appear concerned. Nodding, he said, "I'd risk getting grounded for you."

"I'm all gross from running."

"So am I. Let's go be gross together."

She hesitated then stood. "Okay, but I'm keeping my shirt on."

"Okay, but I'm still going to try to cop a feel."

They held hands as they took the stairs. His room was the third door on the left. It wasn't much, just where he'd slept for the past twenty-eight years of his life. It was painted hunter green and the furniture was raw wood, made from a local carpenter. His bed was big, because he was big.

As he opened the door a flutter of something reminiscent of adolescence tickled his gut. He couldn't remember the last time he had a girl in here.

Turning, he lowered his mouth to Mallory's and kissed her softly. "This is my room."

"Mmm." She said against his lips. "Nice."

"I think I left that pin on my bed somewhere."

She giggled. "I'm sure we can find it if we look hard enough."

He led her to the unmade bed and pulled her down. She pushed him and he sat on the edge. She straddled his legs and linked her arms around his neck. Her mouth tasted like strawberries and her skin was salty.

He cupped his palms over her back and felt the straps of her bra. It was one of those sporty contraptions without clasps. He didn't have the first clue how women got into them or a clue about getting her out of it. His hand traced over her shirt and he cupped her breast.

"Rounding those bases pretty quick there, Finnegan."

"You know it," he said kissing her neck.

Her nipple pressed against the fabric and he teased the peak. She began to rotate her hips, grinding over him. He wanted to be inside of her then he remembered he'd left the condoms at her place. "Shit."

"Problem?"

"I left the condoms at your apartment."

She groaned and pressed her forehead to his shoulder. "I guess we're just going to have to behave ourselves like teenagers do—with our pants on."

He picked her up and she squealed. "Finn!"

Dropping her onto the bed, he blanketed her with his weight. Through his track pants, his erection was quite evident. He pressed it into the cradle of her hips and she moaned then gasped.

"Good?"

"Yes." She spread her legs. Her pants were those tight black running kind. He could feel her crease through the layers of material. He ground himself into her and she arched. Every rub of friction along his cock felt incredible.

They kissed and made out and touched through their clothing until they were both panting. He was shocked when he felt his climax nearing. Shit. He was going to come in his pants.

She moaned and dug her nails into his shoulders

through his shirt. "Finn." Her voice was breathy, a sexy rasp that whispered to every nerve in his body.

"Fuck, Mallory, I'm gonna come."

She lifted her hips and pressed into him. His spine tingled and he moaned. She tightened her knees around him and tugged at his hair. Her body bowed and she cried out. Warmth seeped over his length as his cock throbbed and pulsed.

He fell to the side and pulled her close. They were both out of breath. "I can't believe I just did that," he admitted and she giggled.

"Me neither. You're definitely giving me your pin now."

He didn't actually have a pin in mind, but when Mallory left to use the bathroom and he changed into some fresh clothes and cleaned himself up, he found the old fishing pin his grandfather had given him when he was a boy.

The door opened and he turned. "I have something for you."

She looked up at him inquisitively. "What is it?"

"Come here." She stepped closer and he pressed the spike of the pin through her shirt. After he snapped it closed he said, "There."

She glanced down at the pin and read, "*Catch and Release.* How romantic."

He kissed her nose. "That's big stuff from a logger."

"I'm sure. I love it."

. . .

MALLORY COULDN'T SLEEP that evening. Her mind continued to replay their weekend like a loop at the beginning of a movie. She watched scenes from the past two days flow through her mind and stared into space, utterly speechless that this was her real life.

The following morning she was tired, but thoughts of Finn worked like espresso for her soul. He texted her throughout the day and she had to try hard to keep a straight face. He was coming over that night and she planned on making dinner for the two of them.

She ran to the market right from work and intended to take a quick jog around the park before he got there at six. She'd been waiting at the butcher counter for her order when someone bumped her cart. Still in the daze she'd been in for the last twenty-four hours, she muttered a quick apology, and pulled her cart out of the way. That was when she realized she'd been intentionally bumped.

Erin glared at her with disdain over a cart only filled with produce and cereal in the child seat area. "Sorry. You seem to be taking up the whole aisle."

Mallory frowned. She *did not* like this girl. The butcher returned and showed her the two cuts of chicken she'd ordered. "Will this be enough, ma'am?"

She glanced at the peach colored meat cradled in the white paper and nodded. When she looked back at

Erin, the girl said, "Cooking for two or just eating more than you should?"

She gaped at her audacity. "Excuse me?"

The bitch rolled her eyes. "I don't know what he sees in you, but I'm sure he'll be over it soon."

Her spine stiffened. "Many could say the same about you."

She chuckled coldly. "I doubt it. Everyone knows Finn's been in love with me since high school. Don't get too attached." With that, she wheeled her cart away, shaking her petite little butt for everyone to see.

The butcher handed her the wrapped poultry and she quickly darted to the checkout.

When she returned home and unpacked the groceries, she should have changed and left for her run, but she couldn't find the strength. She sat on her couch and stared at the blank television screen.

Finn's been in love with me since high school...

Don't get too attached...

I don't know what he sees in you.

Mallory let out a shaky breath. "Me neither."

She must have sat there for over an hour. The sky began to fade from blue to violet and when she glanced at her watch it was almost time for Finn to be there. She stood and dug her phone out of her purse. There were three missed texts.

.   .   .

*J*UST FINISHING UP. *See you soon. Xo*

   ~F.

*D*O *you need anything from the store? Leaving in ten.*

   ~F.

*A*RE *you still at the park? You aren't answering. Leaving now.*

   ~F.

T*HE* L*AST* T*EXT* was sent almost twenty minutes ago, which meant he would be there any minute and she hadn't even started dinner. She quickly pulled out the items she needed and turned the oven to preheat. Before she had the salad tossed, Finn was knocking at the door.

Brushing her fingers on a dishrag, she went to let him in. He greeted her with a smile and pressed a kiss to her lips. "Hey, beautiful. I missed you."

"Hey. Dinner won't be done for about thirty minutes. You can watch TV if you want."

He frowned. "Did you go running?"

"No." She returned to the salad and continued chopping tomatoes.

"Bad day?"

"It was fine."

She scraped up the tomatoes and dumped them in the bowl. The oven beeped and she carried the dish of chicken over and slipped it inside. The oven door slammed with a little more force than necessary.

"What are you making?"

"Chicken. It's for you. I'm just having salad."

"You sure you're okay?"

She huffed. "I'm fine. Stop asking."

"Do you want me to leave?"

"No," she snapped. "If you leave then the meal is going in the trash. I made it for you."

His hands went up in a defensive motion. "Whoa, Philly, what's going on?"

She fisted her hand on her hip and lowered her head. "Sorry. I'm just…in a mood."

"Did something happen at work?"

"No. Work was fine."

"After work?"

She turned and opened the fridge. "What kind of dressing do you want on your salad?"

He caught the door of the refrigerator, sneaking up on her. "Forget the salad. Talk to me. Something happened and I want to know what."

Was she really going to tell him? What if he agreed with Erin and she saw it in his eyes that he'd eventually return to his ex. No matter what he said, he'd never be able to take back that sort of look once it was out there.

When they first met he'd planned on marrying that girl. "Nothing. A cart hit my car at the market. It put me in a bad mood. I'm sorry. Let's start over."

"Is it bad? I know a mechanic that does bodywork. I can take it over there for you and have him look at it if you want."

Jesus. This is why you don't lie! "No. It's barely notice-able. I overreacted. Do you want to set the table?"

He smiled, but his eyes looked concerned. "Sure."

By the time they were sitting down to eat, she'd forced all thoughts of Finn and his ex out of her mind. Finn told her about his day and complimented her cooking. He gave her a lecture when he noticed she was eating her salad without dressing, but she was sick and tired of people using her weight against her. She was going to get skinny if it killed her. And if she failed… well, then she'd sit on little bitches like Erin and beat the crap out of them.

She needed to calm down.

After dinner Finn helped clear the table and kept stealing little touches here and there. She kept shouldering him off.

His arms wrapped around her waist and she felt like she couldn't breathe with him holding her like that. He wasn't suffocating her, but she didn't want him to touch her at the moment, didn't want him to feel her, if that made any sense.

She nudged him away and he pulled her back,

pressing his lips to her shoulder. "Want to go watch some TV?"

That wasn't what he was asking. He wanted to fool around and while that had been her plan all morning, things had changed.

"I'm not really in the mood."

He frowned. "What do you want to do?"

She sighed. "I need to get stuff ready for work and…stuff."

His gaze scrutinized her. "Do you want me to go?"

"It's late." She didn't want him to go. She wanted him to stay and hold her while she cried about how badly his miserable ex hurt her feelings that afternoon. She wanted to tell him how much he meant to her and how afraid she was that he would leave her eventually.

Needy much?

"Mallory, if I—" His words cut off as his phone rang. He rolled his eyes and let out an aggravated sigh as he answered it. "Hello?…Again?…I'm sort of busy…"

She didn't think it was anyone in his family by the tone of his voice. To give him privacy she started on the dishes, but she could still hear him talking to the person on the phone.

"Can't you call your brother?" There was a long pause. "Fine. I'll be there in twenty minutes. Stay in the car and lock the doors."

He ended the call and she shut off the water, grabbing a towel to dry her hands. "Everything all right?"

"I have to go. That was Erin. Her car broke down and she's in the middle of nowhere."

Her jaw must have hit the floor. *"What?"* She was doing this on purpose. She knew Mallory was cooking him dinner tonight. That...*Bitch!* "Don't go," she suddenly pleaded, completely changing her tune from minutes ago.

He frowned. "Mallory, I have to go. She's stranded and her brother isn't answering the phone."

"So? Doesn't she have other friends she can call?"

"I guess not. She called me. I'm sure I wasn't her first choice."

Wanna bet? "Finn, I think you should call her back and ask her to call someone else. Doesn't she have parents?"

He scowled at her. "Mallory, she called me. You have to get ready for work anyway. It would be different if we had plans, but you just told me to basically leave. I might as well go help her."

She couldn't help the begging tone in her voice. "I don't want you to go."

He sighed and ran his hand through his hair, gripping the back of his neck. "Mallory, please don't be like that. I pride myself on being a guy people can count on. She's a girl and she's broken down on the side of the road. Don't be like her. Don't make me choose."

Her breath caught. He *did not* just say that. No, she

wouldn't make him choose. She couldn't. She was too afraid of what his choice would actually be.

Her expression blanked. "You better go."

"Please don't be mad."

"I'm not." *I'm afraid this is the last time I'll look at you and be able to call you my boyfriend.*

He kissed her and she pulled away too soon. After he left, she stood by the window and listened as his truck roared to life. Her throat tightened as she watched his taillights fade down the dark road—on the way back to his ex.

FINN FOUND Erin's car on the shoulder just after the exit out of town. The road was dark and the glass was foggy from her waiting inside. He pulled up behind her and grabbed the tools out of the back of the truck. As soon as he fixed her car he needed to have a talk with her about calling someone else the next time something like this happened.

It wasn't fair for him to upset Mallory, but what else could he have done? He couldn't leave Erin stranded. He walked to the front of the car and banged on the hood. "Pop the hood."

The latch under the hood released followed by the soft pinging of the driver door opening.

"You should stay in the car," he called as he lifted the

hood and turned on his flashlight. She, of course, ignored him.

"I don't know what happened. It just made this horrible noise and stopped."

He shined his light over all the major things that usually went wrong, but everything looked tight. "It just stopped? How did you get over to the shoulder?"

"Well, it sputtered, like." She stepped closer and he smelled her perfume. He preferred Mallory's perfume and found Erin's to be the type to give him a headache. "I really appreciate you coming to help me. I hope I didn't interrupt your night. Were you doing anything?"

"No. It's fine. Why don't you try to start it?"

"You're always so wonderful, coming to my rescue and driving me when I need a hand."

He turned and felt his brows lower. He wasn't buying this sweet act. "You really need to start calling someone else for this kind of thing. Either that or get some roadside assistance."

"I know. I'm sorry. I was scared and I knew I could count on you." Her hand landed on his where it rested on the car.

He glanced down at her manicured fingers. "Go start the car, Erin."

She looked at him for a long moment then nodded. She seemed to take a long while getting the key in the ignition. When the engine turned over it purred like a kitten and he cursed.

"Son of a bitch." He slammed the hood. "Sounds fine to me."

She left the car running and got out again. That was when he noticed her outfit. She was wearing the jean skirt he used to like her in and a cropped little top. It was too cold for an outfit like that.

"I don't know what happened. Maybe we should just wait here a few minutes and let it run. You know, to make sure it doesn't shut off again."

He doubted it would. "Do you think I'm an idiot, Erin?"

"What? Of course not. Finn, I swear, it just stopped."

"Yeah, cars do that when you take the keys out. Do me a favor and play your games with someone else."

She scoffed. "Because you're too busy to help your friends now?"

"That's the thing, Erin. We aren't friends. Friends don't trick each other to play games and cry wolf. Did it ever cross your mind that I might have been in the middle of something when you called?"

She laughed dryly. "Yeah. Maybe I thought *I* was rescuing *you*."

He scowled at her. "What the fuck is that supposed to mean?"

"Oh, come on, Finn, everybody is talking about it. Do you really think a girl like that is going to compare to a girl like me?"

He stepped back. Never before had he had the urge

to hit a woman. "No, I don't think there's any comparison. Mallory is nice and sweet and honest and doesn't have a nasty bone in her body. You on the other hand…"

"She's fat, Finnegan!"

He grit his teeth and gave her a look of absolute disgust. "You can call her whatever you want. Your opinions don't matter. But for the record—regardless of whatever label you throw at her—I find her way more beautiful than you. It's not always about the package, Erin. Maybe you should look at your reflection from time to time and figure out when your personality turned ugly. You used to be sweet." He turned and marched back to his truck.

"Asshole! Just wait, Finn. You'll see. You'll be back!"

He left her there and drove the long way home, needing the time to cool off.

When Mallory's phone rang around ten-thirty that night she was surprised and relieved, but before she answered it those emotions were replaced with darker ones. Was this it? Was he calling to break up with her?

She answered the call. "Hello?"

"I'm sorry. You were right. I shouldn't have gone."

Her stomach knotted with fear. "What happened?"

"Let's just say I made it clear from now on she needs to call someone else if there's an emergency."

She lowered herself to her bed. She'd been pacing her room since he left. "Are you just getting home now?"

"No. I've been home for about an hour. I went for a drive. I needed to think. I'm really sorry if I upset you."

She smiled sadly. He had upset her, but she mostly upset herself. She needed to stop being so insecure and give Finn the trust he deserved. It wasn't that she didn't trust him. It was that she didn't trust his ex. "I'm sorry too. I was awful tonight. I shouldn't have taken it out on you."

"Well, we all have bad days. Listen, if you want me to take your car over to the mechanic's tomorrow to have their dent guy look at it, I can swing by the school on my lunch, probably have it back before you're done for the day."

She was a terrible person. "Yeah, about that…"
"What?"
"Um, my car's fine. There's no dent."
"Then why did you say—"
"I lied." The line became silent. "I didn't mean to, I just didn't want to explain what really happened. I was embarrassed."

He didn't sound happy, but he asked anyway. "What really happened, Mallory? I gotta tell you, I'm getting a little tired of being lied to by women today."

His comment stung. She wasn't a liar. She hadn't meant to make up a story, but her self-preservation took over. "When I was at the market I ran into your ex."

"Erin? You saw Erin?"

"Yes. She wasn't nice to me. She said some really mean stuff and I left right afterward. I was so upset I came home and just sat here."

"What did she say?"

"I don't want to talk about it."

"Mallory—"

"No, Finn. It hurt and I can't say her accusations weren't true. I just want to forget about her."

He cursed under his breath. "I don't know what's going on with her lately, but she isn't someone you should put a lot of stock in. I'm sorry she was mean to you, but next time, please, just tell me if something like this happens. If I'd known that earlier, there would've be no way I would've helped her."

She didn't know if that was necessarily true and there was no way he could know that either. "Let's not talk about her anymore."

"That sounds like a good idea. How about tomorrow I come to your place and *I* make you dinner?"

The rest of their conversation was nice and had nothing to do with miserable exes or hurt feelings. By the time she hung up with him, it was almost midnight. She'd barely slept the night before and needed her rest.

•   •   •

THE FOLLOWING MORNING, Mallory stared at the scale and scowled. She'd gained a pound. It was stupid to care about one silly pound, but she did. There were always days that her weight fluctuated. She was due to get her period that week, and that was likely the cause. Nevertheless, she had only six more pounds to go until she reached her first goal.

September was almost over and before she knew it, it would be Thanksgiving. If she kept at it, she might even be able to lose forty pounds by then. What would that look like?

That day at work, she had a visitor in the office. Samantha McCullough popped in and surprised her by inviting her and Finn to dinner.

"Colin and I would love to have you two over. We could play a game or something along those lines. Maybe this weekend?"

"Sure. I mean, I'll have to talk to Finn, but that sounds great."

Samantha gave her a wide smile and nodded happily. "Great. I'll tell Colin to call his brother and set it up. Let them handle the details."

That night she told Finn about the invitation to have dinner with his brother and sister-in-law. Finn laughed and she felt like she was missing something.

"What's so funny?"

"This. They think they're so slick sending Samantha in to do their dirty work."

"I don't understand."

He tossed some sliced peppers into the pan with the shrimp. "It won't be dinner with just the four of us."

"I know. Tallulah will be there too. I want to meet their daughter."

He sighed. "They'll all be there. First my parents will hear about it, then my sister, she'll tell my brothers, and soon they'll all be there."

"But Sam made it sound like it would just be a quiet night with the four of us."

"Where there're McCulloughs, there is no quiet. You should remember that."

"But I already met most of them."

"You haven't really met Kate and her brood yet. She's the overprotective older sister. There's no way she'd miss this."

"You say that like it's a science fair."

"That's because they'll all be judging you."

She shrunk back. "Maybe I'll tell Sam we can't make it."

"Too late. She'll guilt you. She's a McCullough by injection and a fast learner. We're going. Might as well suck it up and deal with it."

The following Friday, they pulled up outside of Samantha and Colin's home. It was a sweet house with green siding and black shutters. Candles burned in each window. She would have noticed the yard or perhaps any gardens they had, if not for the dozen cars crowding every free space of ground.

Finn shut off the car and she sucked in a breath. "You okay, champ?" he asked as she gripped her knees.

She shook her head. She didn't feel like being inspected and judged. "Yes."

He laughed. "Your mouth says yes, but your head says no."

She continued to shake her head. "I'm okay."

He patted her knee. "Come on. They're all probably watching you from the window anyway. Let's get this over with."

He came around to her door and helped her out of the truck. Her steps were slow. Before they even crossed the first porch step the door swung open and Colin stepped out. He held up his hands and said, "I had nothing to do with this."

Finn chuckled. "Possession is nine tenths of the law, Colin. You're housing them."

"I was told we were going to play cards and eat. Sammy never said anything about the rest of them showing up."

The door opened and they all turned to see a little boy step onto the porch. "Uncle Colin, Tallulah stinks. Aunt Sam said to find you and tell you to handle it."

Colin sighed and followed the boy inside.

Finn faced Mallory. "Ready?"

She sucked in a breath and huffed it out, steeling herself for what lay ahead. "As I'll ever be."

They entered the house and it was like a scene from Vietnam. Kids raced around the banister yelling, adult voices carried from the kitchen, each person shouting over the next, and in the den—the foxhole—were the men, each one quiet as though waiting out an attack. Finn took her hand and pulled her toward the den.

"Hey," he greeted.

Luke, his twin, quickly put his finger to his mouth. "Shh. Get in here and be quiet. If they know you're here they'll infiltrate our base."

Apparently she wasn't the only one that felt like she'd just walked into a warzone. Finn headed to the recliner in the far corner and pulled her onto his lap. She awkwardly rested her hip on the wide arm of the chair so as not to crush him.

Kelly tipped his beer to her in greeting. "What's up, Philly?"

"Hi, Kelly."

A football game was on the television so his attention was split. He eyed the TV and asked, "You ready for this? It's a whole different game now that they know you and Finn are a couple."

"Game?"

"They're gonna interrogate you," Colin said.

"They?"

"The women," all the men said at once.

She remained silent. What would they want to know? She wasn't all that interesting.

A woman she didn't recognize went to the front door. "Where are they?" she said, directing her voice to the kitchen.

"Here it comes," Frank, Finn's dad, said. He may have shivered.

"So much for the second quarter," Luke mumbled as he aimed the remote at the television and turned up the volume.

The woman at the front door squinted and leaned farther toward the glass. "Wait a minute. Isn't that Finn's truck?" Her gaze shot to the den and Mallory felt the moment she was spotted. "They're here!"

Like a Black Friday rush, the women poured out of the kitchen and converged on the foxhole. Voices carried to the point she couldn't understand a single word being said, and every man seemed to wince and hunch into their chair.

Her nails dug into Finnegan's legs. If he left her side she'd straight up kill him. Who were all these women?

Maureen McCullough bustled to the front of the line and squeezed her cheeks. It was like having her face closed in a bus door. "There you are, loves! Why didn't you tell us you were here?"

She placed a smacking kiss on Finn's cheek and grabbed Mallory's hand, tugging her up.

Oh no! Her grip on Finn was cut off.

"Everyone," Maureen said, turning her and gripping her shoulders. "This is Mallory, Finnegan's *girlfriend!*"

Mallory winced and as all the women shouted their hello. There was an older woman with bottled black hair and bright red lips. She must have been in her seventies. She seemed to be giving Mallory the stink eye under her dark, penciled on brows.

Then there were two women about Maureen's age. One was holding a toddler on her hip. Sheilagh was in the back rolling her eyes. Beside her was the girl who had spotted Finn's truck. She stepped forward.

"Hi. I'm Kate, Finn's older sister. I saw you at breakfast a while back, but we were never introduced."

"Hi," Mallory said, a little shell-shocked.

The only person she didn't see was Samantha. *Oh, you just wait until I find you, Samantha McCullough. Quiet dinner and cards my ass!*

She was dragged into the kitchen. Glancing over her shoulder, she shot Finn a look of sheer terror and mouthed *Help!*

His brows creased with sympathy and he mouthed *love you.*

FINN CHUCKLED AS MALLORY DISAPPEARED. "Kelly, toss me a beer. I know you have a hidden stock in here." As his gaze drifted from the door to his brother and he stilled. They were all gaping at him. "What?"

His dad cleared his throat and shifted. His uncle turned to the television and asked what the score was. Kelly, Tristan, Colin, and Luke continued to stare.

"So…," Colin started. "I guess the decade of Erin is over."

Finn's eyes narrowed. "Yes. And I'd prefer if we didn't mention her name, around Mallory, or otherwise."

Kelly snickered and tipped back his beer.

"What's so damn funny, Kelly?"

"You."

"Me?"

"Yup."

Finn glanced at Luke and Tristan. His twin held up his hands. "Don't look at me. To each his own."

What the hell were they talking about? Was this about Mallory? He didn't understand what just happened. "Somebody better tell me what the problem is. I won't put up with anyone—"

His dad coughed. "I think, Finnegan, we are all just a little surprised to see you tell the girl you love her."

He gazed at the group of them. Each man nodded in turn. Had he said that? Yes, he'd mouthed it to her before she was dragged away like a sacrificial lamb. Finn shifted uncomfortably in his seat. "So?"

Every man mumbled something, acting like it wasn't a big deal, when clearly it was. Luke shot him a sideways glance, his brow arching.

Finn huffed and got up to grab a beer from the cooler by the couch. He cracked it open and sipped. Plopping back in the recliner he informed them, "She's awesome."

"No one said she wasn't," Kelly commented. "But we know how you are."

"What the hell's that supposed to mean?" Finn asked.

"I think we just all think it's a little fast. I mean, you and Erin just broke up," Colin said, playing the diplomat.

"And it isn't the first time you and Erin have called it quits," Luke added.

He was getting tired of hearing his ex's name. "Well, this time was for good. Even if I didn't have Mallory, I wouldn't go back to Erin. I'm done with her."

"Good," all three of his brothers said at once.

Then Kelly pulled out a ten and put it on the coffee table. "I call within a year."

Luke pulled out a ten. "My money's on six months."

Colin placed a five and five ones on the table. "By Christmas."

They were either betting on how long he and Mallory would last—which really pissed him off—or on how long until—

"I say next month there's a ring on her finger," his dad said, tossing a pile of bills on the table.

Finn stood. Well... He went to the table and scooped

up their money. "You're all idiots. But I'll take your money and put it toward the ring."

"Hey!" They all objected, but laughed in good humor.

He stuffed the money in his pocket and headed to the kitchen. All the women were either working at the counter or sitting at the table. Samantha was sitting with Mallory. He shot his sister-in-law a look that promised retribution. Mallory's brows rose and he took it as a sign of exasperation.

"Hey," he said, softly, settling into the chair beside her.

She smiled and said through her teeth, "I'm going to kill your sister-in-law."

Sammy gasped. "I can hear you."

"I know. You should probably lay low for a while," Mallory warned.

Sammy looked a little scared and got up to help the others. Finn leaned in and kissed Mallory's cheek. "How you holding up?"

"Well, I just had to give my life summery in ten minutes and that old woman keeps staring at me."

"That's Italian Mary. She's a bit overprotective of us McCulloughs."

"Should I be afraid?"

"Nah. Maybe a little. I'm sure you'll be fine."

"All right, you two love birds, it's time to eat," his

mother said, holding an enormous bowl of ham and cabbage.

Everyone filtered out of the kitchen and into the dining room.

His mother yelled into the den. "Come on, boys. Get off your arses and carry something to the table." His nieces and nephews charged down the stairs and rushed into the dining room.

He pulled out a chair for Mallory, and they settled in. Colin had a large dining room built in their house, because he often hosted events for the church. Everyone quieted as his older brother tapped his fork to his glass.

Colin cleared his throat and bowed his head. "Lord, we thank you for this amazing feast and for bringing Mallory here to meet everyone. We hope that she enjoys herself and blesses us with many more nights filled with family, laughter, and tradition."

As Colin went on with grace, Finn reached for Mallory's hand under the table and squeezed. He hoped the same.

After dinner they sat at the table and he suffered many stories—mostly of the embarrassing sort—of his childhood. They got out of there around nine. All in all, the night wasn't too bad. Mallory seemed to hold up well. His parents had pulled him aside before they left to tell him how much they liked her. His brothers took every chance they had to make him feel whipped and rib him.

As he parked outside of her apartment he shut off the truck and waited for her to invite him up. "Did you have fun tonight?"

"It was definitely an experience. You weren't kidding when you said your family's like locusts."

He laughed and rubbed her knee. "That wasn't even all of them. Wait until you meet all the cousins."

"Your sisters are nice."

He eased back in his seat and looked at her. She had such a pretty smile. "You're nice."

Her cheeks darkened and she grinned shyly at him. "Would you like to come in?"

God yes. "Sure."

They walked up the steps and she unlocked the door. Once inside he waited to see what she wanted to do. They both stood in the living room as though waiting for the other to suggest something.

Their eyes met and the energy crackled. Two seconds later, they were wrapped around each other, kissing fiercely. She tugged at his shirt, tearing open the buttons, and his hand slipped under her shirt and found her breasts.

They shuffled into her bedroom, never once taking their lips off each other. They laughed as they toppled to the bed. She spread his shirt wide and bit his chest. He jerked and tugged her shirt over her head. She wore a purple, lace bra and he stilled. Her breasts were magnificent.

"God, you're beautiful."

She froze and lowered her lashes bashfully. "No, I'm not."

"Yes," he said, sternly. "You are."

His fingers pulled the cup of her bra down and out popped her soft nipple. Leaning up, he pulled it into his mouth and she moaned, her thighs tightening on his hips. She braced her arms at his shoulders and he cupped her breasts, filling his palms, and tasted her flesh.

She rocked over him as her moans grew. Suddenly, she sat up and scooted lower. Her fingers worked the buttons of his jeans and the zipper came down in a fast zip. Her warm hand curled around his flesh and pulled him out. Then her mouth was on him.

Breath sucked deep in his lungs. He arched and folded his hands behind his head, eyes shutting in bliss. "I love this."

"Mmm," she said, her muffled reply vibrating along his flesh.

Her hand pumped as her mouth suctioned up and down over his length. Jesus, she was good at that—a little too good. His hips bucked and he felt himself getting close.

"Hold on, Philly, I want inside of you."

She tightened her grip and worked him faster. He

was going to come. His spine tingled and it was too late. His release filled her mouth and she never stopped. No one had ever done that to him so enthusiastically, so perfectly.

He panted as he came down from the sudden rush of endorphins and she came to rest by his side, her fingers trailing over his pecs and sending shivers and chills up his arms.

"Marry me." The words fell out and she laughed.

"What is it with guys and blow jobs?" she asked.

"You're incredible at that."

"Well, I usually don't like doing that, but with you it's different."

That's how he felt about her too. Everything was going so fast with them, he wondered if it was a bad thing. His family broke his stones, but none of them seemed overly concerned.

Once he caught his breath, he turned to her and smiled. "Your turn."

She squealed as he undid her pants and yanked them off her legs. His hands spread her thighs and his thumbs opened her. She was all pink and glossy and plump. He dove in for a taste and she cried out. He gave as good as he got, rushing her to climax until she was shouting his name.

He scrambled up her body and reached for the condoms, but his cock made contact with her sex and they both froze and sighed at the incredible feeling of skin on skin. She moaned and wiggled her hips. The tip of his erection settled at her opening and their eyes met. Fuck, she felt good.

They breathed and she lifted. Heat engulfed his length and he was halfway in. He'd never had sex without protection. He should be the sensible one and pull out now, get a condom on, and get back to business, but then she did something crazy with her internal muscles and he nearly came out of his skin.

"My period's due tomorrow or the next day. I think that makes us safe," she said under a sweet pink flush.

His breath shook. Maybe just a little. He pressed deeper and they moaned. "You feel incredible right now."

"I've never done it without…"

"Me neither," he confessed.

"I trust you, Finn."

"We shouldn't."

"Okay," she said softly, but he thrust again and she made a sound of absolute pleasure.

Again. Just a few more times in and out and then he would grab a condom. Her body tightened around him and he continued. He couldn't seem to find the will to leave her heat. His body began to tingle and he knew he didn't have much time. The fact that she made him come once, bought him some stamina, but she was so incredible it wouldn't last.

He let his mind go. Filling her, loving the way she

tightened around him, they went at it. Nails dragged over skin. Hair was pulled. His name on her lips was pure poetry to his ears.

Before he knew what happened he felt his release bursting out of him. She tightened and cried out her own release. In the last second, he had the good sense to pull out. He spilled his release over her soft tummy and breathed hard. As he stared down at her, he saw perhaps the prettiest expression he'd ever seen her make. She was so damn sexy.

The only thing that broke his mood was the crashing realization that he might have just majorly fucked up. "I'm sorry. That was my fault. I shouldn't have done that."

"Finn, it's fine. I'm sure it's fine. You didn't finish in me and, I told you, I'm not ovulating right now."

He felt terrible. He was usually responsible. "Are you sure?"

"Yes."

He kissed her. "Let's take a shower together and I'll clean you up."

Her expression shuttered. "I'll just take one by myself real quick. I don't mind."

He frowned. "But I want to take one with you."

"I don't do that."

"What, shower?"

"Not with others. Gravity is not my friend."

"Stop. I've seen you naked. You're naked now. What's the difference? I'll be naked too."

"No."

He saw there was no convincing her otherwise and he was disappointed. He wanted to touch her and play under the water, but this was one of those silly hang-ups she had. He didn't feel like getting into how ridiculous that was, so he let it go and kissed her on the cheek. "Fine. Hurry up, though. I'm not done with you."

CHAPTER 14

The following weeks, Mallory knew, would forever be categorized as the best time of her life. She and Finn saw each other every day. He had become a necessary part of her life.

The parts of her life that didn't necessarily include Finn were doing wonderful also. She loved her job, had forgiven Sammy for setting her up with the family dinner, and, on October seventeenth, something incredible happened. She got on the scale and read a number she hadn't seen since her early twenties.

Since then, she had dropped another eight pounds. It was insane to her that she would soon be a weight she hadn't seen since she was a teenager. Her body was still a work in progress, but she felt incredible.

She could carry groceries up her apartment steps without getting winded. She could dance for hours on end. And she was becoming quite the acrobat in the bed sport department.

She and Finn went climbing often. Today she was determined to ring that bell at the top of the tree.

She laced up the boots Finn had surprised her with last month and grabbed the flannel he'd left at her apartment. It was her flannel now. She wasn't giving it back. As she ran down the stairs he was waiting in his truck. It was damp out. Rain misted in the air, too insignificant to form actual drops.

She hopped in the truck and buckled up.

"Ready, champ?" Finn asked as he leaned over to greet her with a kiss.

"That bell is mine," she declared proudly.

As they drove to the lumberyard, the wipers swiped over the windshield every few minutes as mist gathered. The ground was muddy, but she was determined this was her day. Thanksgiving was just around the corner and, while the Rocky steps were on her bucket list, tree climbing came first.

Finn grabbed the equipment and helped her climb into the harness. He cupped the apex of her jeans and teasingly suggested he'd be ringing her bell later. She swatted him away, all business, and proceeded to buckle up her spikes.

She got the rope around the trunk on the first swing and took a deep breath. Her spikes cut into the bark and she hoisted herself up. Shimmying the rope and taking small steps, she was soon twenty feet off the ground. Getting down was the hardest part, but she'd learned not to look at the ground.

Her muscles shook the higher she climbed. Sweat gathered under the leather of her gloves. A strand of hair tickled from under her helmet, but she blew it out of her way.

It was November and the temperature had lowered quite a bit. That was why today was important. It would be snowing in Center County soon and she didn't want to have to wait until spring to try and ring the bell again.

Unfiltered winds gusted at her, strong and steady, the farther up she climbed. She squinted through her protective glasses toward the top. It was difficult to see, since the misty air had started to form drops on her lenses.

"You're almost there, babe!" Finn shouted from far below.

She dug in her spikes and took another step. Glancing up, she spotted the old rusted bell at the top. Winded, she took a few minutes to gather her wits.

"You all right?"

"Yes," she shouted back.

Once she caught her breath, she whipped the rope up and took two more steps. A little closer. She breathed and grunted as she whipped the rope up again. Two steps and she reached, but she wasn't there yet. Bracing herself, she shimmied the rope again and shut her eyes. The treetops were a daunting reminder of how far she was from the ground. Step. Hoist. Kick. Step.

Looking up, she spotted the weathered tail of the frayed rope hanging over the sprout of an old branch. She reached and her leather-clad fingertips teased the threads closer. Her fist closed over the rope's end as her weight leaned into the harness. She tugged and the loud clank of the rusted bell echoed through the forest.

Finn whistled and clapped and cheered and a rush of pride had her blinking back tears. She did it!

Taking a deep breath, she stood there for a moment. Her gloves wiped across her glasses and she took in the magnificent view. The green horizon met blue sky. It was likely the closest she'd ever come to flying.

Peace settled over her and she suddenly felt very close to God. As though she had His ear for that brief moment in time, she whispered to Him. She could have asked for something, but that wasn't what she wanted. Rather, she stared at the heavens and told Him, "Thank you."

As she climbed down, she focused on making it to the ground safely. By the time she was below the canopy of trees her legs were practically numb. Her steps grew clumsy and her fingers were slowly starting to slip.

Sweat beaded at her forehead and trickled into her

eyes. There was nothing she could compare to the rushing sense of relief she felt the moment Finns arms closed around her.

"I got you," he whispered and her limbs nearly gave out as he helped her down.

The ground met the bottom of her cleats hard and she suffered the quick bite of vertigo as her equilibrium reacquainted itself with the earth. She turned and pulled off her helmet and glasses. "I did it!"

Just then the sky opened up and cooling rain began to pelt her shoulders. Finn smiled and hugged her tight. "Yeah you did!"

They spun in the rain, laughing and kissing. She was so proud of herself.

"I knew you could do it," he said, his lips pressed to hers. "You're amazing!"

She sealed her lips to his and pulled him tight. She had yet to catch her breath. The kiss slowed and excitement bubbled in her belly. Her clothing clung to her body, damp from the rain.

"Come on, let's get out of the rain," he said, taking her hand and running toward the truck.

Thunder cracked and she jumped. "Wait. I can't run in these spikes."

He stopped and pulled her under a nearby tree. Bending to one knee, he quickly unlatched her spikes. She leaned into the trunk of the tree, her legs still burning from exertion.

He glanced up at her, his face wet with rain, a smile splitting his face. "I want you, Philly. Now."

Breath sawed out of her lungs. How could she say no to him? "You have me."

He reached up and undid the leather harness around her hips and thighs. His fingers pulled at the buttons of her jeans until he had the zipper flayed wide. His warm mouth pressed into the silk patch of her panties and he tugged the denim down her thighs.

Rough bark bit into her palms as she braced herself. Once her hips were exposed she shivered. The rain was cool and although her skin was hot, the temperature was low.

His thumb followed the seam of her panties and tugged it aside. He lifted from his heels and brought his mouth to her sex, piercing her folds with his tongue. He growled. "You taste so fucking good."

Her head fell back, her hair catching on the bark of the tree. She breathed fast as he licked, kissed, and fucked her with his tongue. Thunder rumbled followed by the unmistakable rip of silk. He used both hands to part her folds and teased at her clit. Her knees bucked, but he held her there, pinned to a tree, in the middle of the woods as rain pelted them from every direction.

Her voice echoed through the forest over the shelling sound of rain. He pressed a finger into her sex, then two, and she tightened. His mouth was relentless.

Heart racing, she shook and shivered as the first wave of her climax crashed over her.

"Finn!"

He continued to draw out her orgasm until she could take no more. As she caught her breath, he stood. "I need you now, Mallory."

She yanked her pants somewhat back in place. He laced his fingers in hers and tugged her toward the truck. It was really raining now. Their clothes were drenched and she struggled to yank her soaked jeans over her hips as they ran.

Every few steps Finn glanced back at her from over his shoulder. She knew she'd always remember the way he looked in that moment, happy, intense…in love.

They reached the truck and he spun her so her back pressed into the metal. His lips tasted of her. Her fists closed over his saturated shirt. "Fuck me, Finnegan. Now."

He growled and threw open the driver door. The keys were still in the ignition and the mechanism made a repetitive ding. He tugged her wrist. "Here, lay down. No, on your stomach."

She rested her arms under her chest as she bent over. He yanked her jeans down and rain spattered over her ass. She heard him fumbling with his own clothes and then he kicked out her booted feet. She could only spread her legs so much with her jeans twisted around her knees.

"Shit. No condom," he suddenly said.

"I don't care." She needed him.

"Me neither."

His lips pressed into the cheek of her ass and then the blunt tip of his erection parted her folds and filled her in one deep thrust. She went up on her toes as he thrust again and again, taking her hard.

Her fingernails bit into the leather upholstery of the seat and she panted, crying out with each hard thrust. Her body contracted and clamped down on him, a rapid thrumming starting somewhere in her womb and bursting outward. He cursed and fucked her harder. As her second climax peaked, he filled her completely, his body stiff yet quivering, and warmth bathed her channel.

His body fell onto hers and she shivered. His lips kissed her cheek, the other side of her face stuck to the seat of the truck. "I love you, Mallory, so much."

She loved him too. So much it terrified her. She blinked back at him and smiled. "Ditto." As she saw his hair she laughed. "You're soaked."

"I don't care."

"Come on, get in the truck." She wiggled, but he growled in protest as she tried to peel apart their bodies.

Once she climbed into the passenger seat, Finn ran off to get the equipment. The rain let up and returned to the soft misting it had been all morning. He climbed in the truck and slammed the door. They studied each other and burst out laughing. They were soaked to the bone.

"Here," he said reaching behind the seat. He produced a gray blanket. "Let's get out of these wet clothes."

He peeled off his flannel and she did the same. Even the thermal she had underneath was wet. Finn started the truck and turned on the heat. He placed their wet clothes over the heater vents.

She unfolded the blanket and he helped her wrap it around her shoulders. Tucking the edges close to her neck, he pulled her close and fit her right in the crook of his arm. They were down to their undies, hers partially shredded, and there was no place else she'd rather be.

The windows fogged as the scent of rain and heat filled the air. "I can't believe you made it to the top. I mean I can believe it, I'm just so proud of you," he said, brushing a damp curl from her forehead.

"I'm proud of me too," she admitted.

"You should be. Not just because you rang the bell. I know you had a lot of goals when you moved here and you haven't reached them all yet, but you're doing a damn fine job of getting there, Philly. I never knew a woman with a stronger will. You figure out what you want and you take no prisoners. I admire that."

Her lips trembled as his words sunk in. So many

times in her life she felt less than everyone else—or in her case *more*. Things were different. She wasn't perfect. She still had a boatload of flaws, but she liked herself in a way she'd never been able to claim before. Finn did that.

It wasn't that she only found value in herself through Finn, but he showed her she was valuable in a way she couldn't find on her own. He was like her beacon in the night. He made her happy and made her see reasons to celebrate herself and the little victories in life. He even got her to eat ice cream again, small bites, but she realized she could have a little and that was enough.

Bottom line, she loved him more than she'd ever loved anything in the entire world. "Thank you."

He wrapped his arms around her and squeezed. She was thanking him for the sweet compliment, but also thanking God again. Never had she imagined this sort of contentment. She was finally at peace with herself and believed life didn't have to be so lonely or hard. There were good days and there were bad, but she'd take days of bad for even a few minutes of good, especially when the good included Finn.

The following week was Thanksgiving. She was a little high strung. There was a fine line between excitement about seeing her Philly friends and vomiting all over her suitcase from nerves. Finn had been very understanding all week. She had no idea how he remained so patient with her when she was acting like a complete psycho.

As he sat on her bed eating a banana, she rummaged through her closet and tossed various pieces of clothing around her room. She'd have to refold everything.

"Do you realize you've been packing for five days? You're only going home for four."

They were leaving Thanksgiving morning. One, because she didn't like driving at night and two, because it was widely known the Wednesday before Thanksgiving was the biggest bar night of the year and the worst for travel.

She and Finn were leaving at six a.m. and returning to Center County on Sunday. It was Tuesday night and she had packed and unpacked more times than she could count. "I don't know what to bring. I don't know if we'll be going out and if we do I don't know what to wear."

"Just bring two nice outfits and a bunch of casual stuff. I'm bringing jeans."

"All you own are jeans," she huffed, digging through her shoes. "These or these?" she asked, holding up two pairs of pumps.

"Mmmm, the red ones." She studied the shoes and tossed the red ones back in the basket and opted for the black. He laughed. "I'll never understand women."

"You don't need to understand women. You only need to understand me."

"True."

Once she had her suitcase packed with everything but her sneakers, she carried it to the front door. She wanted everything loaded up Wednesday night so she could run out the door first thing Thursday morning. But she needed to run one last time before she packed her sneakers.

"You should bring your stuff over tomorrow so I can load the car," she suggested.

"Hey, OCD, relax. We'll have everything loaded up and ready to go in time. Stop obsessing. Everything will be fine."

She took a deep breath, fighting the urge to vomit again. She was ridiculously nervous. Maybe it was because she was finally bringing home a guy. Maybe it was because she'd lost thirty-seven pounds since leaving home six months ago. She needed to calm down.

"Sorry. I don't know why I'm acting like this."

"I think you need to get your mind off things. How about tomorrow we go out? Braydon will be home from college, so it should be a fun night."

"But then we'll be hung over."

"I'll drive and you don't have to get wasted. Let's just go out and have fun. Then before you know it we'll be driving to the city and you won't have to worry.

Remember that saying, it's not the boom, but the anticipation of the boom? You're just going to keep working yourself up over nothing."

"Okay," she whined, leaning into him. "Thanks for understanding I'm crazy and still loving me."

"Hey, being around family is stressful. I know."

"Are you nervous to meet my parents?"

"A little."

She laughed. They'd love him. Sure, her dad would threaten disembowelment and castration if Finn hurt her, but that's only because he was an Italian father of two daughters, born and raised in South Philly. It came with the territory. But she had no doubt Finn would win over her mother and father in a matter of minutes. "They'll love you as much as I do."

"I hope."

The following night, Mallory needed to run. Her nerves were making her crazy and she couldn't seem to settle her stomach. She ran six miles and was feeling every ache by the time she got into the shower. Maybe she'd skip the bar that night and just go to bed early.

When she was drying her hair her phone buzzed. She had a voicemail from Finn. She hit the button and listened to the message.

"Hey, babe, it's me. Braydon needs to take his car into the shop and wants me to drop him off. I told him since I'd be away all weekend he could use my truck. I'm going to drive him into town now. Why don't you just meet me at O'Malley's to save time then we'll stay at your place tonight? Don't worry I'm all packed. Love you. See you soon."

She put down her phone and sighed. She supposed her plan to skip the bar wasn't going to happen. Venturing to her closet she dug out something to wear.

WALKING into O'Malley's with Braydon was like walking into *Cheers* with Norm. Everyone cheered when they saw the blond McCullough son had returned home and women flocked to him. Finn patted his brother's shoulder and went off to find Mallory. The lot was packed and he didn't see her car, but that didn't mean she wasn't there.

Kelly was busy at the far end of the bar, but they had a new bartender working—Sue or Sally or something. He approached the edge of the bar and muscled his way to the front.

"Can I help you?"

"Can I get a draft?"

She disappeared and returned a moment later with his beer. "Hey, you're Kelly's brother, right? One of the twins?"

"Yeah. I'm Finn."

"Finn? There was a girl here looking for you a few

minutes ago."

He paid for his beer and left the change on the bar. "Do you know where she went?"

"She headed in the backroom, I think."

"Thanks." He nudged his way through the crowd and headed toward the back where the pool tables were. As he ducked into the room he saw a few guys having a game and a couple people sitting in the booths along the wall. Then he saw her. Erin.

"There you are," she purred, abandoning her drink on a tall table.

Great. This was the last thing he felt like dealing with. He scanned the room for Mallory. "Hey, Erin. Have you seen Mallory?"

She stepped close and smiled. "Not here. She's pretty hard to miss."

He grit his teeth and took a step back. She cornered him against the pay phone. He needed to get rid of her before Mallory showed up. "Well, it was nice seeing you."

As he turned she snatched his beer out of his hand and took a swig. "Wait, I was looking for you. I need to talk to you."

She could keep the beer. Their days of sharing beverages were over. God only knew where her mouth had been. "What, Erin?"

She pouted. "You never have time for me anymore. I remember when I was all you thought about."

"Well, those days are over."

"Right, because you found yourself someone new. I have to admit, she's a whole lot more woman than I ever was."

His eyes narrowed. "Don't start."

"Sorry. You're so touchy." She stepped closer. Her finger plucked at the collar of his shirt. "I couldn't sleep last night. Wanna know why?"

"Not really." He caught her wrist and shoved off her touch.

"I couldn't sleep because I was up all night thinking about how good it used to be with us. Remember how hot we were?"

No. He didn't remember. They ran lukewarm at best. They were always fighting and Erin was the unforgiving type. For as volatile as their relationship had been, they didn't even have good make up sex. She used sex to get things, like her way, which she got a lot.

"Don't do this, Erin. I'm not in the mood for games."

She lifted to her toes and whispered in his ear. Her breath smelled like she'd already had a few drinks. "I used to love sucking your cock. I bet she can't do it like I can."

Gripping her hips to push her away, she turned and caught her mouth with his. He jerked, but his head hit the wall. Her arms laced around his neck and he dug his fingers into her hips to rip her off.

. . .

MALLORY SAW Finn's truck and knew he was there. The parking lot had cars everywhere. She'd never seen the bar so busy. As she pushed her way inside she searched for him, but didn't see him. She saw Braydon, but only women surrounded him.

Heading to the bar, she found Kelly. "Hey, Philly. What can I get you?"

"Hey, Kelly. Can I just have a ginger ale?"

"Sure, love. You feeling all right?"

"Yeah, just sore and my stomach's upset."

He used the soda gun to fill a glass. She handed him a few dollars and he shook her off. "Don't worry about it."

"Thanks. Have you seen Finn?"

"Yeah. I think he's in the back."

"Okay. I'll see you later."

Getting to the back of the bar was no easy task. Some guy nearly spilled his drink down her front and twice she got elbowed in the boob. *Assholes.*

The back room wasn't as crowded. She stepped through the door and saw some people sitting around and playing at the billiards. She scanned the room for Finn and there was a loud shatter.

Something told her it was her glass of soda, but she didn't know. Her eyes were glued to her boyfriend, cozied up at the back wall, kissing his ex.

Her chest ached as she breathed rapidly. *No. This isn't happening!*

The crash of her glass must have drawn some attention. Everyone looked at her, including Finn, but all she could see through the haze of betrayal was that slut's lip-gloss covering his mouth.

A gasp left her mouth and she shook her head. She needed to get out of there. He pushed Erin away and cursed. "Mallory! Wait!"

No way. She turned and pushed her way through the crowd. She nearly slipped on the dance floor and some guy caught her arm. "Hey, cutie, where you rushing off to?"

"Let go of me!" she snapped, ripping her arm out of his grip.

"Don't let her leave!" Finn yelled over the crowd. She turned and saw him practically climbing over the mob of people separating them. "Mallory! It wasn't what it looked like!"

A sound of absolute distress left her and she shoved her way to the door. Those were the last famous words of every cheater.

When she reached the door her hands slammed into the handle and she propelled herself into the parking lot. She rushed to her car and yanked her purse over her shoulder. As she dug for her keys the bag fell to the ground and if things fell out she didn't care. She saw her keys, grabbed them, scooped up her bag and made it to her car.

The door to the bar burst open and Finn came

flying out. "Mallory, wait a minute!"

Her hands were shaking so badly she couldn't get the door unlocked. He grabbed her shoulder and her purse fell again.

"Wait a damn minute, will you? It's not what it looked like!"

"Fuck you, McCullough!" She ducked and snatched up her purse, this time not sparing a minute to repack it. Her door unlocked and she threw all her crap inside, not caring where it landed. She slid behind the wheel and jammed the key in the ignition.

Finn caught the door. *"Wait!"*

"No! Get away from me! How could you?"

"I didn't do anything! She kissed me! I was shoving her away!"

"I saw you!"

"I was pushing her off. I was only back there because I was looking for you."

"Yeah, you were really looking hard." Her hand swiped under her eyes.

"I was! Damn it, Mallory, I wouldn't cheat on you. I fucking love you!"

"Right, until something better comes along."

"Wrong. There is no one better than you. You're all I want. What do I have to do to prove that to you?"

"I don't know. Don't make out with your ex!"

He growled. "I wasn't fucking making out with her. I can't stand her."

"Four months ago you intended to marry her."

"Well, a lot's changed. Come on, Mallory, don't leave. Please. I swear it wasn't what it looked like."

She sniffled. She was pretty sure her heart was actually breaking. "See, Finnegan, that's the difference. I would never let another man get close enough to me for there to be a question of what 'it looks like'. You let her get to you. You had your mouth against hers. God, all I can see is your hands on her!"

"I was pushing her away!"

"Please let go of my door."

"No. I don't want you to drive this upset."

"Well, there's no fixing that now."

His voice softened. "Come on. We're supposed to have a fun night and leave for the city tomorrow."

"Well, I've had all the fun I can take."

"Don't do this," he begged. "Please."

She saw him, but her mind's eye was torturing her. She shook her head. Her heart was being ripped through her chest. "I have to go."

"No, you don't."

She put the car in drive. "Yes. I do." As she hit the gas he cursed and let go of her door.

She should have just gone home, but he would have followed her there. She took the main road out to the highway and cried the entire four and a half hours back to Philadelphia.

CHAPTER 15

When she parked her car outside of her childhood home, she simply sat there with her head resting on the wheel. Her phone had been going off the entire first hour she'd been on the road. Eventually, she shut it off and was currently too tired to look at all her missed calls and texts from Finn.

Leaving her luggage in the car, she grabbed her purse and headed up the stoop to her parents' house.

Her keys slipped into the lock like feet slide easily into a favorite pair of slippers. The door opened and she stepped into the dark living room.

"Who's there?" Her father's voice called from the top of the steps where the bedrooms were located.

She stepped into the glow coming from the hall. "Daddy?"

"Mallory, is that you, buttercup? I thought you weren't coming until tomorrow afternoon."

Something broke inside of her. As she stood there in her home, surrounded by the scent of her childhood memories and the sound of her father's voice, she shattered and fell into a fit of tears.

Her dad rushed down the steps and wrapped her in his arms. "Sweetheart, what happened?"

She sobbed into his soft chest and hiccupped out words that barely made sense. The light flicked on and she heard her mother's voice. "Vince, you better not be picking at those pies!"

"Mallory's here," he called as he ushered her to the sectional sofa that was badly out of date.

"What? But she's not coming until tomorrow."

Her dad sighed. "I know, but she's here now. Get down here. She's all upset and I can't understand her."

"Let me get my housecoat."

Her mother appeared a moment later. "Mallory? Is that you, baby? What happened to you? I barely recognize you."

The comment about how different she looked should have registered, but it didn't. None of it mattered. "Oh, Mom," she cried. "He kissed her."

"Who?"

"Finn! I caught him kissing his ex. He's not coming and…I think…oh God…I think we broke up."

Her parents glanced at each other like they had a secret and then calmly rubbed her back. "Mallory, baby, we never expected you to bring a boy home. It's okay. We were excited just to have you."

She frowned and wiped her eyes. "What?"

Her dad cleared his throat. "Buttercup, we sort of assumed you'd be here by yourself."

"You assumed…why?"

They looked guilty for a second then shrugged. "Well, it's just always been you."

"But I told you about Finn."

They gave her a skeptical glance.

She gasped. "He's real!"

"Of course he is, sweetheart," her mother crooned.

"He is!"

"It doesn't matter, pumpkin. You're home now. Your mom made a bunch of pies and I think she should let us tear into one now, with you being upset and all."

"Vincent!" he mother snapped.

She stood. "I don't want any pie. I think I just want to go to bed."

They stared at her as if she'd grown a second head. How pathetic was she that even her parents didn't believe she had a boyfriend? Well, she didn't anymore. Today was officially the worst day of her life.

. . .

THE NEXT MORNING, she woke up and smiled as she realized she was in her old bed. The scent of turkey cooking was incredible. *Ahh, Mom's cooking.*

Knowing today would be an ordeal involving lots of food, she went to clean herself up in the bathroom. She looked wretched.

She headed out to her car to grab her suitcase. After lugging it up the stairs she changed into her stretch pants and a sweatshirt. She might not be able to control certain parts of her life, but she still had control over her own choices and today she chose to do something that made the move away from her childhood home worthwhile.

She laced up her sneakers and skipped down the steps. "Where are you going?" her mother called from the kitchen. Mallory turned to say good morning and her mom dropped the saltshaker right in the gravy. *"Mallory?"*

"Yeah?"

"You look so…your legs…I've never seen you so…"

She smiled. "Thanks, Mom."

"Are you eating out there?"

She laughed. "Yes, I'm eating. I've just been exercising."

"How much have you lost?"

"Only thirty-seven. By the doctor's standards I'm still obese, but no longer morbidly so."

"Well, I think you look gorgeous. I mean, you've

always been beautiful, but you look really good, sweetie. I'm proud of you."

"Thanks."

It was odd. She expected some sense of accomplishment to accompany those words, but she felt the same. She knew she looked better. She felt better. She had more energy and her self-esteem was a little stronger. Her parents' praise didn't seem to matter. What mattered was her own opinion of herself.

She stood, in the kitchen where she had consumed countless meals, and realized that being home didn't matter. Her family wasn't the most sensitive crew, but…none of it mattered. She'd already proven her value to herself. She didn't have to be skinny to be happy. She'd always thought that was what it would take.

It wasn't about reaching a certain size or weighing a certain amount. It was about liking herself. At some point over the last few months, she'd begun to like herself and see that she deserved to be happy as much as anyone else.

Today she was going to make herself happy. "I'll be back in a little bit, Mom."

"Where are you going?"

"I need to run out for a bit. I should be back in an hour or so." She grabbed her keys and a bottle of water and headed out the door.

As she pulled her car into the street, she took the

one way and turned at the intersection toward Market Street. She parked on the corner of Thirteenth and Market, grabbed her iPod, and stuffed her keys in the pocket of her sweatshirt.

She stretched for a few minutes then hit play. The horns started and then came the drums. Her feet hit the pavement and she was off.

Her pace built as she turned and ran under the blue rails of the El. Her heart was really pumping as she cut the corner by the brick row homes, slapping her hand against the stained concrete that marked Rocky's home. When she spotted JFK Plaza, she grinned and picked up her pace. Almost there and she was barely breaking a sweat.

Her iPod was set on repeat and as the theme song continued she continued to push herself harder. She could do this. Nothing was stopping her. Nothing!

It occurred to her that she didn't need to hide from the world to prove something. She only needed to shut them out. All of the media and trendy pop culture that was jammed down her throat on a regular basis made it impossible to see beyond her shortcomings.

Center County had given her the escape she needed. Moving had silenced the judgmental world, hidden her from the critical onlookers, and helped her see *her*. She finally saw herself as a woman capable of anything.

The peaks of the cathedral showed on the horizon

and she was soon cutting around the curve of Race Street. Then she was almost there, on Ben Franklin Parkway, the fountain flowing behind her.

The Philadelphia Museum of Art stood like a castle in the distance. To her right was the famous statue of the boxer. Mallory panted and threw up her arms, mimicking his cast pose, gloves held high.

Just a little further and she would have done it. Her sneakers smacked over the pavement. At the top of those seventy-two concrete steps were Sylvester Stallone's shoe prints and she wasn't stopping until her feet filled the marks.

Her thighs burned as she took the stairs hard. Skyscrapers towered behind her, but nothing stood as tall as her in those moments. She crossed the first landing and was climbing again. The next landing arrived and she lengthened her strides. So close. More steps. Her blood was pumping. The bass was thrumming in her ears. There was no stopping her. She was a machine. She was doing this, doing it for herself and she was almost there.

The peaks of the museum crested the horizon the higher she climbed and then the long columns. Just a few more steps and she'd be there. Looking down, she watched her feet cross those last few steps, her arms pumped at her sides as her lungs sawed in her chest and she was finally—

She slammed into some asshole that was standing in her spot!

Her knees hit the pavement hard. Who the hell was standing on her Rocky footprints? She yanked her ear plugs out of her ears, cutting off her awesome theme song, and turned, prepared to give someone hell for screwing up the biggest checkmark on her bucket list yet.

The guy was down. She crawled to her knees and froze in the process of getting to her feet. She knew that flannel.

Oh my God.

He wasn't moving. She rushed to his side. "Finn? What the hell are you doing here?"

He grunted. "It was the only place I knew to find you."

She shook her head and panted. "*What?*"

He moaned and sat up. "We have to stop running into each other like this."

"You're in Philadelphia."

"I know. You did the steps a lot faster than me."

This was her happy moment. He was ruining it. The sight of him reawakened all those horrible emotions she'd put away to do something nice for herself. "Why are you here?"

He sat up. "You left before I could give you something."

"Did you drive all night?"

"I left around three in the morning when it occurred to me I'd probably find you here at some point. I'm glad you didn't make me sleep on the steps."

"You were going to camp out at the Museum of Art? Why?"

He met her gaze and smiled sadly. "Because I love you."

Oh no. She started to blink rapidly and her throat tightened. "What did you have to give me?"

"This." He reached in his pocket and pulled out a small keychain with a little pink Converse sneaker on the end.

"You drove all this way to give me a shoe?"

"It's also a keychain." She frowned at him and he said, "It has a zipper. Open it up."

She took the little shoe—it was actually kind of cute—and tugged the little zipper. The sun caught on something and she squinted. Her fingers reached inside and cold metal met her fingertips. She gasped as she pulled out a solitaire diamond ring on a platinum band. "What is this?"

"This is what I was trying to tell you. I bought it a few weeks ago. There's no one else, Philly. You're it for me. I love you and I want to marry you. Not because I need a wife and want a family, but because I can't imagine one single day without seeing your beautiful face or hearing your laugh. I want to wake up every morning and look into those blue eyes of yours. I don't ever want to have to worry about you being home alone at night, because I want to always be there, keeping you safe and warm and I want you to do the same for me. Keep me warm, Mallory. It's too cold and lonely in this world without you."

Her chin trembled as she stared at him. He was proposing? To *her*? "What about Erin?"

"I have five witnesses that will tell you she's the one who cornered me and I was trying to get away from her the moment I saw her. I was looking for you. I'm always looking for you. You're who makes me happy, happier than I've ever been."

Her fist closed over the ring and she shut her eyes. "I'm glad you asked me now."

"Why's that?"

"Because I'll always know we got married because you wanted *me* and not for any other reason."

"What other reason would there be?" he asked, his brow crinkling.

She smiled. "Remember that time in the woods with the rain?"

"How could I forget?"

"I think I'm pregnant."

"*What?*"

She held out her hand as his eyes went wide. "I'm not sure. It just occurred to me this morning as I was lying in bed. My stomachs been upset and—"

He kissed her. He kissed her long and hard right

there on Rocky's footprints. "You could be carrying my baby?" he asked, his smile pressing against her lips and his hand curving over her belly.

She grinned and kissed him some more. "Maybe."

"Oh, you're definitely marrying me now, because if you're not pregnant I'm gonna get you so."

She giggled. "I didn't say yes yet."

He tickled her side. "Say yes."

"Maybe."

"Say yes." He tickled her some more and she laughed.

"Possibly."

"Mallory Fenton, you agree to be my wife right now or so help me I'll make a scene."

She snickered, slyly slipping the ring onto the finger of her left hand. "I guess I could marry you."

He cupped the back of her head and with his lips still planted against hers, he asked. "Is that a yes?"

"Yes."

And that was when he stood, arms thrown in the air, fists held tall, and bounced on the footsteps permanently engraved in the steps of the Philadelphia Museum of Art, cheering like an idiot. *Ah, my future husband.*

When his lunacy had carried on long enough she cleared her throat and stood. He looked at her, smiling like a boy who was just given the best thing in the world and she told him, "Um, you're sort of stealing my thunder."

He stepped aside and fanned out his hands. She grinned and fit her shoes right over the ones printed in the cement. She was indeed a champion of the world.

Pregnancy was great. She never felt fat. As a matter of fact, when she went to the doctors to confirm her suspicions, he spent a good ten minutes remarking about how proud he was of her. It didn't matter. She may have started out doing it for him, at some point she was doing it for her friends at home and her parents and her sister, who would always be dramatically smaller. At one point, she was even doing it for Finn. But in the end, she did it for herself.

She did it because she felt better. She did it because she finally was comfortable in her own skin. She did it for the two little boys growing in her womb. She did it because she was tired of sitting on the sidelines. She wanted to live and that's what she had done, started living.

She still ran almost every day. Not as hard as she

once had. The doctor said it was fine so long as she didn't overexert herself. Now, at six months along, running was becoming more and more difficult. She and Finn would often walk the field at night and on the way home they'd check on the construction of their new house. It would be done sometime next month, just in time for their sons' arrivals.

That Thanksgiving last fall had been quite interesting. She'd left for a run, her parents thinking her desperate enough to make up a boyfriend, and she returned with a fiancé. She did eat pie that day, right after she served them up a big slice of the humble sort.

She and Finn got married two weeks later at Colin's church and Erin finally stopped sniffing around. Rumor had it she was now working at the Dairy Queen and had put on a few pounds.

Mallory had no idea what her body would be like after the twins. She really didn't care. As long as she felt good and her babies were healthy, she'd figure out the rest later. Finnegan was continuously doting one her.

They made love often and she finally agreed to shower with him. He even bought her clothes now and then. After everything she had put herself through, she realized she would always be her hardest critic. Finn loved her, it didn't matter what shape, size, or color she came in. He loved *her*, the real her, the one he saw every time he looked into her eyes and she loved him that much more for it.

The End

309

If you enjoyed BEAUTIFUL DISTRACTION, you will love IRISH ROGUE, the next story in the McCullough Mountain Series.

Skip ahead for a sneak peek inside

Never miss another book release!
Click here to sign up for Lydia Michaels' Newsletter.

Follow Lydia Michaels on Instagram and Facebook!

What to Read Next?
Click here to claim your FREE Book from Lydia Michaels!

Billionaire Romance
Falling In | Sacrifice of the Pawn | Calamity Rayne

Small Town Romance
Wake My Heart | The Best Man | Love Me Nots | Pining For You | Almost Priest

Emotional Favorites
La Vie en Rose | Simple Man | Wake My Heart | Sacrifice of the Pawn | Forfeit

Romantic Comedy

<u>Calamity Rayne</u>

Erotic Romance
<u>Breaking Perfect</u> | <u>Protégé</u> | <u>Falling In</u> | <u>Sugar</u>

First Books in Binge Worthy Trilogies and Series
<u>Almost Priest</u> | <u>Falling In</u> | <u>Wake My Heart</u> | <u>Forfeit</u> |
<u>Original Sin</u>

Paranormal Vampire Romance
<u>Original Sin</u> | <u>Dark Exodus</u> | <u>Prodigal Son</u>

LGBTQ+ & Menage Romance
<u>Broken Man</u> (MM) | <u>Breaking Perfect</u> (MMF) | <u>Forfeit</u>
(MMF) | <u>Hurt</u> (Non-Consensual) | <u>Protege</u>

Sexy Nerds & Second Chances
<u>Blind</u> | <u>Untied</u>

***Teacher Student, Workplace, and Age-Gap Love Affairs...
Oh my!***
<u>British Professor</u> | <u>Pining For You</u> | <u>Breaking Perfect</u> |
<u>Falling In</u> | <u>Sacrifice of the Pawn</u>

Single Dads & Single Moms
<u>Simple Man</u> | <u>Pining For You</u> | <u>First Comes Love</u> |
<u>Controlled Chaos</u> | <u>Intentional Risk</u>

Dark Psychological Thriller & Tortured Hero Romance
(TRIGGER WARNING)
Hurt

Non-Fiction Books for Writers
Write 10K in a Day: Avoid Burnout

About the Author

Lydia Michaels is the award winning and bestselling author of more than forty titles. She is the consecutive winner of the 2018 & 2019 *Author of the Year Award* from *Happenings Media,* as well as the recipient of the 2014 *Best Author Award* from the *Courier Times*. She has been featured in *USA Today, Romantic Times Magazine, Love & Lace*, and more. As the host and founder of the *East Coast Author Convention*, the *Behind the Keys Author Retreat*, and *Read Between the Wines*, she continues to celebrate her growing love for readers and romance novels around the world.

In 2021, Michaels released the groundbreaking, non-fiction series, **Write 10K in a Day**, to commemorate her career in the publishing industry. She looks forward to many more years of exploring both fiction and non-fiction writing, teaching about the craft, and learning from the others in the author community.

Lydia is happily married to her childhood sweetheart. Some of her favorite things include the scent of paperback books, listening to her husband play piano, escaping to her coastal home at the Jersey Shore, cheap wine, *Game of Thrones*, coffee, and kilts. She hopes to meet you soon at one of her many upcoming events.

You can follow Lydia at www.Facebook.com/LydiaMichaels or on Instagram @lydia_michaels_books

Other Titles by Lydia Michaels

Wake My Heart

The Best Man

Love Me Nots

Pining For You

My Funny Valentine

Falling In: Surrender Trilogy 1

Breaking Out: Surrender Trilogy 2

Coming Home: Surrender Trilogy 3

Sacrifice of the Pawn: Billionaire Romance

Queen of the Knight: Billionaire Romance

Original Sin

Dark Exodus

Calamity Rayne: Gets a Life

Calamity Rayne: Back Again

La Vie en Rose

Breaking Perfect

FREE! - Blind

Untied

Almost Priest

Beautiful Distraction

Irish Rogue

British Professor

Broken Man

Controlled Chaos

Hard Fix

Intentional Risk

Hurt

Sugar

Simple Man

Protégé

Forfeit

Lost Together

Atonement

First Comes Love

If I Fall

Something Borrowed

Write 10K in a Day

SAMPLE IRISH ROGUE

reshman Year

"Bray!" Kelly hissed his brother's name as he nudged his shoulder. "Bray, get up."

"What, Kelly? What time is it?"

"Three in the morning. Wake up."

Braydon roughly rubbed his hands over his face and scooted into a sitting position. His eyes narrowed when he focused on Kelly. "Where were you?"

Kelly grinned wide and gave his brother a telling look. "At the pavilion. I snuck out and met Rachel."

Bray's eyes widened. "If mum catches you she's gonna beat your ass."

"They're asleep. No one knows." He bobbed, his

heart still racing with adrenaline from the crazy night. "Bray…we did it."

"*It?*"

"Yup."

"What was it like?" Bray whispered in the dark.

"It was…*awesome*. Sort of confusing at first, but we figured it out. You have to do it."

His brother's mouth opened as he stared into the dark, a slice of moonlight and an expression of awe clear on his face. "Did Rachel like it?"

"Yeah. I mean, I think so."

Of all his older brothers, Braydon was the only one Kelly felt safe sharing his news with. Colin wouldn't be able to relate, being that he was away in seminary becoming a priest. Luke definitely wasn't a virgin, but he was more of the private sort and would kick Kelly's ass for asking. Finn…Finn was with Erin, and Kelly assumed any couple together for a year would do it, but he wasn't quite sure. Finn was so good and respectful and Erin didn't really put off any come hither vibes.

"Did you use a condom?" Braydon asked.

"Do I look like an idiot? Yes, I used a condom. The last thing this world needs is another me running around, although, he would be a cute little bastard."

"I can't believe this. So…are you guys, like, a thing now?"

Kelly shrugged. "Dunno."

"You're going to be gettin' it all the time, you lucky bastard."

His smile widened. Yeah, he could definitely do it again. Now that he'd opened Pandora's box he wanted to set up camp and do more. There were all sorts of things he wanted to try and he couldn't wait to get to it. Maybe tomorrow after school…

"What was that?" Bray hissed, and they both froze.

A door in the hall opened and closed followed by heavy footsteps. Holding his breath, Kelly watched his brother's door. The knob slowly turned and he snatched off his hat and kicked off his shoes so it wouldn't look like he'd just gotten in.

The door pressed open and their father's gaze met his, blue eyes narrowed with suspicion. "Kelly? What the hell are you two doing up? Go back to your own room. It's late."

"Sorry, Dad. We were just talking about the game."

Frank's lips pursed. "I'm sure. Get your arse in bed and go to sleep. It's a school night."

Their father shut the door and they were silent for a minute. When he met his brother's stare they both stifled a laugh. "Get out of here, Fabio. I got a test tomorrow."

Kelly grabbed his shoes and hat and said goodnight.

The following morning he woke and bounded down the steps for breakfast. He was anxious to get to school and see Rachel, maybe make some plans for that afternoon.

Feeling like the king of the world, he slid into his seat across from his little sister and grabbed the box of cereal. Oats went scattering across the surface of the table when something hard cracked him in the ear. After shaking off the unexpected blow, he turned and found his mother scowling at him, both hands fisted and wedged into her rounded hips. "Ow, Ma!"

"What did you do?" she snapped.

"What was that for?"

"Don't you go playing all innocent with me, Kelly McCullough. A mother knows."

Sheilagh snickered over her bowl of Frosted Flakes. He met Bray's wide eyes and quickly turned back to his mother. "I didn't do anything!"

Her green eyes contracted into small points hidden behind her fiery red lashes. "I can tell when one of my sons is up to something."

"I'm not up to anything."

She rolled her eyes. "You're so full of shit your breath stinks. Whatever you're acting all cheeky about this morning, you better knock it off."

He turned back to his bowl and scooped the spilled cereal inside. Mumbling as he poured the milk, "Christ, can't a guy be happy in the morning?"

"All of your life you've lurched into this kitchen like a zombie. Today you come bounding down the steps like you're leading a bloody parade. Not in my house, young man."

"Fine. I'll go back to being a grump in the morning."

"Damn right, you will. And whatever you're up to knock it off."

The rest of breakfast passed in silence. He wasn't sure how his mother sensed what he'd been up to, but she knew. By the end of the week there was a surplus size box of condoms in his sock drawer, right where she put his fresh laundry.

Talk about awkward. He couldn't meet her gaze for almost a week. When he finally built up the courage, she'd stared at him in such a knowing way paranoia had him blinking away. How the hell did she know?

The following weekend, just as Kelly was rushing out the door to meet some friends, his father stopped him. "Kelly."

He skidded to a halt at the front door and hooked a left into the den. "Yeah, Dad."

"Sit down for a minute."

Hitching his thumb toward the door, he said, "I'm meeting some friends—"

"I said sit."

Recognizing the stern tone in his father's voice, he dropped onto the couch.

"I got a call last week from Jerry Blackwell."

Oh, fuuuuuudge. Jerry Blackwell was Rachel's dad.

"Apparently, Rachel's been sneaking out at night.

She won't be doing that any more now that her parents caught her."

"Dad—"

"It's different with boys. You five do stupid stuff all the time. Even Colin had his moments of idiocy. But I keep thinking about Sheilagh. Next year she'll be in high school, just like Jerry's daughter. I look at my little baby and I try to think what I'd do if I found out she'd snuck out with some punk kid."

Everything in his gut solidified, as he understood the implication. Sheilagh was their baby sister and if anyone ever—ugh, he couldn't even think it. "I'm sorry, Dad."

"I don't think I'm the one you should be apologizing to. Is this lassie your girlfriend, Kelly?"

He shrugged. They were friends. They had fun together. They liked fooling around. "Not really."

His father leveled him with a hard stare. "Then I'd say it's not really right for you to be touching her. I'm not ready to be a grandfather."

"I was safe."

His father's large hand pinched the bridge of his nose. "Kelly, sex isn't about getting in and getting out clean. That's important, but it should be more than that. It should mean something. Now, I know your mother's upset. Colleen convinced her to get you some condoms, but I'd rather see you practice abstinence. You're young. You have your whole life ahead of you. Having a child changes everything. It ties you to that person for the rest of your life. What happens when that person isn't the woman you love?"

He understood what his dad was trying to say. Kelly barely knew Rachel. They were fourteen. The rest of their lives was a long time. "I hear ya."

"Do you?"

"Yeah." He nodded. "I'll be more careful."

Frank stared at him for a long moment. "Boys will be boys, Kelly. I remember what it was like. Just… don't mislead anyone and don't do anything you're not prepared to take accountability for. Carelessness comes with consequence and if you screw up, you're responsible for the mess. Don't volunteer if the repercussions are too much to handle. As an Irish Catholic family, you know certain things are off the table and not an option."

He swallowed. "I know."

Later that night, after hours of considering what his father said, he found some of his excitement evaporated. He didn't want to ruin his future by having a baby when he was just a kid. Rachel wasn't around because she was grounded for sneaking out. Guilt for getting her in trouble wasn't pleasant.

He and his friends met up at the local pizza parlor in town and he wasn't really feeling social. "Hey, Kelly."

Kelly looked up from his soda and grinned at Lauren. "Hey, Lauren."

She slid into the booth, her dark hair tickling his arm. "What are you up to?"

"Nothing."

The rest of their friends were crowded around the video games at the back of the restaurant. "I'm bored. You wanna go somewhere?"

He was bored too. He didn't have money to waste on games and his head hurt from thinking about his father's lecture. "Where?"

She shrugged. Her shoulders showed in one of those neat shirts that tied around her neck. "Let's go for a walk."

Kelly nodded and followed her out of the pizza shop. They walked for a while and wound up at the elementary playground sitting on the swings. Lauren was easy to talk to. She didn't say much, but she laughed at the stupid things he said.

When it got dark they seemed to run out of things to discuss. Lauren climbed off her swing and slowly came to stand in front of his. "I like you, Kelly."

Taken by off guard by her confession, he stared at her for a moment. Lauren was really pretty. Her full lips and big brown eyes shined under the moonlight. Her darker Cherokee skin was flawless.

The scent of her hair surrounded him as she leaned lower and brushed her lips over his. They tasted like cupcakes. She must have put some sort of vanilla lip stuff on. He licked his lips slowly. "You taste like sugar."

She giggled quietly and stepped over his knees. His sneakers pressed into the sand as his fingers tightened on the chains of the swing. Her body lowered, fitting perfectly over his lap as her mouth found his again.

They kissed for a long time, losing themselves in so many new and exciting sensations. His hand slid into the back pocket of her jeans and she moaned into his mouth. It was dark and the only light was several yards away.

Lauren leaned back, her hands disappearing beneath the curtain of her black hair. When she lowered her arms, the ties of her top came with them.

"Christ."

She smiled and he lowered his head, placing his lips on the soft swell of her breast and kissing over the lace of her strapless bra. Kelly should have been thinking about lots of things in that moment, but the only thing on his mind was Lauren. His body was rock hard and screaming for more. He never expected to get more, but when Lauren stood and led him to the tunnel in the jungle gym, he didn't have the sense nor inclination to say no.

"You're a pig!"

Speechless, Kelly stared at Rachel as the entire cafeteria went silent. "Rachel—"

"How could you?" Her lips thinned as she shook her head in disbelief. "I gave you everything," she whispered. "And none of it mattered to you." Leaning close, she hissed so only he could hear, "I haven't even gotten my period yet!"

His blood ran cold. "Are you late?"

She shrugged and stepped back. "I won't know for another week or so. If you were so concerned maybe you should have kept it in your pants." Her blond ponytail whipped into the air as she pivoted and marched out of the cafe.

The whispers of onlookers slowly climbed to the ordinary roar of the lunchroom. Girls watched him and whispered behind the backs of their hands as guys smirked and nodded his way. He glanced around, knowing the back of his neck was bright red, and stilled when his gaze collided with Lauren's. Those brown eyes were no longer big and soft. Her face was pale and she quickly stood, carrying off her tray and leaving the room without notice.

A shadow fell over the table and he turned to find Finn standing there. "Wanna get out of here?"

Kelly swallowed. "Yeah."

His brother nodded and Kelly followed him out of the cafeteria and right to Finn's pickup. They didn't talk until they drove some distance and wound up at the hunting cabin on the outskirts of their property.

"Come on. Dad and Uncle Paul were here last week

fixing the water heater. Chances are there's probably beer left over."

Kelly nodded and followed Finn inside. His brother was right. The old fridge was stocked with bottles. Kelly made to toss one to Finn but paused when his brother waved him away. "One of us has to drive home."

Nodding, he cracked open the beer and took a long swig.

"Wanna tell me what's going on, Kelly?"

"Not really, but I will. I had sex with Rachel Blackwell."

"You did?"

Finn's expression gave away quite a bit about his brother's long-term relationship with Erin. "You've done it, right, Finn?"

His brother flushed and rubbed the back of his neck. "Not yet, but Erin says we will soon."

"Oh." It was odd, lapping his older brother in such a rite of passage.

"What's it like?"

Kelly smirked and peeked up at Finn. "It gets better the more you do it."

"You slept with her twice?"

"Not exactly." He fidgeted and took another sip of beer. "I slept with Lauren Sweeny too."

"Jesus, Kelly!"

"I know!" He drew in a frustrated breath. In a

smaller voice, he said, "I know. I don't know what I was thinking. It just happened. I didn't plan it. As a matter of fact I planned to not do it with anyone again for a while, but then Lauren whipped out her boobs and all common sense left."

"Kelly, you gotta slow down."

His fingers fisted through his hair and he tugged. "I know. I feel like crap. Mum's mad at me. Dad's worried I'm gonna make him a grandfather—"

"Mum and Dad know?"

"Yeah. She actually put a huge box of rubbers in my drawer. But she's pissed. And worst of all, I hurt Rachel and Lauren. They're sort of friends, you know? I don't want to be an asshole."

"Then don't be. Kelly, you're responsible for you. Everything has a consequence. See how we're sitting here now? Well, tomorrow we're gonna get suspended for skipping. I knew that before I asked if you wanted to bail. Sometimes the consequence is worth it and sometimes it's not. You have to think ahead."

"When you and Erin do it, you let me know if you can think of anything else. It's hard to say no when it's right in front of you."

"I'm aware. We say no for a reason."

"What? *Why?* You guys have been together since eighth grade."

"Because we aren't sure if we want to wait."

"Wait for what? Finn, you live once. *Do. It.*"

He lifted a shoulder. "We probably will soon. Like I said, it's hard to say no, but Erin's never been one to easily say yes."

Yeah, his brother's girlfriend was cute, but sort of mean. Kelly sighed and slouched on the futon. "You're probably right to hold off. You know Rachel said something about being late."

"Is she?"

Kelly shrugged, hiding his panic with indifference. "We used protection. She said she's not due for another couple weeks."

"Good luck relaxing 'til then."

"I know. I wasn't really stressed, but now I sort of am. It doesn't help that she hates my guts now either."

"You guys weren't dating."

"I know, but maybe she thought having sex changed things. We didn't talk about it or anything, but girls are weird about stuff like that."

"And what about Lauren?"

"I don't think she'll be showing me her boobs again anytime soon."

Finn nodded and a contemplative silence filled the minutes ticking by. He should be in gym class right now—

"Were they nice?"

"What?"

"Lauren's boobs. Were they nice?"

Kelly laughed. No matter how perfect Finn tried to

be, he was still a guy and a McCullough at that. "Yeah. They were real nice."

They didn't leave the cabin until after dark. Kelly convinced Finn to have a few drinks and they both needed to sober up some before either one of them could drive or face their parents. As predicted, they were both suspended for ditching school and, per McCullough law, they were both punished with cleaning the toilets at his aunt's bar and extra chores around the house.

In the weeks that followed Kelly steered clear of all females. Rachel continued to hate him from afar and *luckily* informed him she'd had her period. Lauren never smiled his way again. But as school wound down and summer break took shape, more parties and free time came.

It was Fourth of July, the annual community picnic, when he next screwed up. Her name was Shawna and she did things to him he never knew a guy could experience. He was pretty sure she was responsible for most of the fireworks that night.

After Shawna came Ella and after Ella came Trish. He'd learned a valuable lesson from Rachel and never promised anything in return. No matter who he was hooking up with, they always understood he wasn't into long term.

Sex was a funny thing at that age. It made a guy popular with *all* the cliques. The jocks wanted him to come to their parties. The preppy kids gave him a little more respect. And the girls… it didn't matter what club they belonged to. Even the dorky girls batted their eyes at him.

By the end of sophomore year, he was like Moses parting the Red Sea when he walked down the halls. People stepped aside for him, laughed at all of his jokes, and inquired where he'd be each weekend as though it determined where the current hot spot was. He liked it. He liked it a lot.

His mum seemed to get over her disappointment and accept that her sons were growing up. Kelly was no longer the only one with condoms in his sock drawer. When a woman had five sons it was only practical to accept that boys would be boys.

He was always careful and he never took what wasn't offered. He didn't have to work for it. Not until he met Lexi.

Lexi was a senior and she was hot as hell. Her entire being seemed to throb with sexuality. From her wavy red hair to her long ass legs, she was everything a teenage boy's fantasies were made of. She didn't look like she belonged in high school. She looked like she belonged in a centerfold. The night she approached him at a party something changed in Kelly.

Usually, he called the shots, but not this time. She walked up to him, cutting a path right through the swarm of underage drinkers swaying with their plastic cups and didn't stop until she was staring him right in the eye.

"Wanna come upstairs?" Her voice was like velvet, smooth and sultry.

Kelly sipped his beer and placed the empty cup on the cluttered table. When he stood, she didn't wait for confirmation. With the confidence of a queen, she marched up the steps, never looking back to see if he followed.

It was the first time he'd ever had sex in an actual bed. And like everything else Lexi, there was nothing juvenile about the way she took a man. She seduced him, made love to him, took him to places he'd never dreamed.

Afterward, they lay in the bed naked and talked until the party broke up. He was stunned at how potent she was, how experienced and knowing she seemed. By the time he got home that night he knew something was different. There was no afterglow, only anticipation to see her again.

The following Monday he'd found her in the hall by her locker. Without giving it much thought, he leaned in and kissed her.

She pulled back and frowned at him. "What are you doing?"

He laughed nervously. "What do you mean? I'm kissing you."

She glanced around anxiously. "Well…don't."

His brow tightened. "What do you mean?"

She grabbed his wrist and pulled him into a semi-empty stairwell. "Kelly, the other night was fun, but that's all it was."

"Nothing wrong with having fun twice."

She laughed nervously. "I don't think that's smart."

"Why? You enjoyed yourself."

"Yeah, I did. But I'm graduating soon and in August I'm off to Penn State. There's no point in getting mixed up with a guy like you when there isn't a chance we'll stay together."

He drew back. "What do you mean a guy like me?"

Her mouth opened as she seemed to struggle for an explanation. "Come on, Kelly. Everyone in this school has your number. You're *that guy*."

"What the hell's that mean?"

"It means you were born in Center County and you're gonna die in Center County. High school will always be your glory days. I mean, what's your average? Have you even applied for colleges? You're the guy everyone loves. The bad boy who can show a girl a good time. You're not someone's future."

Blanking his expression, he shoved back the sharp cut of her words. He hadn't applied to college because he'd bombed his SATs and his grades weren't enough to carry his ass. He had no idea what would happen to him after high school, but feared she was right. What if this part of his life was as good as it got? He'd eventually get older, fatter, and lazier.

"Look," she said, as the bell rang. "You're a nice guy, but I can't wait for someone while I'm at college making a future and he's sitting at home reliving his glory days, wishing he could turn back the clock. There's nothing wrong with who you are. People like you and you're really funny, but you're not the guy for me. I gotta go. I'm gonna be late."

She left him there as the halls emptied and quieted. He had to be somewhere, but for the life of him, couldn't think of one good reason to show up. Why bother if he was only ever going to be some has-been in some shitty town?

Turning, he took the stairs at a sprint. His feet didn't stop until he was at his truck. His books were tossed carelessly inside and he peeled out of the parking lot. He wasn't sure where he was driving, but pulled over when he found an empty section of road. His fingers gripped the wheel as he breathed hard through his teeth.

She hadn't even given him a chance. How many other people saw him as just some nobody holding claim to the current definition of cool that would be outdated tomorrow? Reaching in his pocket he thumbed through hundreds of phone numbers. There was no doubt he'd been around.

With each contact came a memory. After Rachel and

Lauren, he'd learned to make it perfectly clear he was good for a night and nothing more, but after a while that bit of information seemed assumed. It was like that was all *he* was really wanted for, nothing more.

Everyone wanted a piece of him, but none of the girls ever asked him out or showed any interest in anything long term. Even Rachel was involved with some college guy and Lauren was over a year deep with the class president. It was as though he'd literally screwed over all the good girls. But they were fine with that. They'd gotten exactly what they wanted—a good time—which was pretty much all he was worth.

After sitting on the side of the road for some time, he finally looked around. He was in his Aunt Colleen's neck of the woods, close to her bar, O'Malley's. He glanced at the clock. It was still early. She was probably just opening up. Throwing his truck in drive, he headed that way.

When he reached the pub, the lot was empty aside from his aunt's car. He parked in the back and used the kitchen entrance. His aunt came into the kitchen, appearing startled, with an empty pitcher in her hand. "Kelly love, what are you doing here? I was about to brain you like a burglar."

"Sorry, Aunt Col."

She tipped her head to the side. "Why aren't you in school? Is everything all right?"

He shrugged.

She placed the pitcher on the large cook counter and said, "Come along. I'll get you a soda and you can tell me what's going on in my favorite nephew's life."

"You can get shot for making a comment like that. You have other nephews."

"You won't tell, and if you do I'll deny it."

He smiled and followed her to the bar. They used the pub for family parties, but other than that none of the younger McCulloughs were allowed to hang out there. "When do the customers start showing up?"

"The regulars will be shuffling in shortly. Tell me what's going on." She placed a soda on a napkin and came around the bar to sit beside him.

"I had a bit of a wakeup call this morning."

"Did something bad happen? Were you in an accident?"

"No, nothing so dramatic. It's about a girl."

"From what my kids tell me, you have quite a few female admirers, Kelly."

"Yeah. Well, things sort of spun out of control."

His aunt pinched his cheek. "Breakin' hearts left and right, I bet." She hummed happily. "Such a wee rogue, you are."

He arched a brow. "Nothin' wee about me, Aunt Col. I'm a McCullough after all."

Her hand slapped his cheek as she giggled. "Smartass."

They laughed for a moment and then he sobered. "I don't know what I'm doing."

"You're seventeen, love. What's there to know? Seems to me you're doing just fine."

"I am. For now. But what happens next year when I graduate? Everyone thinks I'm something great, but soon they'll all go off to college and become doctors and other important things and I'll still be here, only there will be nothing impressive about me then."

"You'll always be impressive, Kelly. There's something special in you. You just have to find it yourself. A lassie can try to show you how great you are, but unless you're ready to open your eyes and see what you have to offer in this world, you'll never believe it's in you."

"I don't want to be a logger," he blurted.

"So don't."

"But what else is there?"

"Well, what do you fancy? What are you good at?"

"Nothing that means anything."

She tsked. "That's not true. You have a wonderful sense of humor, a big heart, you're loyal, and people feel special when you look at them. Not everyone can do that to others."

"Yeah, but where does that get me as far as a future?"

"You need a job that requires people skills, Kelly, because you're a people person."

"What sort of job's that? I can't get into a decent

college and, honestly, I have no desire to continue with school after graduation. I've never been good at it."

"Well, we all can't be like your sister, Sheilagh. The world is an extraordinary place because ordinary people keep coming, Kelly. If there were only lawyers, doctors, and teachers, who would do the plumbing? Who would fix the electric when it went out? Who would plow the roads when the blizzards come so the surgeons can make it to the hospitals to save lives?"

"Are you suggesting I become a plumber or buy a snow plow?"

"No, I'm suggesting you not worry about being successful, but worry about being happy. Find something that makes you happy and success will come easily enough."

"All my friends are going off to college. Luke's gone. Bray's leaving. Colin's been gone. We all know Sheilagh's on her way."

"No one said you couldn't join them, Kelly. There's always a way. What about your art?"

He shook his head. "That's private. It's something that's mine. I don't share it and there's no way I can make a career out of it."

"I think you need to get out of your fishbowl. Living up on that mountain, you're only surrounded by McCulloughs. Then you head off to school and see everyone following the tide. It's okay to move on without them before they leave you behind."

"What do you mean?"

She spread out her fingers over the bar. "You see these hands? I remember when they were young and beautiful. I don't remember them getting freckled with age or wrinkled by time. I just looked down one day and there they were, old and ugly.

"I've been working in this bar since Paul and I rented the apartment upstairs right after we got married. We couldn't afford a house until Italian Mary came to live with us and helped us with the down payment. It was a struggle and everyone thought we were crazy, but we loved the atmosphere, and over time O'Malley's became the place to be.

"We could afford several houses now and I think we're going to buy one in Outer Banks soon for summer vacations. The problem is, this damn bar demands so much of my time I can't take off for weeks at a time. The locals would rally. Sooner or later I'll need to sell it."

"You can't sell the bar. We haven't even had a chance to enjoy it."

She smiled. "I know, love. So my only other option is to find someone to run it for me. They'd have to be someone easygoing, trustworthy, and good with people." She gave him a sidelong glance.

Kelly's expression flattened. "Me?"

"Why not? You could do it, Kelly. You could even move upstairs eventually, if you fixed it up a bit."

"How…how would that work?"

"Well, you wouldn't be able to serve until you were eighteen, but if you wanted to learn the ropes you could start out bussing tables. I could teach you the things I don't normally show the other employees, like how I manage the suppliers and the bookkeeping. Once you're an adult, I'll teach you how to tend bar. Give it a year after you graduate. Let this be your job and see how you like it. If you like it and you're interested in taking over, we'll talk about getting your name on the mortgage."

"Are you serious?"

"As serious as a rodeo clown in a red speedo."

He laughed. "Not very serious then."

"Oh, I think once that bull came chargin' out of the shute that clown would be pretty serious. Life can be serious *and* funny. Yes, I'm serious, Kelly. If you want the job, it's yours."

This was unbelievable. O'Malley's was legend. It was the number one place to be in their town. He couldn't believe she was actually offering it to him. "I'll take it."

"Good. This weekend you can start by cleaning the toilets, because no doubt my sister will punish you when she finds out you skipped school again."

He nodded, glad to clean to toilets. Holy shit, he'd just been handed a future.

"And, Kelly?"

"Yeah."

"Whatever that lassie said to you, she was wrong. Just because you aren't running off to college with the rest of them, doesn't mean your future's any less bright. The trick is to find someone who sees the light in you even during life's darkest moments. That's what real love is."

He didn't want love. He just wanted to know someone saw potential in him. It hurt being told he wasn't good enough. If he could, he'd rewind the day and go back to when he thought everyone loved him. But that would mean missing out on the opportunity his aunt just presented.

It had started as an ordinary day, but changed the rest of his life. He finally knew what he was doing with his future. He also learned a valuable lesson about girls. If he never expected anything more and gave them exactly what they expected from him, everyone wound up happy. That was the trick, wasn't it? Find happiness and the success and everything else would eventually come.

Don't stop there! It gets so much better...
Download Irish Rogue now!

www.lydiamichaelsbooks.com